Celeste

Marie O'Regan

Contents

For my family, with thanks for their patience with me.

Chapter 1

Clive listened for any sounds of Celeste stirring and breathed a sigh of relief when none came. The house stayed quiet. Celeste could be vicious when she was fading, and he'd learned to stay out of her way as best he could. So many times he'd been too close and paid the price. So here he was, sitting slumped at the kitchen table, nursing a glass of vodka and orange at a quarter to ten in the morning. He rubbed his hand over the table's worn wooden surface, feeling every pore of its grain. Looking around, he grinned ruefully. Every crack in every tile, every bump and imperfection in this kitchen—hell, in the whole house, was as familiar to him as his own skin. He knew it better than Celeste ever had, even though she was the one who thought she knew everything.

His throat burned as he downed his drink, grimacing as he placed the glass back on the table. Clive rubbed his hand across his mouth to dry his lips, blew on his palm, and sniffed. Celeste would know he'd been drinking, but he didn't want to rub her nose in it by stinking of booze. He never drank so much that it was noticeable; at least he didn't think so. He drank just enough to stiffen his backbone a little.

At nearly ten, the ancient brass bell above the kitchen door jangled roughly, heralding some demand or other from his mistress. With a groan, he stashed the vodka bottle in the cupboard under the sink and rinsed his glass under the tap, leaving it on the drainer. Then he put the carton of orange juice in the fridge and straightened up, wincing. The pain in his lower back was a near-constant reminder of the last time he had crossed her. He'd taken just a minute too long to answer her summons and, furious at being kept waiting, she'd pushed him down the stairs. She'd laughed as he fell all the way to the bottom, clapping her hands at the crack of vertebrae fracturing. He'd been in traction for two months.

Clive pulled his black butler's jacket from the back of the door and put it on, casting a last glance around the kitchen to make sure everything was neat and tidy. She'd only check later on, and any mess would be punished.

He left the kitchen and made his way up the stairs to her bedroom, where she spent most of her time these days. As usual, she was half-buried under the rich, crimson bedding, lying propped up on her pillows and watching the monstrous television set that stood on a mahogany chest at the foot of the bed. He hoped she'd stay there, this time. If he was lucky, she'd be sick of the dance; she'd let herself fade just a little too far to be able to get back again, and maybe, just maybe, he'd finally be free.

She stirred, struggling to sit up tall in her nest. "You took your time, Clive."

"It takes me a bit longer these days, Miss Celeste; that's true." He stayed as near the door as possible, wary of getting too close. There was a glint in those bright green cat's eyes he hadn't seen in an age, as if she was daring him to come closer. *Careful, Clive*, that glint said. *I still bite.* Safer to stay where he was, for now. "I'm not as young as I used to be."

"No, you're not." She watched him carefully before losing interest and gazing at her hands, seemingly entranced by their outline, the now wrinkled flesh marred by myriad age spots dotted across the backs of her hands. "But then again, neither am I."

He said nothing, just waited for what he knew was coming. This was not the time to break the cycle after all; she was too strong, even in this state. She beckoned him to her, and Clive moved reluctantly nearer to the huge four-poster and its decayed drapes.

"I can't let you go, Clive. You know that, don't you?" She clasped his hand, and he marvelled at the fragility of her grip. The skin was papery to the touch, mottled with grey here and there. The bones felt like twigs in his grasp, brittle and ready to snap at the slightest pressure. He wondered if her neck would snap just as easily and resisted the temptation to see.

Clive was surprised to hear a note of sadness in her voice; he'd never heard that before. Touched, he looked up, hopeful that he could change her mind this time. She dipped her finger to the tears welling up and touched it to her lips, seemingly surprised to find her eyes wet. There was an unaccustomed sympathy in her expression as she stared at him.

She patted the edge of the bed, motioned for him to sit down. Tired or not, she was still going to go through with it, even after all this time. "It's time to turn the wheel once more, old friend."

Clive resisted. "Not again, ma'am, please. I'm too old."

She squeezed his hand, pulled him closer. "Not for long. We can do it, Clive. Don't you want to be young again?" Clive stayed mute and she faltered, her face falling. "You still love me, don't you?"

He groaned, aware that she knew it and was playing him, as she always had. Clive hated that wheedling tone she adopted at such times, knowing he always gave in, always gave her what she wanted. He couldn't help himself. However twisted it was, he loved her and always would. "Yes, ma'am. I do. God help me, I do."

"That's all I want." She cupped his face in her hands and smiled. "That's all I ever want." His flesh stirred at her touch, and he felt a whisper of shame as she responded in kind.

Clive could feel the old familiar energy starting to flow as she kissed him, building in the air around them. He breathed deep and felt the air's heat, felt it scour his insides, igniting appetites long since dormant.

Hot breath whispered against his neck as she drew him down into her embrace. "It'll be all right You'll see."

The dance began.

Chapter 2

Clive woke to a different world. The bedroom was back to its former ostentation, the drapes around the bed and at the windows made once more of heavy crimson velvet, the tiebacks trimmed with gold braid. The rest of the room echoed these two colours, and the air was fragrant once more—a bunch of blood-red roses blooming furiously on the bedside table, heads wilting under the flowers' weight. He grinned. Understatement never had been Celeste's style.

For a moment, he felt almost glad to be alive. He lay on his back breathing deeply and cleanly for what felt like the first time, with no sign of his usual coughing. His joints were supple once more, the pain in his back gone, his lungs clear of the emphysema that had been slowly sapping his strength for the last five years. Yesterday, he had been an elderly butler with a bad chest and the beginnings of arthritis. Today, he was a young man again. To an outsider, he would have looked thirty at the most—a tall, muscular man who moved with an easy grace that had always been his trademark. More than one girl-friend had remarked on it. He'd accepted such compliments as his due, making no comment on them. Now it was time to be young again, and in a way, he supposed he was glad. He wondered, though, how high the price would be this time, and who would have to pay it?

Clive stiffened as he heard Celeste sigh beside him and roll onto her side, stretching, catlike. He closed his eyes, not ready to see.

She touched his shoulder. "Clive."

Her voice was back to that velvety drawl he remembered, strong and vibrant.

"I know you're awake." Her tone was playful, but he knew better than to trust that.

"Ma'am?"

"Turn the television on; I want to see what's going on in the world."

He got out of bed and went to the dressing table, grabbed the remote and selected the news channel she liked. Turning back to the bed, he saw her face and stopped dead. She was magnificent.

Celeste smiled at his attention, fully aware of the effect she'd had. "How do I look?"

Lost for words, he could only nod and smile. She'd know. Her black hair gleamed in a sleek, bobbed cut. Her breasts were full and firm. Her skin was as white as ever, and flawless. Sometimes he thought it was the one constant about her, other than those green eyes. She had no need of make-up. His gaze dropped to her breasts once more. There was no sign now of the cut she had made high on her left breast for him to drink from, closing the circle and sparking the change. He looked down at his own chest. There was no sign, either, of the symbols she had carved there in the night.

She stood and walked over to the full-length mirror, laughing as she pulled him with her. They were perfect. He couldn't take his eyes off her, and when he managed to raise his eyes to her face, he saw a desire to match his own. Smiling, she turned towards him and pressed close.

He could feel her heart thudding against his chest. With a groan he hugged her tight, breathed in her scent. Then he lowered his lips to hers. He reached down and lifted her, carried her to the bed. Even as he was laying her down, she was reaching for him, guiding him into her. She gasped as he entered her and wrapped her legs around him, pulling him deeper. For the first time, Clive felt as if they were making love instead of just rutting like animals. She was tender, even affectionate, and that wasn't something he normally equated with Celeste. He had seen her in all her moods, he thought, but he had never seen her like this.

If she was like this more often, she would have no need of others. Clive would adore her completely, for all time, without a qualm—if only that were enough. The familiar heat was building, Celeste responding, and they climaxed together. He thought it would go on forever. They clung to each other as if their lives depended on it, as if they would drown if they let go. Then it was over.

She touched his face, and he wasn't sure if it was in understanding or commiseration. Then she pushed him aside, got up, and made her way into the bathroom without a word. He was dismissed. He was left to dress and start the day, bereft.

May God forgive me, he thought, *for what happens this time.*

Every time it started, he prayed he would find the strength to end it. Every time, he prayed this time he would be the only victim. And every time he was disappointed.

Either way, he was damned.

Chapter 3

Clive had been left on his own for the day. Celeste was in the mood for some "serious shopping," as she put it. Their lovemaking had not been referred to again, and Clive reluctantly acknowledged that any signs of affection he thought he'd seen had been designed to entice him, nothing more. She had come out of the bathroom only to flounce in front of the mirror and dismiss virtually everything she had to wear.

"My clothes are all out of date, Clive. Old woman's clothes, and I'm young now."

"Shall I order you a cab to Knightsbridge, Miss Celeste?" He had kept his tone carefully neutral, not wanting her to see she'd hurt him yet again.

"I don't want to go to Knightsbridge, Clive. I want to go somewhere new."

Clive waited. She was leading up to something definite, he knew.

"What about one of those new things, Clive. What are they called?"

"You mean shopping centres? Malls?"

"That's it. What's the nearest one of those?"

"The nearest, miss, is Brent Cross. It's not far from here, only around twenty minutes in a cab."

She had positively glowed at the thought of a whole collection of shops, all under one roof. With Celeste, the love of shopping was eternal. And so she had ordered a cab to Brent Cross. Clive knew she wouldn't be back until seven o'clock at the earliest. Shopping for her had always been an all-day event. She had left instructions that the house be cleaned from top to bottom and aired out while she was gone.

Since she had last faded, the house had assumed a musty, ancient atmosphere—more like a mausoleum than a home. Now, as Clive walked through the house, he drew all the curtains and threw windows open wide in room after room, letting sunlight flood in and fresh air start to blow through. His skin prickled in the sunlight and he smiled, happy to feel so alive after all this time. Perhaps he'd been wrong to hope this last period of seclusion would be the final one.

Once all the windows were open, he made his way up to the top of the house, originally used as servants' quarters, and started the long, arduous process of cleaning windows, vacuuming, dusting, and polishing. He knew from experience that the curtains—all fixtures, in fact—would repair themselves, becoming plusher and richer of their own accord, almost as if travelling backwards through time as the house completed its rejuvenation. The dust, however, was another matter. The only thing that would effectively remove the patina of age was polishing, lots of polishing.

Echoes of past activities in the house echoed around him as he worked, reminding him of the hustle and bustle of a bygone age. These days it boiled down to just one servant—him. But in its time, the house had been filled with maids, cooks, groundsmen...all with their own jobs to do.

It took Clive most of the day, but finally everything was done. Exhausted, sweat dripping down his bare torso, he walked slowly from room to room once more, closing windows where necessary, proud of what he had achieved. He knew he was tied to the house as inexorably as Celeste. It had sustained them both far beyond their natural span, and he felt the least he could do was cherish it, make sure it looked its best. He finished his checking and headed for the lower floor —his own rooms, which adjoined the kitchen at the back of the house and allowed him a view of his beloved garden. He just had time to bathe and put on a fresh uniform before Celeste got back.

1893

Clive was twenty-two, born six years after the abolition of slavery in 1871 but well aware of his position as Colonel Parker's butler. He might be a citizen of the United States, same as his employer, but there any similarity ended. The colonel's daughter, seventeen-year-old Celeste, flirted with any man in sight, even him, but he knew that to respond to or even acknowledge her advances would spell trouble. So he went about his duties, proud of the position he had achieved, occasionally dallying with one of the kitchen girls.

Celeste was another matter. She was unusually tall for a woman, maybe five foot nine, and beautiful—with sleek ebony hair and brilliant green eyes. The local lads had swarmed around her as soon as she was old enough, eager for her favours. At least to begin with.

Then word of her behaviour began to spread. How she was wild, much too forward. Some even said she was unhinged.

It was a bitterly cold morning, barely a week before Christmas, and he was woken by the sound of raised voices, glass smashing, women crying. As quickly as he could, he dressed and crept down the stairs, trying to avoid any boards that creaked. Halfway down, he saw that Miss Celeste's door was open, and that was where the noise was coming from.

He heard the colonel's voice, thunderous with rage. "I will not have my daughter consorting with...with negroes!"

Clive flinched at that, but stayed quiet. He knew better than to alert them to his presence at such a time.

"But Papa..."

"Hush! That woman is a witch, child, pure and simple. The whole town knows it! Same as the whole town knows you've been going out there to see her!"

"So what if I have? Bess is just an old woman who's good with folk remedies, is all—"

Her voice was cut off suddenly as the sound of the colonel's cane sliced through the air, stopping with a slapping sound as it encountered soft flesh. Clive had to give her credit. For a soft, rich white girl, Celeste showed a lot of courage. She didn't cry out once, though it was surely the most painful thing she had ever experienced.

"You will not go there again. I forbid it! Do you hear me?" Another whack with the cane when she refused to answer, then another. "I said, do you hear me?"

"Yes, Papa."

She spoke quietly, her voice barely audible but still managing to convey defiance, with not even a hint of the pain she must feel.

Her father stormed out of the room and headed off back down the hall, passing out of Clive's sight. Moments later, he heard the colonel's bedroom door slam. Then it flew open again as Celeste's mother, sobbing, fled to her daughter's side. Clive heard her fussing over Celeste, cleaning and dressing the welts left by the colonel's cane, but Celeste was immovable. Through it all, he only heard Celeste speak once. Her voice was tightly controlled, icy in its vehemence, and it chilled him to the bone.

"I'll get him. You'll see, Mama, and you'll know." Just that, no more. But sentence had been pronounced.

A fortnight later, her father announced that he had been offered a position in London, England. "An ambassadorial post for the company," he said. They would leave in six weeks. Other staff would be hired for them there, but Clive must go with them. Clive made the appropriate grateful responses, which he knew they expected of him, but he had decidedly mixed feelings. His family were here, all that he knew was here.

What did he know of England, of its ways? He knew that, technically, he didn't have to go. He wasn't a slave; he could always get another job. In practice, it wasn't going to be that easy. Blacks with a good job, like his, tended to hang onto them. No, best to stay where he was, wherever it led him. His mother tried to persuade him otherwise, unwilling to lose another son—his brother Matthew had died but a short time before, and with Clive gone she would be alone. Clive stood firm and carried the knowledge with him that he'd broken his mother's heart.

The colonel set Clive to watch Celeste, make sure she didn't get into any trouble. He knew what that meant. If she was to see Bess again, it would have to be soon. Celeste claimed she was only a wise woman, a healer...but they all knew how far that was from the truth.

Old Bess, as she was invariably known, was renowned locally as adept in what the whites called voodoo. She could kill you with no more contact than someone procuring a hair from your head. She had been credited, rightly or wrongly (Clive knew what he thought, but wisely kept it to himself—she had a long reach), with at least a dozen deaths over the last three years; not to mention the withered limbs, sicknesses, and God knew what else. Oh, there were the good stories, too...the babies saved, barren couples suddenly blessed with children after years of trying, illnesses cured. But they weren't quite so plentiful. And she was well rewarded for such largesse, he was sure.

"Just watch her, Clive," Celeste's father had said. "Make sure she doesn't go anywhere near that woman. You have my permission to stop her and bring her home." He had given Clive written instructions to that effect, in case he was stopped while in her company. He may have grown up in the colonel's service, but anyone stopping him wasn't to know that.

As it happened, for the first five weeks she showed no signs of going anywhere. Later, Clive realised that messages must have been to-ing and fro-ing the whole time, but he had seen no sign. And he had watched carefully, he was sure of that. At the beginning of the sixth week, Celeste became more blatant. Or maybe it was desperation. Every time she came near the front or back door, she would find Clive engrossed in some menial and seemingly absolutely vital task nearby. She would then feign a nonchalance completely alien to her normal character and saunter off in a different direction. Again—to begin with—Clive had assumed success. Still, he dared not relax. Not now. Three days before their departure he realised how wrong they had all been in assuming they'd won.

Passing a window, he happened to glance out and saw Celeste far off, hurrying for cover under the trees that bordered the property. Somehow, she'd managed to slip out without him noticing.

He set off after her. By the time he got to the trees, he figured she was no more than two minutes ahead of him. Clive slowed down slightly, not wanting to make any noise, striving to adjust his eyes to the gloom.

There she was.

He could just make out a pink blur, moving far ahead of him. He tracked her, gaining ground slightly, but trying not to get too close. The figure ahead stopped moving, and Clive began to circle around, trying to see what she was doing from a safe distance. She was standing by the wrought-iron fence, talking. Clive couldn't make out who her companion was to start with, so he tried to edge closer.

Even as he realised it was Bess, he was grabbed from behind by someone with enormous strength and marched towards them. Without even looking up, Bess spoke. Her voice was thin, sibilant, reminding Clive of a snake.

"So now you know. And what will you do with this knowledge, Clive?"

Bess looked at him, and Clive felt all the strength drain...no, *gush* out of him, at the malice evident in those obsidian eyes. If it hadn't been for whoever was holding him up, he would have fallen to the ground in a dead faint.

"Nothing. I won't do anything."

He was crying now, his promise to the colonel forgotten. All he wanted was to live. What did he care for them? He had a life!

"How do we know that for sure?" Bess asked.

She was enjoying this, revelling in his fear.

"I swear. I—"

He was interrupted by the sound of Bess laughing at him, a dry, rasping sound totally devoid of humour.

"You don't need to swear, boy," she drawled. "You belong to us, now."

Clive felt a sharp pain in his wrist and looked down in time to see Celeste wiping off the blade of the pocketknife she had used to make a small diagonal cut across his flesh. The blood was flowing freely, and she was holding a wax doll underneath it. He didn't need to ask who the doll was meant to be. He recognised the cloth wrapping it as part of a shirt he had thought lost. She was right; he didn't have the strength to fight that. He might as well surrender to the inevitable.

Clive just hoped it was quick.

She spoke sharply to his captor. "Let him go."

The arms supporting him fell away at her command, and his captor took a step backwards. Stumbling, Clive chanced a look over his shoulder and gasped. His brother, Matthew, stared blankly back at him, no trace in his unseeing eyes of the life that had ended three months before.

Clive stood trembling, unable to even cry. Matthew just stood there, inert—but not, Clive thought, completely unaware. Some part of him, at least, knew what had happened to him. What was still happening. His flesh was grey and dead—patches of skin sloughing off here and there. Clumps of hair were missing, and Clive could see things crawling in his mouth as it hung open.

The mouldering shirt he wore was squirming slightly, and Clive knew without a doubt that Bess had called Matthew back for the express purpose of aiding in the domination of his brother. Securing the hold.

He heard someone laughing behind him. Whether it was Celeste or Bess, he neither knew nor cared. He screwed up his courage and took a step towards his brother. The laughter cut off suddenly, and Clive sensed their eyes on him, the expectancy in their gaze.

Matthew watched him, dead-eyed, as he edged his way forward. Reaching him, Clive put out his hand and caressed his brother's cheek, fighting the revulsion as he felt whatever was underneath wriggle frantically away from his touch. It made his brother's expression flicker grotesquely, as if he were about to spew forth something vile.

No matter what Matthew was now, Clive still loved his brother. He had to hope something of Matthew's love for him remained, too.

Even as he stroked Matthew's cheek with one hand, he punched his way into his chest with the other, praying nothing would skitter up his arm as he did so. He heard the splinter of bone and the dry rattle of whatever was left in Matthew's lungs escaping. His fingers clenched convulsively around his brother's heart and wrenched it free. With a whisper that might have been Clive's name, Matthew's features sagged, his flesh losing the unholy spark that animated it—and he collapsed to the ground; no more now than a pile of rotting meat. The heart pulsed in Clive's hand for a moment, then lay still. Already liquefying, sending a cloud of putrescence up into the air.

Clive gagged and collapsed to his knees, sobbing. He felt hot and sick, weak with reaction. His brother was free, and he had to be content with that.

It was his last act of defiance.

He remembered very little of the night's events after that. He remembered the blood, the deep ache in his wrist. Although afterwards he had never been sure whether that was a result of the cut itself or the foul-smelling paste Bess had slapped on before binding it. He had felt it burrowing deep into the wound, sealing it by infiltration. At one point, he had roused himself enough to become aware of his surroundings, only to find Celeste astride him, naked and riding him hard. He remembered both their bodies had been painted with strange symbols that almost seemed to move with a life of their own. She had been bathed in sweat that dripped as dark as blood, and was moaning in a language that he didn't, couldn't, recognise. There had been a smell of burning, and he had turned his head to see Bess clutching a bundle of grasses, aflame with a green light, which produced a strangely intoxicating smoke. She had been walking in a circle around them, waving the makeshift torch in intricate patterns, voice raised in a strange ululation.

He'd felt his breath growing shorter; felt sick with the overwhelming aroma from the grasses. Clive and Celeste had climaxed together, and she'd collapsed onto his chest. Then there had been nothing, until he woke to find himself in his own bed the next morning. He had been pitifully weak. There was no sign of the cut on his wrist, but he was aware of a burning sensation emanating from it, searing up his arm.

Clive had no idea what had happened, how he had got here. All he knew was that, despite all his fears, he was alive. And if he wanted to stay that way, he had to obey Celeste.

He belonged to her now.

Over the next day or so Clive did indeed endeavour to watch Celeste, as he had promised, but from what he thought was a safe distance. She did nothing, however, to further arouse his suspicion. They both knew the damage had already been done, and this was just a charade. What need did she have now to escape?

The day of their departure dawned without further mishap.

They boarded the ship without incident and, before long, Clive found himself sitting in his cabin waiting to be summoned. There would be calls for clothes to be laid out and such things, but not much else. For the duration of the trip, he would be little more than a valet. He did not find the prospect altogether displeasing; in fact, it would be quite restful. He relished the thought of having some time to himself, especially away from Celeste. His employers were entertained by the captain and kept company with the other travellers. He should be safe enough.

On the third day, there was a violent storm. All day, the air had an unnatural stillness, the heat pressing down on them almost unbearably. The clouds gathered, black and dangerous, and when the storm finally broke, they found themselves tossed around on the furious ocean by waves almost the height of the ship itself. Everyone was ordered to return to their cabins, where Clive spent a sickening afternoon convinced they would all die. His cabin was directly below that of the colonel and his wife, and he could hear the cries and moans upstairs, echoing his own. They were talking, and there was a tension to the conversation that Clive didn't care for. It made his flesh crawl, even though he couldn't make out the words.

Then, in a rush, it crowded in on him; caused him to clap his hands over his ears in pain at the rising clamour. It was Celeste. Somehow, she was allowing him to hear this, warning him not to interfere. He could hear her voice as clearly as if she were standing next to him. Falling to the floor, he lay writhing in pain as the cries seared the inside of his skull. It felt as if his head were full of unnatural leeches, crawling across the surface of his brain, sucking it dry. He could feel them.

Celeste was laughing now, well aware of his pain and revulsion, taking delight in it. There were other voices, too—guttural, hissing voices—inhuman in their cadence.

Clive was dimly aware of the intensity building, the pressure in his head rising until—a crashing sound from the cabin above broke its hold and released him. He collapsed to the floor, shuddering. He felt as if he could hardly breathe. Thunder boomed as if in counterpoint, and the cabin was lent a nightmarish resonance by the accompanying lightning. What had Celeste done? What in God's name had she done?

Then there came a scream from the cabin above. Clive struggled to his feet. He had a horrible feeling that Celeste had just made good on her threat. Reeling, he clung to the walls and made his way up to the colonel's cabin. He tried the door and found it locked, started banging on the door for admittance. He could hear the colonel moaning, but he could hear nothing of his mistress. Clive called Celeste, cajoling her into opening the door, or trying to, but she didn't answer. Through it all, he could feel Celeste's satisfaction, festering away inside him.

Suddenly the door opened, and he almost fell into the cabin. The colonel lay on the floor in the middle of the cabin—barely conscious. A large wooden bureau had fallen over in the storm and lay across his legs, pinning him to the floor. Clive staggered over and managed to get a grip on one corner of the bureau. He strained to lift it, muscles standing out in stark relief on his corded arms. His shoulders burned with the effort, and he braced himself anew, trying to gain a little extra leverage. No use. Even with his great strength, it was far too heavy for one man to lift.

Then, rough hands were pulling him back, forcing him out of the way. He stepped away and watched helplessly as four crewmen struggled with the bureau, forcing it upright—revealing the colonel's wife crushed beneath her husband's prone form. He had tried, and failed, to protect her. They moved it back over to the wall, leaving the way clear for the ship's doctor. As the physician bent over the colonel, Clive went across to the bureau. He saw with horror that it had been bolted to the wall in two places. There was no sign of wear; the bolts had simply come out of the wall. Clive knew what had happened was impossible. He felt Celeste's laughter, all but inaudible, and realised he had been right. She had taken her revenge after all.

As for the colonel, his legs had been crushed—and despite the doctor's best efforts, infection set in within days, resulting in amputation in order to save his life. He was never the same after that, and Clive took the blame for that upon himself as well. One day, he swore he would free both himself and the colonel of Celeste. Whatever it took.

Chapter 4

Celeste sat in the cab on the way to Brent Cross, busily absorbing the nuances of modern daily life. She was hopelessly out of touch with the way people acted now—what they wore, how they spoke, everything. Clive had helped her choose an outfit that he thought would fit in in this day and age—one of her favourites from the sixties, bizarrely popular once more, even if the current fashions didn't look exactly as she remembered them.

The cab swung into what looked like a one-way motorway, only smaller, more convoluted. There were less people on the streets here, she saw—the roads between Highgate and here had been swarming with them—far more than she remembered as being normal back in the days before she'd last faded from view. Then, off to her right, she saw it—Brent Cross.

So that was what a shopping centre looked like. From the outside, it looked like a huge concrete cell block. She only hoped the inside was more inviting.

The cab pulled up at a taxi rank not far from the main entrance, near a courtyard full of buses. Celeste watched through the cab window as hordes of people queued up at the various bus stops, jostling for position as the vehicles' doors wheezed open, waiting to be swallowed up within the giant red beasts even as they spewed forth more and more people.

"This okay for you?"

"What?" Celeste stared at the driver, unsure of his meaning.

"I said," he went on, and now his tone was that of a grumpy parent explaining to a small child, "is it okay if I drop you off here?"

"Drop me off?" Belatedly, Celeste realised he wanted her to exit the cab. They were here, at Brent Cross shopping centre, and his job was done. "Oh, I see."

The driver tapped a box on the front of the dashboard, and said, "£15."

Still gazing out at the people rushing past, Celeste dug in her handbag for her purse. She grudgingly paid what seemed to be an exorbitant fare, deliberately ignoring the muttered invective at the lack of a tip, and stepped out of the vehicle to stand on the pavement as the driver pulled away and joined the line of cabs waiting to pick up more fares.

She made her way carefully across the courtyard and walked through the automatic doors into a different world. Cool, air-conditioned...and with wall-to-wall shops. Bliss. She meandered erratically from shop to shop, basking in the variety of fashions these days. Tall and slim, she bought several pairs of black jeans, knowing they would look good. It was a great relief to buy flat shoes and boots, again in black. While she was walking around, she began to feel more and more alive, noting with satisfaction the admiring glances she was drawing. She went into the ladies' restroom in a department store and changed into a tight black shirt and black jeans, with calf-length boots. Studying herself in the mirror, she smiled at the result. Time to turn some heads.

Twenty minutes later, having picked up several more garments, Celeste was heading for the lift when she became aware of someone watching her. People had been openly staring at her all day, so that was nothing new. She'd even been approached by a photographer—what was his name? Terry, that was it—keen to take some "glamour" shots, as he put it. She could see by that he had meant naked, but had no problem with that. Such pictures would mean more "admirers," which meant she would stay young longer. And Terry could be... useful. She'd taken his card, and agreed a time to meet at his studio for a "photo shoot," then moved on, bored and wanting to shop some more. But what she felt now was different and had nothing to do with Terry. The contact this time had been nothing short of electric. She stood still for a moment, trying to locate the direction this unexpected sustenance was coming from.

There. Off to the left.

Turning her head slowly, Celeste scanned the gaggle of shoppers flocking around the lifts, looking for the one that had initiated this euphoria she felt, this almost sexual tension. He wasn't hard to spot.

This man was tall, fair, good-looking—and he was rushing towards her, his face frozen in shock. Over his shoulder, Celeste could see a woman standing there with maybe a dozen shopping bags scattered on the floor around her, her eyes narrowed with intense dislike. The link between him and Celeste had been so strong that he'd just abandoned his partner, left her stranded in the middle of an aisle like a lost sheep.

And she didn't look happy about it, either.

Celeste grinned, enjoying the rush of malice she felt, fresh and strong once more. He was in for a mouthful of abuse from the girl-friend (wife?) and no amount of side-tracking would get him out of it, by the look of things. She was a big, strapping girl; disgustingly healthy-looking with a mass of auburn hair.

She probed his (*Sam, his name is Sam Hansen*) mind, searching out the key to his heart. She probed past his memories of Marianne (funny, she looked more like a Mary or a Brenda), past his experiences—all the accumulated detritus that made the average human mind look more like a lost-property room. She saw him falter slightly as she probed deeper into his psyche, into his fantasies and desires, and moved further in—time was short.

On the face of it, this was a normal guy in his early thirties. He was tall, blond, and definitely attractive. He knew he was and it was a matter of complete indifference to him; something she always found refreshing. So many truly attractive men were really narcissists at heart, finding love of a sort with women that were really their own mirror image, if they would only admit it.

But she had sensed something else within Sam, buried deep inside. She doubted whether he even knew it was there, except in his dreams, when he allowed himself to float free. His soul was deeply dramatic—she saw a love of the twenties and thirties, the finery of the Art Deco period, a longing for a return to that glamour in today's more prosaic world. That was her way in with him, then. She would invade his dreams as she had already appeared; at least in his mind's eye. She knew when he'd caught sight of her, what he'd seen was a twenties-style beauty—black hair cut in a bob, green eyes, red lips. Well then, that was what she would be—at least for him.

She felt stronger already. Confident she had his interest now, she broke eye contact and joined the throng heading for the lift that had just opened. She reached the safety of its interior with seconds to spare, and watched the doors shut just as he got within reach of her, leaving him standing at the lift's entrance, expression vacant and somehow lost. She smiled to herself, secure in the knowledge that even though he'd only seen her for a moment, he was hers now, and she could renew the contact at will.

Chapter 5

"Lift your head a bit, love. That's right. Now look off to one side, right, look at the camera..."

Even as he was reeling off instructions, Terry knew he was onto something special. The camera loved this girl. Really loved her. He had a feeling he was looking at the genesis of the newest supermodel. Move over Kate Moss, Tyra Banks...here comes Celeste. She wasn't telling anyone what her second name was. "Just Celeste will do fine," was all she'd say. She had a voice like crushed velvet, and there was a hint of an accent, wasn't there? He couldn't quite place it, but it sounded vaguely American—from the south, maybe, but very faint. Whatever it was, it was hot. To Terry's experienced, if a little jaded, eye she looked electric, exuding a raw sexuality he had rarely seen exhibited with such force.

And she was well aware of the effect she was having.

This was her first photo shoot. Terry had spotted her while meandering around Brent Cross, and with a lot of fast talking had managed to convince her that he wasn't some sort of pervert, but a professional photographer who could make her a lot of money. When she seemed interested in posing for him, he'd broached the subject of whether she had any objections to more...adult work. She'd laughed and shaken her head. It was then that they'd set up this shoot. She was spectacular, at least his own height of five foot eight, if not taller. And she had sleek, shiny black hair bobbed to jaw length. He wondered whether she had any Native American blood, what with the hair and those high, angular cheekbones. Her skin was milky white, though, and her *eyes*... She had the greenest eyes he had ever seen, almost clear green —like liquid jade.

"All right, love, that's it. We're finished."

She smiled gratefully as he started switching the lights off, no doubt glad to escape the heat. Terry started to pack his equipment away, curiously uneasy. He definitely didn't want to see her getting dressed, which was ridiculous really, seeing as he had just photographed her wearing not much more than a smile. He justified such pictures by saying that everyone had to start somewhere, didn't they? And she certainly hadn't had any objections. Usually it was all just meat—he had seen too much flesh to get turned on by it these days. A picture with a bit of mystery was much sexier, he thought. More of a turn on.

"What's the matter, Terry?"

Startled, he nearly dropped the camera. She had come up behind him. He could feel her brushing against him, felt her breath on his neck. She hadn't made a sound.

"Nothing. I was... I was just putting my stuff away, that's all."

"I thought you seemed a bit nervous."

He laughed and was embarrassed by the high-pitched sound that emerged—nothing like his usual laugh. "No, not nervous. I'm fine."

With the last of his stuff put away, Terry had no excuse not to turn around. Funny, he was almost afraid to. It had been a long time since he had been this uneasy around a girl.

He braced himself to appear disinterested, and slowly turned around, ready to confirm that this was all just a tease. He found himself face to face with her, literally. If there was an inch of space between them, he'd be surprised. Her perfume surrounded him, an intoxicating musk he found as intimidating as it was enticing. He had the impression that had been her intention all along.

"Was I all right?"

"You were amazing, love. You'll go far, I think."

She laughed again, this time sounding surprisingly cynical. "Further than you think, Terry. Much further."

He had no idea what she meant, and he wasn't sure he wanted to. She wasn't the first ambitious girl he'd come across that thought showing everything she had was the passport to superstardom, even if he had needed to use a little persuasion—and he was fairly sure she wouldn't be the last.

"Do you like me, Terry?"

He cleared his throat. "What?"

"Do you like me?"

He paused, expecting a trick and not ready yet to hear the punchline. "Of...of course I like you."

She leaned close and whispered into his ear. "Are you sure?"

"Look, what is this? What do you want?"

Celeste smiled and cast her eyes down, shyly. He had the distinct impression that her shyness was just an act, an opinion that was reinforced when she sighed and bit her lip before peeking up through her lashes. She started toying with his shirt buttons, leaned even closer.

"I want you to like me. At least to start with."

Her hands slipped inside his shirt, pushed it down his arms, leaving his chest bare and his arms pinioned. He closed his eyes and felt her fingers trace their way across his chest and down to his stomach. He felt her undoing his jeans and knew he ought to stop this, say something, *anything*. She couldn't be more than seventeen, far too young for him. She was scarcely more than jailbait, for God's sake. Then he gasped in shock as her hands slipped into his jeans and she took hold of his erection. His eyes flew open as she kissed him full on the lips, tongue darting into his open mouth and teasing his tongue.

Marie O'Regan

When she broke the kiss, he saw a grin, wicked in its lasciviousness, appear on her sweet, innocent face.

"When I'm finished, you'll adore me."

Chapter 6

Sam was lost from the very first time he saw her. She reminded him of an actress from the silent movies—lambent skin, so cold and white, like a pearl in clear water. Eyes you could drown in and a mouth that promised delights to be treasured, if only they could be endured.

He just caught a glimpse of her, that first time. She glanced sideways for a moment before stepping into a lift, and he was willing to swear she looked straight at him; her eyes glowing like green fire. Her mouth curved upward in the hint of a smile, and she held his gaze just a bit too long for the connection to be chance.

He started forward, pushing through the crowd, desperate to stop the lift before she got away—to say, "Hello, don't I know you? *I love you...*" Madness; especially as he'd left Marianne behind so he could chase this creature. This *vision*.

Marianne, he knew, would be less than overjoyed at being left standing, stranded in the middle of a department store surrounded by a sea of carrier bags.

He managed to catch her eye just before the lift doors closed; caught a quick glimpse of the beginnings of a smile as he opened his mouth to finally speak, and then she was gone.

Sam was bereft. He stood there, panting, gazing at the lift doors like an abandoned pup...and then he remembered what he'd done. Gingerly, he stole a sideways glance at Marianne, unsure exactly how much trouble he was in.

A lot. She was standing there, arms folded, with all her weight on one leg, tapping the other foot. A stance Sam knew only too well. He made his way sheepishly back to her and started to pick up the bags littering the floor by her feet. He figured he was dead anyway, but it made sense to at least try and minimise the damage.

Marianne unpursed her lips enough to spit out a question. "Well?"

He affected an air of innocence. "I thought I saw someone I knew."

"*Good* friend, was she?"

The suspicion in the air was palpable, and Sam was amazed at people's ability to sense an argument brewing, almost as if they could smell it in the air. A circle cleared around them as if by magic, people unwittingly diverging as their paths crossed the danger zone, like ants avoiding an obstacle. Sam wouldn't have been surprised to see a neon sign above their heads, emblazoned with the legend "DANGER: ROW IMMINENT." He'd have to be careful. Marianne had a famously sharp tongue, and she could be brutal. Should he admit it was the girl he'd been chasing? Or should he press one of the other occupants of the lift into service?

No contest.

"I wasn't chasing *her!*" Sam assumed a tone of righteous indignation, but at least had the decency to feel slightly ashamed of himself. "I was chasing Simon."

"Simon who?"

"Simon Morrison. I used to work with him, up to about a year ago. Then one day he just didn't turn up."

"I can't wait to hear what happened."

Neither could Sam. Marianne's voice was dripping sarcasm, but it was too late to change stories now. He pushed on blindly, just hoping he could remember his lies if he had to restate them later.

"Neither can I. The bastard owed me £150 when he left. I want it back."

Marianne was still unsure, but Sam thought she was beginning to thaw. "What on earth did you lend him £150 for?"

"So he could get his car fixed. It was only a week 'til payday, so I thought it was a safe bet." Sam kept an eye on her as he carried on retrieving the bags. He knew she was thinking it over, looking for loopholes in the story. So was he, but he couldn't see any. She thought she knew Sam pretty well, and she did in many ways. They both knew he tended to overcompensate by being excessively defensive when lying.

Not this time. Please.

"Where to now?" Sam stood, waiting for Marianne to make up her mind. There was one thing about her he could always rely on: the woman loved to shop. She could spend an entire day at the mall and come home with nothing more than a pair of tights and a beatific smile at the memory of all the things she had rummaged through, tried on, and generally had a good time with. More often than not, though, she came home laden with bags and with her credit card smoking at the edges. Distracted, she looked around, getting her bearings. Sam knew she was mentally listing all the shops she hadn't had a chance to get through yet. Glancing at his watch, he saw it was twelve fifteen. Time to put them both out of her misery.

"Tell you what. Let's go and have lunch. My treat."

She hesitated, gazing at all the shelves as yet unexamined.

Time for the ultimate sacrifice. "We can always come back afterwards."

That did it. She smiled happily and followed him to the little restaurant set down in the middle of the shopping centre's main aisle. There, diners could watch the browsers as they chewed, whilst those accompanying avid shoppers could envy those eating—nothing like a little mutual coveting to whet the appetite.

Lunch was pleasant enough, and Marianne was back to her sparkling best, but something was missing. The stranger had disappeared into the depths of the shopping centre and no doubt had finished her shopping and escaped by now, as they would in due course.

Life would go on.

At the moment though, it all seemed a little flat.

As he put the key in the lock that night, Sam still felt a little weird. Dislocated. Nothing looked quite right; everything he touched seemed to resonate with an echo of what might have been, had things taken a different course. Stupid. Whatever he was yearning for had never existed, and never would, which was exactly as it should be. He was happy with Marianne, and life was good.

So why didn't that make him feel any better?

The lock finally decided to cooperate, and he flicked on the light as the front door finished its swing inward. Usually, Sam got a buzz from coming home. It was their first home, in an Art Deco block of flats in Muswell Hill, full of period features, and they'd spent ages getting it just right. Pale walls, huge black leather sofas...posters on the walls from some of his favourite movies: *Brief Encounter, Pandora's Box, An Affair To Remember*...but tonight he felt nothing. Tonight it seemed cold and vacant, as sterile as a waiting room in some indeterminate corporate monolith.

Marianne pushed past Sam, impatient to deposit her booty in the living room, ready to be exclaimed over once more. With her inside, the flat seemed to regain some of its usual warmth and he started to relax, grateful for the force of nature that was forever Marianne.

He dropped his share of the bags and went to pull the curtains closed. The living room looked out onto shared gardens at the back of the block, and they were screened from the surrounding buildings on either side by a dense layer of trees. It gave the illusion of living in a much quieter area than they actually did. Something moved in the shadows, just at the tree line, and he froze.

It was her. Even though all he really saw was a flash of white and the impression of a face that etched itself onto his mind even as she drew back under the trees, her presence was unmistakeable. The air was suddenly, impossibly, heavy with her perfume, and he inhaled deeply, savouring the aroma. Then she was gone, and Marianne was beside Sam at the window, eager to see what had so captured his attention.

She pressed her nose against the window, breath misting the glass. "What is it? What's out there?"

Her breathless curiosity broke the spell, and he came back to reality with a bump. The trees were their usual prosaic selves once more, the eldritch atmosphere gone.

Forcing a smile, Sam turned to her. "I thought I saw a fox."

She frowned, tried to block the room's light out by covering her brow with her hands so she could see outside more clearly. "Really? Where?"

He gave her a second to see and then pulled the curtain shut. It wasn't an experience he felt like sharing. "It's gone now."

Marianne looked at him oddly, but said nothing. She probably thought he was just in one of his moods, fed up after a day following her around shop after shop. She was partly right, at that. Sam left her unwrapping her treasures and made his way to the bathroom, muttering something about taking a shower.

Marianne barely even looked up.

Alone in the bathroom, he finally allowed himself to relax. The afternoon's encounter had rattled him more than he'd realised, and it had been a strain hiding that from Marianne. Theirs was what you might call a volatile relationship, but it was a strong one, for all that—perhaps even *because* of that. The rush of desire Sam had felt today, for a complete stranger, had been totally unexpected and had left him feeling sleazy, and somehow unclean.

He turned on the shower and undressed quickly, musing idly on how a day's shopping made him feel dirtier and more rumpled at the day's end than virtually anything else. He stepped into the water and felt the stress melt away as he grabbed the soap and began to wash, noting the strong lemony smell that wafted up, held by the clouds of steam. Marianne and her toiletries! She did love her lotions and potions, and the stronger they smelled the better it seemed to him.

Sam let his mind wander over the encounter in the department store. *Encounter.* Now there was an evocative word. It sounded as if they should be surrounded by clouds of steam, and the world should be a chiaroscuro creation of light and shadow.

She was beautiful.

In black and white, she would have been out of this world.

Her hair was pure black, shining like moonlit water—cut in a bob, very sleek. She reminded him of someone, but he couldn't put his finger on it.

It couldn't have been her in the woods. He was just being stupid. Sam made a conscious effort to put her out of his mind as he rubbed himself dry and made his way into the kitchen, a towel around his waist.

There was no use asking Marianne what she had planned for dinner. She was so busy going through her new magazines that she hadn't even noticed him coming back in. Who was he kidding? She probably hadn't even noticed him leave.

Sam picked up the phone and dialled their local pizza place, ordered the usual. Moving into the kitchen, he took a couple of beers out of the fridge and headed back into the living room. Handing a beer to Marianne, he let her off the hook.

"I've ordered pizza."

She grinned up at him, relieved. "Thanks. Cheese feast, I hope?"

"Of course."

"Garlic bread?"

"And Diet Coke."

"Great. I'm starving." She gestured at the magazines and bags littering the sofa and floor around it. "Help me put this stuff away, would you?" The expression on her face was comical.

"Is putting it away that bad?"

"I suppose not." She grinned suddenly and inflicted the coup de grâce without a hint of remorse. "There's always next time, isn't there?"

Laughing, Sam hauled her upright, and they took the bags through to the bedroom. It took over half an hour to put everything away, and they were just finishing when the doorbell signalled the arrival of dinner.

Marianne went and paid while Sam scuttled into the bedroom in search of pyjamas Then they adjourned to the sofa and curled up to scoff pizza and channel hop; a perfect end to a day's purgatory.

Sam woke up at two in the morning, sure he had heard something. His head was hanging over the arm of the sofa, and his neck felt as if it was broken. He felt something weighing down his torso and forced his head upright, only to see Marianne sprawled across his lap, comatose, her head lolling on his chest. Sam groaned. Marianne was a very heavy sleeper. He tried shaking her gently. Nothing. He eased her head up as gently as he could and slid out from underneath her, lowering her carefully back down before settling onto the floor. She barely even twitched.

The television was still on, but there was nothing coherent to watch. The screen was full of static, casting the room in a flickering light that made Sam feel as if he were in the cinema, waiting for the main feature to come on. He reached forward to turn it off and stopped, suddenly sure he could see something taking shape in the prickles of black and white.

Ghost images superimposed themselves over the snow on the screen, like the continuation of a dream. The only problem was, he couldn't remember the first part.

A girl was running down a long hallway, although whether she was running to something or away from it wasn't clear. The music was crashing and discordant, a maelstrom of brass and percussion accompanying her steps into light, then dark, as windows flashed past, signalling both her progress and the length of the apparently endless hall she was racing down. He realised it must be an old silent movie when it dawned on him that there was no sound of her breathing, of her feet slapping against the flagstones. No screaming, even though her mouth was stretched wide in terror as she hurtled on, banging against walls as she went.

Then she turned around.

It was her. Same ebony hair, same enormous eyes. It was impossible, but there she was, and all of a sudden it hit him. Louise Brooks. That was who the woman he'd seen reminded him of.

Half smiling, Sam settled down to watch. So it wasn't old. It was some arty effort made recently. Who cared? He could sit and watch her to his heart's content and find out her name at the end.

The girl turned a corner and stopped short, her face a mask of fear. Sam could see her chest heaving as she fought for breath. The camera cut quickly from her face to a view of what it was that had so terrified her.

It was just an empty room. Why was that so scary? She was in a bedroom, old and neglected. It was dominated by an ageing four-poster bed, its drapes rotting away. In places, it looked more like cobwebs than the velvet it looked to have been originally. The decaying curtains hanging from the tall, dirty windows had obviously matched them at some time. There was a mouldering rug on the dusty wooden floor, and a large chest of drawers stood against one wall. Otherwise, the room was bare, except for the patina of dust that covered everything. It was strange—there were no pictures, no mirrors, no flowers, nothing.

Then the camera zoomed in on a door, hidden in the shadows. The music became more threatening, and Sam groaned. Yet another movie where a beautiful girl was lured to her death by her insatiable, unbelievable curiosity, when anyone with half a brain would get the hell out of there.

Sure enough, she inched forward, music growing more and more menacing. Whoever had directed this certainly believed in milking a scene for all it was worth. Sam was a little embarrassed to find that, even though he could see how blatant the device was, he'd succumbed and was now hunched forward, trying not to breathe as he watched. Now the camera zoomed in on the door handle. Her hand came into shot, reaching for it. Violins screeched in the background, shouting a warning to all but her, yet she persisted. The camera flicked back to her face, scared yet determined, as the dark, wooden door slowly opened.

Sam hunched forward a little more, Marianne forgotten. He was spellbound.

The expression on her face shifted from fear to exaltation, making Sam's insides drop, and when the camera cut once more to show what she saw, he saw why.

Marianne.

Even though he saw her there, hanging from a rope in a walk-in cupboard, it didn't register properly at first.

Almost as soon as he'd registered what he was seeing, it was gone. The picture started to flicker and die, replaced by the white noise it had come from—but not before the girl looked straight at him. And smiled.

Sam's stomach did a slow roll as what he had seen finally began to sink in. He shuddered, suddenly ice cold. Wanted to turn around, see if Marianne was still asleep—and felt stupid for being too scared to do it.

"Turn the telly off, Sam, for God's sake."

He must have jumped a mile.

Marianne laughed, stretched, and joined him on the floor. Reaching forward, she turned the television off. "My God, you're shaking like a leaf." She grabbed a throw off a chair and wrapped it round his shoulders, rubbed his arm to try and warm him. "You're frozen!"

Sam put his arms around her and hugged her, hard. Buried his face against her shoulder, pulled the throw around both of them, eager for her heat. He could still feel the desolation—the *heartbreak*—of seeing her hanging there, dead eyes staring from a fly-blown face as she swung gently in a non-existent breeze, and just wanted to hold her close, reassure himself that she was here, that she was real.

She hugged him back, tried to cheer him up, bring him out of this state. "What was it, some ancient horror film?"

"Something like that." He let out a shaky sigh, relieved to hear that his voice sounded relatively normal. He got up, pulling a chuckling Marianne with him, and made for the door. "Let's go to bed."

She didn't argue. They were both exhausted.

Marianne fell asleep almost immediately, head cushioned on Sam's shoulder, legs wrapped around his. He held her as tight as he could without waking her.

Sam jumped as a shadow raked its way across the wall and then laughed, feeling stupid. It was just the branches of the magnolia tree outside their bedroom blowing in the wind; happened all the time. Marianne was safe in his arms, right here with him. So why did he still feel as if he'd lost her?

He had a feeling it would be a very long night if he kept this up, jumping at shadows while he was awake and too scared of what might invade his dreams should he fall asleep.

Chapter 7

When Sam woke the next morning, he was already reaching for Marianne, wanting to reassure himself he'd been wrong about what he saw, vague images from his dreams perpetuating what he'd seen on the TV last night. His hands closed on a crumpled sheet.

He sat up with a start, sure he'd lost her. He heard a woman laugh—not Marianne. It was close; a throaty, sexy laugh—but with a bite. Sam moaned, just as Marianne walked into the bedroom with two steaming mugs of tea. She stopped cold when she saw his expression, making him wonder what his face must have looked like, and who'd got more of a fright.

"Jesus, Sam. What's wrong?" She came over and sat down beside him, putting the tea on the bedside table. He buried his head on her shoulder and held her tight.

"Bad dream, that's all." The words were muffled against the softness of her throat, and she smelt wonderful. Sam sat up, unsure what else to say.

Marianne just grinned and handed him his tea before climbing back into bed with hers. She didn't ask any more about his supposed nightmare, and he was grateful for that. Let her think he'd freaked himself out with a bad horror movie. It wouldn't be the first time. How do you tell your lover that you just saw her hanging dead in a cupboard? They concentrated instead on the mundane and eventually succeeded in banishing the night's terrors.

Mid-afternoon and they were standing at the top of a hill on Hampstead Heath. You could see most of London from here, and it was depressing how much scarcer the trees became almost as soon as you passed the Heath's boundaries. Further in, it was all grey—row upon row of grey buildings with the occasional little pocket of green that was a local park or a grassy area in the middle of an estate, forlornly trying to restore the inner city. Fat chance.

Sam turned to the Heath, instead, which at least gave the illusion of health. The air was marginally cleaner. Dogs were chasing the falling leaves, bounding ecstatically from heap to heap, scattering flurries of red and gold everywhere. The park was full of people eager to escape their homes or just get out and enjoy the day, away from the concerns of home, if only for a while. People needed to recharge, Sam thought, and he'd always believed fresh air was vital for that.

Marianne made for a bench just ahead, and he ambled along after her, content just to let the world go by while they walked off Sunday lunch. Two Afghan hounds were gambolling gracefully towards them, creamy fur swaying as they moved, lending them the illusion of slow motion. Sam looked around for a likely owner, maybe a leggy blonde with a fur coat. He found the fur coat, but it didn't belong to any blonde. It was the woman from the mall again.

She was walking towards him so gracefully, almost as if gliding, enveloped in a huge fur coat so dark it almost seemed to absorb daylight —a perfect match for the ebony of her hair. Her face was so pale in contrast that from a distance it looked like some sort of kabuki mask.

Marianne and a few others were watching her, openly hostile. Sam wondered if Marianne realised it was the same woman they'd seen the day before or whether it was just the fur coat attracting such hostility.

As she drew level with Marianne, the woman glanced her way. Sam was shocked to see her flinch. The stranger leaned in closer to Marianne, her expression savage as she whispered something. Marianne looked terrified, and Sam broke into a run, eager to get to her and make sure she was safe.

The woman with the dogs left her shivering on the bench and was striding towards him. When she was close enough, the woman reached out a tiny hand encased in black leather and placed it on Sam's arm. He yelped and tried to pull it away. She had barely touched his jacket and yet he could feel his skin crawling. The woman leaned in close, her lips brushing against his cheek. She wore a heavy perfume, musky, that made him think of ripping her clothes off right there and then. Arousal began to overtake the fear, and he leaned in closer, breathed in her scent, his head swimming.

She put her mouth against Sam's ear, and whispered, *"Kill the bitch."*

Sam reeled. "What?"

She had already released him, and he stumbled backwards. From the corner of his eye, he saw Marianne spring up and start running towards them. Whoever this woman was, she was leaving.

From a distance of about ten yards, she glanced back and whispered something else. Sam heard it as clearly as if she was pressed up close against him. *"You would if you loved me. We could be together."* Then she was gone.

Marianne reached Sam and snaked her arm around his waist. "What the hell was that?"

"God knows. Some psycho." Sam watched the stranger's progress as she swept down the hill. She didn't look back once, and people were unconsciously swerving out of her way as she passed them, giving her a clear path. The dogs were nowhere to be seen.

Marianne wasn't about to give up that easily. "What did she say to you?"

"She muttered something about keeping you under control." He turned then, looked directly at her. "Why? What did she say to you?"

"Nothing." She wouldn't look at him, but Sam could see she was shaking.

"She must have said *something* to you."

"Well, she didn't, all right? Stop going on at me." With that she was gone, storming off down the hill towards the gate, heading for the car. Sam wanted to follow her, but that probably wasn't a very good idea. She was terrified but not about to talk, and he knew from experience not to push her.

Sam's mind was made up for him when he saw that the woman hadn't left at all; she was waiting at the gate for an unsuspecting Marianne. He started to run, desperate to get to Marianne before this woman could hurt her. It felt like things were spinning out of control, and the smell of her perfume was all around him as he ran. This was *crazy*—they were just out for a walk in the park, for God's sake. Things like this just didn't happen.

When Sam reached Marianne, the other woman was nowhere to be seen. Marianne wasn't talking, but at least she slowed her pace enough that they could walk together comfortably. She was still angry, but not really with Sam. He walked along beside her in silence, content to let her cool down. He was usually a pretty easy-going sort; it took a lot to make him lose his temper. Marianne, on the other hand, was what you'd call hot-blooded. When they first started living together, it was a side of Marianne that took Sam completely by surprise. It was like watching a volcano erupt. She threw things, ranted—and God help you if you got in her way when she was in that state. He'd made that mistake only once, but once was all it took.

Sam had just spotted the car when he felt Marianne's hand sneaking into his. He didn't embarrass her by saying anything more, just squeezed it briefly as he ferreted in his pocket for his car keys with his other hand. He put the radio on as he drove, letting the mixture of inane chat and bland background music defuse the atmosphere. By the time they reached home, she was back to normal.

In bed that night, Sam lay for what seemed like hours, trying to figure out what was going on. This woman had to have come from somewhere. The first time he had seen her was at the shopping centre, then she had been in the woods behind the flat. Then there had been the weird business with the television. Today she had shown up in the park. He was nobody; why on earth would she be following *him*, of all people?

Marianne shifted beside him and rolled over, muttering indistinctly in her sleep. She was the total opposite of this stranger, with blazing curls spread out across the pillows, her cheeks warm and pink. Sam put the stranger out of his mind and cuddled up to Marianne. He loved to lay close to her like this, smelling her hair, which always smelt totally unlike anybody's he'd ever known, full of life. Finally able to relax, he drifted off to sleep.

Celeste had been in England for a little more than twenty years now, and Clive had finally started to see some signs of ageing in his mistress. Seventeen years old when they'd arrived, she had wasted no time in seducing every eligible young man she came across, leaving them broken and weary when she was done. Clive was amused to note that they invariably chose plainer, quieter women to marry afterwards—he imagined it made for a much calmer life. Certainly it would be safer.

The colonel had died some five years earlier, his only comfort seeing the creature that had been his daughter gradually run out of victims as her notoriety grew. In his final moments, he had promised Clive that he would keep watching over him, even after death. "I'll pray for you, Clive," he had said. "I'll pray for your soul." Once he was gone, Clive had been alone with Celeste, and he'd known he was damned.

Celeste had greeted the beginning of World War I with glee. She had gone through one generation's young men and become something of a pariah in the process. She saw the war as a clearing of the decks.

Sickened, Clive stayed out of her way as much as possible. She had taken to her bed to wait the war out, wait for the coming of "fresh meat," as she put it; her next chance to shine.

One morning, Clive woke to the sound of screaming. He quickly made his way into the hall and saw one of the maids heading straight for him at almost breakneck speed. Her eyes were wide with shock. The second maid, a timid little thing who hardly spoke to him at all, usually, was crouching against the wall, shivering. Clive tried to stop the screaming girl, but she shrugged off his hand and kept on running, still keening. She headed downstairs, and moments later Clive heard the kitchen door slam, followed by the scraping of a chair. The screaming stopped abruptly, only to be replaced by long, shuddering sobs. Gently, Clive knelt beside the other girl, put his hand on her shoulder. The stench of urine was overpowering, and he could see the stain spreading across her skirt. The poor girl was deep in shock, so badly scared that she had wet herself and never even noticed.

"Mary..."

Nothing. He might as well not even have been there, for all the notice she took of him. He took hold of her elbows and carefully helped her to her feet, supporting her as best he could. She had no strength in her legs at all; he could have been lifting a rag doll.

A guttural moan came from further down the hall. The effect on Mary was electric. She clung to Clive, sobbing, and buried her head against his chest. He could feel her shaking as he held her, trying to

46

comfort her, calm her down. Gradually, she regained some measure of control, at least enough to respond to his questions.

He led her back into his room, sat her down on a wooden chair by his desk. She sat there, trembling, while he went to the desk and opened a drawer. He took out a bottle of rum and poured her a glass, made her drink it down. She shuddered and coughed, spluttering as the fiery liquid burned its way down into her stomach. But at least she started to get some colour back into her cheeks. Clive sat on the bed opposite and took her small hands in his large ones.

"Mary."

She looked up at him slowly, not wanting to answer.

"Mary, what happened?"

Mary shuddered. "Cook."

"What about Cook?"

"Me and Annie, we heard her choking, see? So we went to her room to see if she was all right..."

Clive heard the panic mounting in her voice again, so he increased the pressure at once, not wanting to hurt her. He just needed the answers.

"Was she? Mary, was she all right?" Of course, she wouldn't be—he knew that. But he had to ask. Tears started to flow once more, but at least she managed to keep it under control this time.

"Oh my God, we left her...the blood..." Mary screamed. "We left her!"

She was off and running up the stairs before Clive could even take it all in. He leapt to his feet and followed Mary, cursing himself for not checking on the source of the moaning earlier. They were too late now, that much was obvious. Cook was lying on the floor, legs twisted in the sheets where she had fallen out of bed, arms stretched out imploringly towards the door. She had died while trying to get help. Her eyes stared blindly at the door, pleading.

The room looked like an abattoir. The whole of the bed was drenched with blood so dark it looked black. Clive could actually taste the coppery aroma, feel it clogging the back of his throat. He forced back the nausea. The front of her nightdress was awash with blood. She lay there, mouth open as if about to call for help, filled with congealed blood.

He heard gagging sounds coming from behind him and remembered Mary. Best to get her out of here. He put an arm around her shoulders and ushered out her out of the room, down the stairs, and into the kitchen. Annie was in there, crying. Angrily, Clive sent her to fetch the doctor—it was the only thing she was any good for. He sat Mary down and gave her a glass of water, ordered her to stay there while he informed Celeste (as if she didn't already know).

As he climbed the stairs to Celeste's room, he mused on the fact that it had been the cook who had suffered Celeste's wrath. Cook had been strong, and wise, too. She had known something was wrong with Celeste. He had known that from the start; it had been evident in the excessive respect she had shown her, verging on reverence. More than once, thinking herself unobserved, Clive had seen Cook cross herself as she made her way back to the haven of her kitchen after an encounter with Celeste. Yet she had said nothing to anyone, not even Clive—though whether out of loyalty or fear would never be known now. He had a feeling that could well have been her downfall.

Entering Celeste's room, he saw he was right. She looked so happy she was almost glowing, delighting in all the commotion. Celeste lay propped against numerous pillows as she always did, to ease her breathing. Yet Clive had the distinct impression that this time she didn't need them. Celeste had an air of being stronger, more aware, with the vitality, if not the appearance, of a much younger woman.

"Get rid of those two, Clive; they're no use to anybody. Completely hysterical, the pair of them."

Clive didn't try to argue their case. It was better for both of them if they did leave—and the sooner the better. He noticed the fact Celeste hadn't mentioned the cook, but said nothing. Her own pride in her amusements would lead her to boast of what she'd done soon enough, remind him she was in charge. Acknowledging her order, he turned to leave. The less he had to look at her, the better he liked it. He felt safer that way.

"Oh, and Clive..." Her voice dripped with spite. Clive found it hard to control his disgust as he turned to face her once more. "Once they're gone and you've disposed of the mess—come and see me."

"Yes, ma'am."

The mess. She hadn't even bothered to disguise her knowledge of what had occurred, just ordered him to dispose of the remains like an old rag. At least he knew now what had happened to the cook's tongue. Celeste's mouth had still been stained with the blood, and she had only swallowed it when he had walked into the room.

Tears in his eyes, Clive heard the front door bang once more. He went downstairs to greet the doctor and show him the cook's body.

The police were called, of course, and they all had to make statements of what they had seen (nothing), what they had heard (nothing), and what they had eventually found. They had poked their noses into every room in the house, banging walls and searching cupboards. The consensus of opinion, backed by the doctor, was that it must have been a wild animal of some sort, maybe a rat, which had entered the room while Cook was asleep.

Clive noticed a studied indifference in their attitudes that was echoed in the demeanour of the maids, in marked contrast to their earlier behaviour. He could sense Celeste glossing over things as usual, working hard to maintain the patina of respectability she needed. Still, the abomination she had worked this morning must have boosted her powers considerably.

"Terrible tragedy, of course, but..." she said, ushering the police out of the house and closing the door behind them.

The girls didn't even make a fuss when he let them go, though by now Clive wouldn't have been surprised by anything. Then they were gone.

The house was empty, though Clive was aware of strange, shifting shapes at the periphery of his vision. He was pretty sure they were the house's "familiars," as Celeste had called them, a mixture of spirits that had died in this house and the spirits of victims tied to her by the manner of their deaths. Were they what she had set on the cook? They were watching him, waiting. He didn't like to wonder why.

When he walked into Celeste's bedroom, he wasn't really surprised to see that she was out of bed, kneeling naked on the floor in the middle of the room. She had drawn a five-pointed star on the floorboards with the wax dripping from a black candle. The smell the scented wax gave off was nauseating, and Clive tried desperately not to be sick. She had drawn the curtains tight shut, excluding all light, save for the little flames here and there. The heat was stifling.

Celeste stood and motioned Clive forward. "Take your clothes off."

Her voice was oddly cold, disconnected, but Clive knew she was merely focussing all of her energies on what lay ahead. There was no way to stop it, he knew. It was best just to go along with her, and less painful. At least now he had an idea of what the familiars had been waiting for. He stripped quickly and, following her direction, lay in the centre of the star, taking care he didn't break the lines of wax anywhere. Not wanting to see what came next, he closed his eyes and lay there, trembling. The dance began again, and it was all he could do to try and distance himself mentally, shut the sensations and the sense of disgust out.

Then it was over, and he felt Celeste stand up and move away.

"Get dressed and get out!"

He did as she said as quickly and quietly as he could, well aware that she was absolutely furious; though whether with him or with herself, he couldn't tell. She was beautiful again, looking even better than she had at seventeen. Physically, of course, she looked much the same as she had at that age, but she held herself with a new maturity now—a self-confidence that belied her apparent age.

She turned and stared at him, panic in her eyes. "Wait!"

"Ma'am?"

"Get rid of the staff, Clive. Too many prying ears and flapping tongues."

Clive stared, aghast. "Are you sure, ma'am? All of them?"

She smiled, then, content in the knowledge of her safety, once he'd done as he asked. "Of course I'm sure. We don't need anyone else, do we? We'll be fine on our own." She'd dismissed him then with a wave of the hand.

Clive shut the door and leant against it, eyes closed. There would be no reprieve now, no let up. Not if they were alone—for God knew how long.

Chapter 8

Celeste spent the next few days wandering around the local area, absorbing the changes that had occurred during the last twenty years or so. She noticed that St. Michael's, the church facing St. Joseph's at the end of Hornsey Lane, was a place of worship no longer; it had been converted into luxury apartments. She smiled grimly. They were probably beautiful, but she had no doubt the very building itself would try and repel her should she try and move there.

Standing atop Archway Bridge, she watched the traffic stream by; the curse of the modern age. She hadn't been out and about for so long now and found the increase in pollution incredible. The most depressing thing of all, she thought, was the speed at which she'd probably get used to it. At the moment, though, the air was so thick she could taste it.

Celeste decided, looking down, to take a walk down Highgate Hill into Archway—see what had happened to the shops down there. From here it looked dingy and seedy, as if it had decayed massively since the sixties and seventies.

She walked all the way down Junction Road as far as Tufnell Park, and at the end of it wished she hadn't. The whole place had a tired, worn-out air that she found thoroughly depressing. Reaching the end of the road, she decided to take a right onto Dartmouth Park Hill and walk back up to Highgate. As far as she could remember, it would bring her out onto Highgate Hill at the junction with Hornsey Lane. She'd be virtually home.

Celeste had only just turned the corner when someone collided with her, knocking her flat. She heard him muttering flustered apologies, but refused to look up at first, concentrating instead on picking up the contents of her bag and trying to keep her temper under control. She didn't have enough power yet to risk everything by annihilating this fool. She needed to avoid attention.

Forcing herself to sound relatively unconcerned, Celeste allowed him to aid in the retrieval of her belongings and help her up. She was by now beginning to see the humour in the situation.

Finally, she allowed herself to look at him. Her anger evaporated in an instant. He was nothing special, certainly not what she'd think of as handsome. He was tall, probably around six feet, with sandy hair and blue-grey eyes, and he carried an air of sorrow that was palpable. Yet there was something about him that appealed to her. There was an air of gentleness, even warmth, that she seldom found in her conquests.

Then again, she had to admit she didn't usually inspire gentleness. Her appetites were usually too voracious, more savage. He looked so careworn, and she could empathise with that, to an extent. Whatever else she was, part of her would always be human, always vulnerable.

The bargain she had struck so long ago had its limitations. "I want men to want me," she'd said. "I want them to adore me." Bess had agreed, knowing full well how things were likely to turn out. What Celeste had really wanted was love. What Bess had given her was a physical need for lust instead. She'd also given her the power to cast a "glamour", making men see what she wanted. She could invade victims' dreams and seduce them there as well, overwhelming their senses until they were hers to play with. Their devotion sustained her, kept her young—but it was far from being loved. Bess had probably gained great satisfaction over the years, thinking of how she had duped Celeste. Just another rich white girl, seeking pleasure with no thought of cost, doomed to forever search for love and only be able to use others.

Men had wanted her, all right. She could number them in the hundreds—and that had sustained her parasitic lifestyle all these years. Without love, however, she had soon come to realise that such an existence was curiously empty. So, embittered, she had taken what pleasure she could in wielding her powers wantonly, destroying many lovers in the process.

She'd even enjoyed it. But this one—Paul—was different, somehow. His stammered request to see her again made her smile. It made a refreshing change to be the pursued instead of the pursuer. She could take time to get to know this one, nurture him. At the very least, she could play at romance for a while. He had potential; she was sure. Maybe, if she was lucky, she had finally found a companion.

Celeste directed him to O'Neill's, a pub in Muswell Hill, enjoying the look of surprise on his face. She had never been there either, but had heard a couple of teenage girls talking about it on the bus and liked the sound of it. It sounded young and vibrant, alive.

She had taken her leave and continued on her walk home, smiling. Things were falling into place.

The photo shoot with Terry had gone well, he said. She laughed out loud at the surprise on his face when she had taken him into her mouth. Considering the photos he had just taken, she wouldn't have thought him so coy. When they had progressed to the bedroom, he had surprised her, in turn, with his staying power. His technique hadn't been at all bad, either.

And then there was Sam.

She had managed to invade his dreams quite successfully, insinuated herself into his desires. To coin a phrase she had heard just recently, she had him by the balls. She liked that phrase. It had a pleasant ring to it. In Sam's case, she realised it was quite literally true. She was pandering to his deepest fantasies, fulfilling his most secret desires. Before long—if all went well—he wouldn't be able to tell what was real and what wasn't. He would be hers, completely.

The girlfriend might be a problem, though. She would bear watching, to see how much influence she actually wielded over Sam. In her experience, Celeste had—almost without exception—found the men to be putty in her hands. It was invariably the women—wives, girlfriends, sisters, mothers, daughters—who first recognised her for what she really was.

The men meant very little to her, usually, apart from the obvious. But strangely, Celeste always regretted having to dispose of the women. She respected them and their misguided attempts to protect their men. Looking back, Celeste couldn't think of a single man she'd seduced that had been, in her opinion, worth the amount of heartbreak they caused.

Her thoughts turned once more to Paul, the man who had swept her off her feet. Literally. She smiled. There was something about him that intrigued her. Something she hadn't come across before. Perhaps, this time, finally things would be different.

Chapter 9

When Paul Marsh left work on that September afternoon, it was a warm and sunny day. Everywhere he looked people were ambling along in twos and threes, enjoying the autumn sunshine. Funny how people automatically cheered up when the sun came out, Paul thought. He wished he could still feel that. He hadn't been able to since...

He veered away from that thought and wondered why he was so cold. It felt as if there was no warmth left for him.

Clare had been gone for six months, and it got harder to bear each day. Whoever called time a great healer was full of it. He had never felt so alone, so *wounded*, in his life. He'd found Clare relatively late, and they'd had twelve wonderful years together, before it turned to ashes.

Their story was a cliché from the start. They'd met at a friend's wedding. He was the best man; she was the chief bridesmaid. It was all over for him the moment he saw her walk up the aisle behind the bride, trying hard to smother the grin that threatened to spread across her face at any moment. They were engaged before they realised their friends had set them up.

For the first couple of years, they guarded their privacy, their time together precious. Then, their thoughts turned to children. It was great fun trying, for a while. When nothing came of it, the doubts started creeping in. Month after month, Clare would watch the calendar. She would convince herself each month that this time it was different. Each time, she was wrong. After about a year, they went to their doctor, and had all the usual tests. Kindly, he tried to reassure them, told them to give it time. Eventually, they gave up trying, and resigned themselves to being childless.

Then, a little over a year ago, their luck changed. He was woken up one morning by the sound of Clare rushing to the bathroom, where she was violently sick.

It turned out not to be the shellfish they'd had the night before, and they started planning. She had a bad pregnancy, and it was a relief when she finally went into labour. It was a month early, but the doctors assured them that wasn't anything to worry about. Everything so far pointed to the baby being healthy; it would probably just be a little on the small side. After she'd had all the initial tests and been hooked up to various monitors, they were left alone to get a little privacy while they could.

Paul finally dozed off in a chair, holding her hand as she rested. He was woken by things beeping and staff flooding into the room. He was still holding his wife's hand, but she was cold, her skin waxy. Paul loosened his grip and stood, leaned over her, ignoring the staff frantically trying to pull him back.

"Clare?" He shook her shoulder, gently, but there was no response. Her eyes remained closed, her expression peaceful. "Clare? Love?"

There was a metallic tang to the air, and he realised with a jolt what had happened when a nurse ran into the room and skidded in the pool of crimson liquid gradually spreading across the floor. He allowed himself to be ushered out and was left to stand in the corridor with no explanation, left to watch and wait as a stream of nurses and doctors swarmed around his wife, barking instructions and calling for blood—always more blood. It seemed like he waited forever.

Hours later, the doctor came out to talk to him. He didn't have to speak; his face said it all. Certain words filtered through: "shock," "haemorrhage," but they were really just dressing. His wife and child were gone, and he was alone. What else needed to be said? He had been allowed to see them both, to say his goodbyes, but it felt as if he was watching someone else do it—some stranger who bore no resemblance to him, to his life as it was supposed to be, at all. Clare looked as if she was sleeping peacefully, their perfect daughter nestled in her arms. A nurse stammered a request for the baby's name, and he named her Hannah, after his mother.

Then he collapsed.

He had no idea what happened over the next two months. Those memories were gone. Obliterated. He just knew that one day he had lost everything, and the next, it was May, and there was a big hole in his life. He knew, of course, that their oldest friends, Bob and Annie, had taken him in for those two months. He could remember little flashes. Drinking late into the night with Bob, talking about Clare, their hopes and dreams. Annie making him eat, shaking her head at his lack of appetite. These things had come and gone, but had left no imprint on his mind, other than the vaguest of shadows.

On that morning in May, he'd woken up in Bob and Annie's spare room, as usual, and stared at the ceiling with shame while listening to them arguing about him in the next room. That had made up his mind.

He walked into the kitchen, sat down to eat breakfast with them, and smiled. Both looked at him, curious, the air still full of their fury and frustration.

"I'm going home," he'd said. "Today."

"Are you sure?" Bob asked.

Paul could see how worried his friend was; even Annie looked decidedly guilty, and he moved to put their minds at rest.

"I am," he nodded. "I don't know how I can even begin to thank you, for everything..."

"You don't need to thank us," Annie said. "We're your friends. We're always here. But—"

Paul smiled. "Annie, don't worry."

She had the good grace to blush, and Bob was looking decidedly uncomfortable. He wasn't happy with Annie's impatience, Paul could see.

Paul tried to put their minds at rest. "I do need to thank you, I know I do; and I hope you know how much all this means to me. But I can't stay here forever." He took Annie's hand and kissed it gently before releasing her. "You're absolutely right about that. I have to get back to the real world. It's time."

Annie wiped her eyes, cleared her throat, and smiled at him. Then she headed back to the safety of the stove where she was cooking bacon.

Bob watched him, still concerned, but only said, "If you're sure, mate..."

"Yep," Paul answered. "I am. Don't worry." Embarrassed, he lifted his tea and took a swig, then attempted to lighten the mood. "You up for a pint or two on Friday?"

Bob grinned. "Course. Usual place?"

And that had been that. With the help of his friends, he'd moved back into his home and started trying to pick up the threads of his life again. He dug out his art supplies and started drawing again, practising in the hope he could resurrect his promising career as an illustrator, but commissions were slow and his heart wasn't really in it. At least, not at first. On weekends, he'd go for a drink with Bob and put the world to rights, and then he'd join him and Annie for Sunday lunch. Routine resumed, of a sort. Except he was alone, and slowly drowning without his family.

Some days he could swear they were still here. He'd wake up to the sound of Clare singing in the kitchen, Hannah laughing and gurgling in her cot, happily playing with her toes. He could even smell the bacon sizzling in the pan. He'd get out of bed and meander into the kitchen or nursery, grinning, and feel his smile die when the rooms were cold and empty, just like him.

He kept the place clean and tidy because that was what Clare would have wanted, but he took no pride in doing so. It was just another function, like sleeping or eating. He supposed he was having a breakdown, of sorts, but it all seemed too remote to worry about. That would have implied that he cared.

He started to come out of it a little at a time, to take more of an interest in things.

Just a little.

But it was a start.

Now, six months later, he was almost back to normal; at least on the outside. He was drawing properly again, and it was starting to come easier. The jobs were starting to flow in a bit more often. On the surface, things were looking up. But nothing could fill the emptiness he still felt inside.

So here he was, walking home with his small bag of single guy groceries on a warm September evening, huddled as usual against the cold he felt inside, thinking about Clare. Then he collided with something and stepped back, stunned into attention.

He had sent the girl he hit sprawling onto the pavement, and she was sitting there, picking up the spilled contents of her handbag. He was relieved to see that she didn't look hurt. He bent down to help her, retrieved a few things that were rolling out of reach. All he could see of her was a sweeping curtain of jaw-length black hair—she kept her head down, muttering to herself; no doubt profanities concerning his clumsiness.

He cleared his throat in a vain attempt at getting her attention, then stuttered an apology. "I'm sorry; I wasn't looking where I was going."

"So I gathered." Her tone was sardonic but not particularly angry, something he was grateful for. The last thing he needed was a slanging match in the middle of the street. She had all her belongings back in her bag now, so he gripped her by the elbow and helped her up.

A few people grinned, probably thinking she was either drunk or stoned. Most just went on by with the peculiarly insular behaviour of city dwellers worldwide; they all lived by the credo of "don't get involved." Life was just easier that way.

Her hand had been grazed, a thin trickle of blood wending its way slowly towards her wrist; but she didn't seem to notice. She still hadn't looked up at him, and he found the whole situation embarrassing. Was she embarrassed? Mad at him? Should he just go?

He dropped her elbow and stood awkwardly by her side, waiting for her to say something, give some sign she was okay and he could escape. She just kept on brushing herself off, as if he wasn't even there. He cleared his throat again, trying to get her attention.

Still nothing.

He made himself speak. "Will you be all right now?"

At last, she looked up, and he felt like a mouse caught in a cat's gaze. She had Clare's eyes—a bright clear green, oddly feral. He couldn't talk, lost as he was in her details. She bore a startling resemblance to his wife. She was staring at him, and he realised he hadn't even heard her answer. She was already turning away, ready to move off once more, when he found his voice.

"Clare!" It burst out of him without him even stopping to think about it, and he was shocked to hear the desperation in his voice. He was even more shocked by the result.

She turned around and smiled at him, her voice full of humour as she replied, "Not quite, but at least you got the first letter. It's Celeste."

"Pretty name."

"Why, thank you." She smiled again, and waited.

There was an awkward silence as he struggled to find the right words. As her smile faded and she started to turn away again, he realised she thought it was a come-on, that he'd probably seen her name on a credit card or something.

Paul had to stop her. He blurted out, "Can I see you again? Please?" and then stood there, stunned by the words that had just escaped his mouth. Where the hell had that come from?

She stared at him for what seemed like the longest time, and he thought he'd blown it. Then she smiled and nodded, and he suddenly became aware of just how fast his heart was beating. Maybe it would be all right.

"Meet me in O'Neill's in Muswell Hill. Do you know it?"

"It's the one that used to be a church, right?"

Her smile dropped. "It did?" She thought for a moment, then continued, "I don't suppose it'll matter, not if it's been a pub for a while." She stared at him. "See you there tomorrow? At seven?"

He nodded dumbly, and she walked away, leaving him standing in the street, staring after her like a lost soul. He couldn't believe he'd just asked a girl out, let alone that she'd said yes. Life was spinning out of control, and he realised he liked the feeling. He liked *feeling*.

The next day was Saturday, and Paul surprised himself by sleeping in until almost eleven o'clock. It was the first decent night's sleep he'd had in ages, and he felt a hell of a lot better for it. He hauled himself out of bed and wandered into the bathroom. Standing in front of the mirror, he took a long, critical look at himself, ready to assess the damage his self-neglect had wrought. He was forty-two years old and looked at least fifty. His hair was heavily flecked with silver now, much more than he remembered it being when Clare was alive. He couldn't remember the last time he'd had a haircut, either, and it definitely needed a wash. His skin looked grey, as if he was recovering from a long illness. In a way, he supposed he was. His eyes were bleary, with dark bags underneath them, and the rest of him hadn't done any better. He must have lost at least a stone. He could count every rib and couldn't believe how bad he looked.

Time to take action.

Stepping into the shower, he stood under the hot spray for a few seconds and then turned it to cold, eager to shock his circulation into action. Next, he washed his hair, conditioned it, and scrubbed himself all over. That was all he could do for now. He padded back down the hall and pulled on a baggy blue shirt and faded jeans, then ate a solitary breakfast of coffee and toast while zoning out to morning TV before heading for the barbershop.

An hour later, he stepped out into the morning sunshine, blinking. He felt as if he was changing, getting ready to be reborn. It was a sensation he wasn't entirely comfortable with, but he was prepared to go along with it, for now. He'd had his fill of the alternative. That path was headed towards ending everything, to suicide—a notion he'd been toying with for a while. If only he'd been able to make himself care enough to actually do it. He wanted to feel alive again, that was all. Whether it turned out to be good or bad was something he was content to leave to fate.

Seven o'clock and he was threading his way carefully through the crowd at O'Neill's, scanning the crowd as he searched in vain for the girl. When he reached the bar, he managed to wedge himself between two young guys without aggravating either of them—no mean feat in such a small space. And when he gained the attention of the barman, he ordered a lager before turning to face into the pub, reluctant to give up his hard-won space.

The noise hit him like a wall, the music's beat thudding through everything. He could feel it filtering up from his feet. Everywhere people were shouting themselves hoarse, trying to look as if they weren't struggling to be heard.

They'll be deaf before they're forty, he thought, then winced at the unintended echo of his father.

This place made him feel old. In the last few years, he'd gravitated towards pubs with little or no background music, just clusters of tables, plenty of bar staff and sawdust on the floor. He remembered Celeste's concern at the building's original function and wondered why she'd thought it would matter.

There she was.

The moment she walked in the atmosphere changed, an undercurrent of tension pervading the room. She slipped through the crowd like a blade through silk, heading straight for him. Her green eyes shone bright as she kept focus on him throughout. He had a brief moment to register the fact that people seemed to be giving her an unusually wide berth. Then she was there, and everything else just faded away.

"I wasn't sure you'd come."

She smiled, tilted her head to one side, and gazed at him. She was making him nervous. "Aren't you going to buy me a drink?"

Immediately he felt clumsy, like a sixteen-year-old on his first date. "I'm sorry. Yes, of course. What would you like?"

"I'll have a Bacardi and Coke, please."

He nodded at the barman, and gave the order. She was smiling at him again, and he had a feeling she was really enjoying his embarrassment. The drinks came, and they began the usual polite chitchat of finding out about the other person. The rest of the evening passed in a blur, and he was conscious of a growing warmth that overtook his embarrassment as he realised the attraction was mutual.

They left the bar early, much to Celeste's apparent relief. "Too loud," she'd said, and he'd been only too happy to concur.

Somehow, they got from the bar to his flat, and then quickly to bed. He relished her heat, the feel of her skin against his, and the smell of her. There was no time to think as he drove into her; her cries told him all he needed to know. The night became a blur of sensation, and he gave himself to it gladly. The only thing he was conscious of was the realisation that he could, at last, *feel*.

Chapter 10

Tommy raced up the stairs to his room, intent on hiding his purchase before his mum found out about it. She'd kill him for buying such a thing. Sure enough, her radar kicked in as soon as he entered the house and headed for the hall.

"Tommy, is that you?"

He reached the safety of his room and slammed the door shut, hoping to gain a few extra minutes. At least he'd hear if she followed him. Good thing she wasn't light-footed. Her voice came again, closer this time though still muffled. He could picture her now, standing at the foot of the stairs, hands—or should he say fists—planted on her ample hips, ready for battle.

He banged his head against the door, lightly, sick of the endless questions. "Yeah, it's me, Mum."

"What did you race upstairs for?"

"I needed the loo."

Opening the door as quickly and quietly as he could, he raced his way down the hall to the bathroom almost on tiptoe, magazine tucked into the waistband of his jeans. Reaching the bathroom, he was glad to find the door already ajar. He took the door handle and crept inside, holding the door handle down until it was safely closed. Then he bolted it.

Just in time.

He heard his mother's heavy footsteps as she climbed the stairs, heard her plodding down the hall towards him until they came to a stop just outside the door.

"Are you all right in there?"

He could hear the suspicion in her voice. Tommy wondered what she imagined he could be doing that was so bad—and what it said about the state of her own mind that she was so quick to suspect misbehaviour. The lack of trust hurt him sometimes. He didn't think he was a bad kid, really. He didn't steal, smoke or do drugs. What was the harm in a few magazines? He realised his silence would only breed more suspicion, so he cleared his throat and answered as calmly as he could.

"Yeah, just got a bit of an upset stomach, that's all."

She flicked the next question at him with the speed and accuracy of a whip, expertly wielded. "Why? What have you eaten that would do that?"

Perish the thought the culprit might have emanated from her kitchen. The whole house was clean, always. But the kitchen was never less than immaculate. Tommy had the idea germs wouldn't dare incubate in her kitchen, and she certainly didn't trust anyone else's.

Inspiration struck. "It must have been the kebab I had on the way back from Mark's house last night."

His mother sighed. "Oh well, if you will eat that rubbish. If I've warned you once, I've warned you a thousand times about buying food in those sorts of places. I'll see if we've got any tablets for it in the kitchen." She made her way back down the hall, back to her beloved kitchen.

Tommy breathed a sigh of relief. She was happy now, suspicion averted, all that remained was to find the appropriate medicine—and he was sure she would. The medicine cabinet was like an Aladdin's

Cave of remedies. It was so easy to play her, Tommy realised. All he had to do was pander to her prejudices, which were legion—though she'd never admit it. Unbuttoning his jeans, he pulled them down along with his boxers and sat down on the toilet. Picking up his magazine, he leafed idly through the pages, smiling, occasionally turning it this way or that to look at a picture better.

Then he came to the centrefold.

She was absolutely stunning. Beautiful wasn't a strong enough word to describe her. Her pose was explicit to say the least, sitting on a chair facing the camera—legs akimbo, fingers at play. All of that Tommy hardly noticed. All he really saw was the jet-black hair that skimmed her jaw line, the high cheekbones, scarlet mouth pouting provocatively, and her eyes. They were a vivid green, so light they almost seemed to glow, as if backlit. She was slim, too, with large firm breasts. The perfect teenage fantasy.

Tommy reached down with his right hand, still looking at the picture. He grasped his erection and, in his mind at least, embraced his fantasy woman.

Chapter 11

For Paul, the next few weeks passed in a blur—a heady mix of cosy lunches, long walks in the park, and evenings spent deep in conversation in old-fashioned pubs. He fell in love with a speed that would have terrified him if he had been able to see it clearly. He told Celeste everything there was to know about him, laid himself bare without a thought of how much she could hurt him should she wish.

She, in return, told him next to nothing. When he tried to find out some detail of her past, she would smile and gloss over it, before turning the conversation to some other, safer topic. All he knew was that she was an only child, and that her parents were dead, nothing more. That would have to do for now. He was just happy to be near her, to have someone, although he did find himself wondering about her reluctance to share things with him. The rest could come later.

Paul woke up one morning in his own flat, with nothing much to do as Celeste was busy. Away from her influence for the first time in weeks, he saw the flat with clear eyes and was shocked. An air of neglect hung over everything. Dirty clothes were draped over the chair and spilled over it onto the floor. The room—no, the whole flat—smelt stale. He saw the photo he kept by his bedside, the one of his and Clare's wedding, covered in a patina of dust so thick he could hardly see their faces. Blinking back tears, he picked it up and rubbed it clean with his sleeve before putting it back.

"I'm sorry, love," he said, and ground the heels of his hands against his eyes to dry them.

He cleared his throat and got out of bed, wandered down the hall to the bathroom, noting the cobwebs that seemed to be proliferating in every corner, the mustiness of the air. The flat felt like a mausoleum. He stood outside the nursery, scared to go in and see the forlorn little cot in the corner, thick with dust, evidence of his abandonment. His wife and child deserved better than this, didn't they?

Paul's thoughts turned to Celeste and he realised for the first time how mysterious she was, how unconcerned with any aspect of his life that didn't affect her directly. Somehow, she didn't seem quite so attractive when he managed to achieve a little distance from her. Instead, she seemed selfish and self-absorbed. Paul resolved to end it, to stop fooling himself. She liked to be pampered, that was all, and he'd been the willing fool. But it had felt so good, to be with someone —not to be alone, for once.

He tried to take hold of the doorknob and laughed in disbelief when his hand wouldn't obey his command. "Come on," he muttered to himself. "Don't be such a wuss."

He forced himself to try again, his hand shaking—but at least this time it did what he wanted. The doorknob felt cold and brittle in his grasp, and he groaned along with it as it turned and the door slowly opened. He hesitated, just for a moment, and stepped forward.

It smells like death, he thought, and laughed nervously at such stupidity.

But it did. There was an air of abandonment here that went beyond mere disuse. What he could smell was neglect, pure and simple, and the loneliness in the room tore at his heart. The puffy pink rabbit that he'd hated on sight but Clare had adored still sat in the corner of the cot, waiting for Hannah. And she'd never know.

Feeling physically sick, he sank to the floor, ashamed. Things had to be put right.

The rest of the morning passed quickly as he cleaned the flat from top to bottom. The smell of lemon hung in the air as he dusted and polished and vacuumed. A cool breeze blew in through all the open windows, clearing the air. The washing machine hummed constantly in the background.

Finally, he was satisfied. He stood in the centre of the living room, sweat cooling in the draught from the windows, and smiled. The place felt like home again.

Starving, he went into the kitchen. He found the menu for what had been their favourite takeaway clipped to the fridge with a magnet, a huge smiley face that Clare had put there, claiming it was guaranteed to cheer them up when they looked at it. Grinning at the memory, he took the menu down and phoned in an order for what had been their favourite takeout meal. Chicken chow mein, egg fried rice, and Coke. While he waited for it to arrive, he busied himself around the flat, closing windows. It was getting cold. Winter wasn't too far away now.

And he was back. where he belonged, instead of in some twilight world where only he and Celeste existed.

Chapter 12

Terry was shattered. Celeste lay curled on her side in the bed next to him, fast asleep, a contented smile on her face. She looked so innocent, he thought, lying there like that—the face of an angel. And yet she was such a bitch, underneath. He shifted in bed, wincing at the pain even that little movement caused. He was too old for all this shit. Handcuffs and whips, for God's sake. His wrists were bleeding slightly, chafed by the friction of the cuffs. He had begged her to loosen them, but she only laughed. From the start he had been ambivalent about all this. Now he was certain. Never again!

He couldn't understand how people got turned on by stuff like this. Celeste definitely did, that much was obvious. To begin with, that alone had been enough to turn Terry on. But not anymore. He eased out of bed and lumbered to the bathroom. He felt ten years older, and for what? Sure, she was beautiful, and being seen with her did wonders for his ego; but he knew better than most that beauty was only skin deep. He had come to realise that, inside, she was evil—her heart probably some blackened, misshapen lump, like a piece of coal. If he never saw her again after this, he'd be happy. He'd be better off on his own. At least he'd get some peace.

Stepping into the shower, Terry groaned as the water hit his battered body. Even tepid and on the lowest power—scarcely more than a trickle—it stung like mad. Looking down, he saw thin streaks of blood staining the water.

"Ter-ry..."

God, he was sick of that tone. That teasing, come back to bed voice. Funny, he had found that exciting at first. *God save us from the male ego*, he thought. What on earth had he been thinking? He ignored her and concentrated on cleaning himself of all traces of her as gently as he could.

Drying himself off, he wrapped a towel around his waist and reluctantly walked back into the bedroom, dabbing at the still seeping scratches with a damp face cloth.

Celeste was leaning back against the headboard, propped up by pillows, stark naked. She was also fingering herself.

Terry kept his eyes firmly averted, determined to finish things before it was too late. He retrieved her dress from the floor and threw it at her, then turned on his heel and headed for the relative safety of the bathroom once more. "Get dressed, Celeste." He slammed the bathroom door shut as he delivered the parting shot. "Then get out."

Terry stared at his bedroom in disbelief. He had waited in the bathroom, only slightly ashamed of himself for not having more backbone, until he heard the front door slam. Then he'd ventured out, only to find himself in the middle of a scene of absolute carnage. He felt like an utter coward, but had faced and admitted the fact that she had systematically beaten all the fight out of him.

She had completely trashed the place. His wardrobe doors were wide open, clothes flung everywhere—what was left of them, anyway. Sleeves were ripped off, and there were great rents in all the clothes he could see, where she had taken a knife or scissors to them.

Feathers were strewn across the floor, escaping from the duvet and pillows, all of which had been thoroughly shredded. The mirror on the dressing table was smashed into a million pieces, shards of glass littering the floor around it. She had probably used one of the shards from the mirror to shred everything else. He groaned when he saw his mobile phone on the floor, smashed beyond repair. He'd just have to phone the police from the landline in the kitchen.

He hadn't heard a sound. *How the fuck had she done all this without making any noise?*

Wandering through the wreckage that had been his house, Terry saw she had certainly made a thorough job of it. There wasn't a single breakable object left intact. He couldn't understand it. It hadn't taken her more than fifteen minutes to dress and leave; he was sure of that. All he had heard was the sound of her muttering as she pulled her clothes on. Yet the house looked as if a cyclone had been through it. At least she was gone. The thought of taking her to court and suing her for damages crossed his mind, but he rejected the idea. Best to make a fresh start, cut his losses.

He headed into the kitchen to see if the kettle was still functioning. Desperate for a cup of coffee, sweet and black. Once the kettle was on, he'd phone the police.

Celeste was standing there, cup in hand. "Here you go. Black and sweet, just how you like it." The phone was still attached to the wall beside her, but the handset was lying on the countertop, the scissors she'd used to cut the wire placed neatly beside it.

He raised his hands in what he hoped was a placatory gesture. "Celeste, calm down. There's no need for..."

She snarled then, actually snarled—like a rabid dog or something. Terry let his hands fall. His mouth dried in an instant, and he couldn't speak. She screamed and flung the contents of the cup in his direction before launching herself forwards, arms raised, eyes glittering with rage. She bore little resemblance now to the woman he had been so besotted with; this thing was barely human.

Before he even had time to shout, she was on him, both arms

flashing down as she buried a kitchen knife to the hilt in his chest, working it, twisting it in an attempt to force it deeper. The pain was immense, causing him to forget the hot coffee—the sting of that was nothing in comparison. His pulse became more erratic, weaker, and he struggled to grip the hilt. He tried to move it with hands he couldn't feel anymore and could barely lift, and his lifeblood welled even faster from the wound, making him let go. He was lost. There was no way to survive this, he knew, but he still couldn't fathom how it had come to this.

Celeste moved into view, smiling. He groaned as she slid a finger along the blade towards his chest, then pushed it into her mouth, sighing in delight as she sucked the crimson fluid.

To Terry, in his final seconds, it seemed as if she was flickering, somehow. The face he knew was changing; other faces, eerily similar, superimposed on it. All of them were enjoying the feast, and his pain.

The darkness, when it finally descended, came as a relief.

Chapter 13

S am woke with a start and sat up, aware of a cool breeze playing on his sweat-soaked skin. The only problem was, this wasn't his bedroom. The ceilings were too high, all the walls were painted stark white, and white muslin drapes were billowing softly back into the room, away from the open French windows. Somehow, he *knew* there was a balcony out there trimmed with black wrought iron railings, although he had no idea what lay beyond that, or even if anything did. He could see a vast expanse of floor, very cold-looking, elegant, gleaming black and white marble tiles that seemed to go on forever.

Sam looked around, trying to find something familiar in all this. The bed was a massive four-poster—fluted ebony pillars rising to a frame, again draped in white muslin. Even the bedclothes were all white—silk, if he wasn't mistaken.

By way of contrast, the girl lying beside him was swathed entirely in black silk.

Well, almost.

It was her, the girl from the mall, and the park. The fur freak.

She smiled at him, reached her hand out and ran one incredibly long, well-manicured fingernail down the length of Sam's torso.

Following her scarlet nail on its journey (the only splash of real colour so far), Sam realised he was shirtless. From what he could tell, he wasn't wearing anything further down, either.

Spellbound, Sam watched as she sat up and moved closer. She took his hand and placed it on her icy breast, smiling encouragingly.

Sam cupped it in his hand, marvelling at how full it was, the unexpected weight of it. He could feel her nipple hardening under his touch and rubbed gently, aware of his own body responding. She moaned and arched her back slightly, forcing the swell of her breast against his palm. He slipped the thin straps off her shoulders, allowing her nightgown to fall, laying her breasts bare. Gently, Sam leant forward and tongued them, the taste as sweet as nectar. So far, not a word had been spoken, or needed to be—there was no sound at all. There was a remote, surreal quality to all this, which only made it more enticing. Words would have been intrusive.

Then things changed.

She drew back, lifted her nightgown back up and over her head and discarded it, leaving herself completely bare. Full-breasted and curvy. Her head was bent, her helmet of dark hair obscuring her eyes. When she looked up, the fall of light across her face gave her a vaguely oriental aspect. Another splash of colour, just as out of place, her eyes were the now-familiar green fire.

Throwing back the sheet, she straddled him, and all was lost. The dream (surely that was what it must be) lost coherence, and all Sam knew was the bed and their bodies as they made love.

Then it was over, leaving him wondering what the hell had just happened. Sam turned to her, brushed her skin with his lips.

"Celeste." The name fit like a glove.

She raised her head and smiled, her words dripping sugared poison. "Kill Marianne for me, darling. We don't need her."

Sam jerked awake with a cry. Christ, what a dream! He tried her name again, Celeste, and relished the sound of it, its rightness. Marianne turned towards him, snaked her leg over his, and he nearly died of shock at the rasp of her warm skin against his. Fully awake now, he lay back, breathing hard. Marianne was like a rag doll as he hoisted her enough to worm his arm underneath her and pull her close. He felt the warmth of her breath against his neck and felt himself starting to calm down. She was here, and she was safe.

He didn't sleep again.

The next few days passed in their usual fashion, at least on the surface. Sam and Marianne each went to their separate jobs as usual, functioned as usual, came home as usual.

Sam was hoping Marianne hadn't noticed that anything was different about him. The morning after his nocturnal seduction he woke up stiff and sore. Disentangling himself from a still sleeping Marianne, he crawled out of bed and headed for the bathroom. Peeling his pyjamas off, he caught sight of his back in the bathroom mirror. There were deep red scratches running right down it, and the surrounding skin was raised and caked with dried blood. When he stepped under the shower, it stung like hell.

For the next few days Sam was careful not to let Marianne see him with his top off. It wasn't too hard. They were both snowed under with work, so were in and out at all hours, barely even meeting. Marianne worked as an estate agent. Sam worked for the Department of Health and Social Security, spending his days assessing people's claims for benefits. He didn't fit in too well, as he didn't have the necessary ruthless streak. He probably erred too often on the side of the claimants, not a trait his superiors looked on kindly; it didn't reflect well in the figures.

By evening, both Marianne and Sam tended to be too tired to do more than collapse in front of the TV. Then it was a race to see who fell asleep first.

But in his sleep, he'd see Celeste.

No sooner would he close his eyes than there he was, back in that black and white bedchamber, where he would spend what seemed like hours tasting the delights of her flesh. And oh, the secrets she knew.

Slowly but surely, hating himself for it, Sam began to find Marianne dull by comparison. It was unfair and he knew it, but he couldn't help himself.

Celeste, of course, was openly scathing of Marianne, "that great cow," as she called her. Indeed, beside Celeste, Marianne did not compare favourably. How could she? Such a blatant creature of daylight, with her copper hair, always rampant—blazing curls escaping no matter how she tried to tame them. Marianne was almost as tall as Sam and voluptuous.

Celeste was something entirely different.

She was... She was like the moon, her black hair seeming all the darker against that pale skin. Even as they made love, her hair never seemed to be unruly. She used some exotic, heady perfume that made Sam's senses swim. Marianne was his real love; he knew that on some level, no matter what happened. He felt tied to her, by bonds of love as well as life. But Celeste was nothing if not persuasive, pandering to Sam's every desire. Being submissive then dominant in turn, her changes of mood so quick they were beyond anticipation, yet quickly welcomed. There were no limits.

After two weeks of all this sexual activity, either real or imagined, Sam was completely drained. He wasn't functioning quite so well in the real world, now. Little things, mostly. He found himself wool-gathering when he should have been interviewing claimants. Time and again, he came to himself to realise he was facing another pissed off, cynical claimant, having just confirmed the fact that, in their opinion, they didn't matter. They were just numbers.

He was starting to snap at Marianne, too. Not often. But enough for her to notice something was wrong.

Sam's denials only made him feel even guiltier, which made him snap more, confirming her half-formed suspicions that maybe there was someone else. She was losing him. Knowing everything he knew about Marianne, he expected her to put up a fight, confront him. Then she'd kick him out.

Instead, she withdrew slightly, became a touch more distant. To an outsider, there would have appeared to be little or no change in their relationship. But Sam knew better.

They had always been a very tactile couple, lots of hugs and kisses, confident with each other's bodies. That was gone now. There was a reserve, a distance. It got to the stage where Sam could have screamed at her, just to get a reaction. When it came down to it, what could he have confessed? That he'd been unfaithful in his dreams?

He hadn't even met Celeste in the flesh yet, not properly. He wasn't sure he wanted to. As it happened, things came to a head somewhat sooner than he had expected.

Sam was back in Celeste's room, but it was empty; he couldn't find her. He could hear muffled sobbing, but couldn't figure out where it was coming from.

"Celeste?"

No answer.

He called again, but still no reply. She was near, though. He could *feel* her. The air was thick with her perfume, as if she had just wafted by. Sam's nerve endings tingled with the nearness of her touch. But she wouldn't come to him.

He could still hear someone sobbing, but he didn't think it was Celeste any more. It didn't sound like her, somehow. Whoever was crying, they sounded desolate—loud braying sobs and sniffles. Sam couldn't imagine Celeste crying like that.

He'd never been out of the bedroom here before, wherever *here* was. He wasn't even sure there *were* any other rooms; this was a dream, after all.

Sure enough, thought became deed. Whoever was controlling this dream was certainly in tune with Sam's desires. He didn't like to think it might be him that was controlling things, on some level.

It had to be Celeste, didn't it?

A door Sam had never noticed before swung open, revealing a dimly lit hallway—candles flickering in wrought iron sconces; very gothic. The crying sounded louder now. He crossed the bedroom and stepped cautiously into the doorway, looked from side to side. All he could see in either direction was a dim, winding passage, lit only by the occasional flickering candle. To the right, the hall angled gradually back, fading into blackness. To the left, it was much the same—angling gently back out of sight.

Only this way there was no gradual fade to black. One of the candles seemed to be moving slowly away from him, its glimmering light fading as it went. Intrigued, he set off in pursuit, not yet thinking it might be dangerous. He had a feeling the rules of this dream had just changed, and was excited at the prospect.

There was an undercurrent of unease running through everything, making him tread carefully. It was cold, and Sam could feel a draft, distinctly damp, chilling him. His nakedness didn't exactly help matters.

The hall kept on leaning to the left as he went on. He couldn't see any other doors, or even any windows. Yet he could hear the wind moaning and the distinctive sound of rain lashing against glass, for all the world as if there was a massive storm straight overhead.

Right on cue, the hall was momentarily lit by a stark flash of lightning, illuminating everything as brightly as a magnesium flare.

There she was.

Celeste was the one holding the candle, far ahead, just as Sam had expected. She was forever moving out of sight, turning artfully around corners just slowly enough for him to catch a glimpse of her. He quickened his pace, then, trying to catch up. No use. She didn't appear to be moving any faster, but the distance between them stayed just the same. The storm continued unabated—thunder crashing and lightning flashing despite the distinct lack of windows. Sam was rapidly beginning to suspect this hall would go on forever.

He must have been walking, following the light, for nearly ten minutes before he realised the floor was gradually sloping upwards. They were climbing a huge spiral.

The walls felt like stone, cold and unpleasantly damp. When the lightning flashed, it was almost blinding, as the white paint reflected the glare. The fact that Sam could now see the lightning didn't register at first. By the time it did, it was too late. What was she playing at? If all of this was designed to make him feel uneasy, then she'd overdone things badly. He'd gone from being unnerved to plain pissed off in very short order.

He continued for maybe three or four turns of the spiral, then the hall began to widen out. Sam turned the last corner and stood trans-fixed, the shock rendering him speechless.

The room he was in now, if you could call it anything as simple as a room, was enormous. It felt as if he was standing in the middle of a cathedral. The walls were barely visible, far off in the distance, and they were made of sheer glass, soaring up to what looked like a mass of iron-grey thunder-clouds. Sam surmised it was merely a ceiling of grey marble, matching the floor. The overall effect was that of standing on clouds in the midst of a thickening, swirling storm, surrounded as they were by nature's fury on all sides. If she wanted to impress him, then she'd certainly pulled that off. Sam felt like Thor, god of thunder, the heart and soul of the anger.

Celeste was standing far off, etched in silhouette on glass by an incandescent flare of lightning. She was watching him, waiting to see what his next move would be.

Sam decided not to approach her. Not yet, anyway.

The hallway he had been climbing so slowly opened out into the centre of this monumental room. Carefully, trying to look as if he hadn't yet noticed her, Sam made his way over to the nearest window...or wall—whatever you wanted to call it. The view was imposing, to say the least. Thickening bulkheads of cloud were clustering around them, drawn to their presence in this beleaguered glass tower. It came to Sam that they were in a lighthouse, of sorts.

Lo and behold, the sound of waves beating furiously at the jagged rocks far below crashed down on his ears, almost deafening him to the sobbing that was still coming from somewhere infuriatingly close by.

Almost, but not quite.

As Sam's eyes slowly became more accustomed to the storm-lit landscape outside, he beheld the inevitable cliffs stretching off to either side as far as he could see, which admittedly was not too far. It came to him that this entire experience was in monochrome, confirming it was Celeste and not Sam who was orchestrating all of this. He usually dreamt in vivid colour and had been known to wake up convinced that his nocturnal escapades had actually taken place.

Not this time.

Celeste was obviously growing impatient with his voyage of discovery. She was eager to move them along to the next scene.

Lightning flared once more, accompanied by a crescendo of thunder. The glass shook with the resonance of it. There, off to Sam's left, was a promontory he could have sworn was new. He certainly hadn't seen it when he first looked. He felt, rather than saw, her smirking and refused to give her the satisfaction of reacting.

That was when she brought Marianne into the picture. There she was wearing the obligatory floaty white dress. It streamed out behind her as it was buffeted in the wind, her flaming curls flying back from her face—in colour, he noted, the overall effect like a halo of fire.

It was Celeste's doing. Sam didn't doubt that for an instant. She wanted him to recognise her nemesis—his lover, in fact, not fiction, plummeting to her death from the storm-blown cliffs onto the hungry rocks waiting below. Why else would she have left Marianne's hair with its customary blaze of colour when all around was black and white?

"Marianne!" Sam called her name again and again until his lungs burned, ripping as much volume as he could force from his tortured throat.

He could feel the malice emanating from Celeste, her satisfaction at the sight of him hammering on the glass, trying to attract Marianne's attention, screaming her name. All to no avail.

She couldn't hear him. Sam's cries just kept blowing back, mocking him as they were flung back by the wind. The same wind lifted Marianne's sobs and threw them back at Sam like a slap in the face, ever louder and harder. He turned to Celeste, intent on making her stop.

As he rushed across the tower towards her, she just laughed, and he quickly realised he would never get any closer. The distance between them never diminished for a moment, though Sam never stopped running. Her mocking laughter scaled up and up to the limits of sound it seemed, becoming a shrieking cry of alarm and joy...

Reality crashed down, and Sam sat up in his own bed, gasping, instinctively reaching for Marianne.

She wasn't there.

Sam's face was wet with tears, and he couldn't stop shaking. Marianne's loss felt like a physical blow, a dull, grim ache in his heart. He had lost everything. He stared stupidly at her side of the bed, barely registering anything—let alone the fact that he had woken—until the insistent shrill of the telephone impinged on what he supposed passed for his consciousness. Sam fumbled for the handset, nearly dropped it, and finally succeeded in bringing it to his ear, cutting it off mid-scream.

Marie O'Regan

"Sweet dreams, lover."

Sam slammed the phone down on her gloating laughter, shuddering as he realised that, for a moment, he had been holding a big, black dial telephone. Not the trim, white digital phone he was so accustomed to. He wiped his hand on the sheets, feeling vaguely dirty. When he looked again, it was back to normal. But he could still hear crying.

This was too much. Things were back in colour now, true, but Sam was still far from sure he was actually awake. This wasn't just another of Celeste's games; the disorientation was total. He had no idea of what was real or what was imagined.

Still, what choice did he have but to proceed on the assumption, at least, that this was real? Sam could feel the breeze drying the sour sweat on his face and chest, making him shiver. He could feel the carpet, warm and soft under his feet, tickling his skin. Funny how walking barefoot on carpet always set his teeth on edge, like the screech of nails on a blackboard.

Pausing in the bathroom doorway, Sam looked around, trying to pinpoint the crying. It was Marianne. It had to be. Celeste had just phoned Sam, after all, so she couldn't logically be here too. The trouble was, logic didn't strictly apply to Celeste. He still hadn't had any real contact with her in the flesh, so to speak. Just a few words thrown at him in passing on Hampstead Heath. He knew her intimately only in his dreams. Sam wasn't sure he wanted things to progress any further between them in the real world. The hallway was dark, the sobbing muffled. Sam was badly unnerved, now. The barrier between waking and dreaming seemed to have been lowered, somehow. He had a morbid fear of what might be waiting, hesitating for the right moment to burst through the barriers and trample roughshod over the real world.

It was bad; he knew that much. He could feel that knowledge, deep down, like a nugget of ice, pulsing waves of fear through him.

A thin line of light was visible under the living room door. Padding softly down the hall, Sam was gripped by the vision of finding Celeste in there, standing triumphantly astride the sobbing form of her crumpled competitor, Marianne—an innocent in all of this. Steeling himself, Sam threw open the living room door and all but hurled himself inside, ready for battle.

There was only Marianne, curled up in an armchair, crying.

She was crumpling up soaked tissues and chucking them in the bin as if it was some sort of race. The pile of tissues in and around it showed she'd been there for quite a while.

Sam stood just inside the door, feeling slightly stupid. He'd burst into the room like Errol Flynn, only to be confronted by nothing more threatening than a box of tissues.

Marianne glared at him, her eyes full of accusation. Sam just wished she'd tell him what it was he'd done. There had been nothing concrete, not really. The beginnings of a smile played around her mouth. She tried desperately to stifle it. She was laughing at him! Still, he had to admit he must have looked ridiculous bursting into the living room like that.

Sam closed the door behind him and made his way sheepishly over to the sofa, guessing rightly that he'd be a less than welcome visitor to the edge of the armchair. She was guarding that space religiously.

"What's wrong?"

"You tell me," she said.

Sam tried to adopt a nonchalant, innocent expression. Not surprisingly, it didn't fool her for a moment. She wasn't stupid, and it was an insult to her intelligence to assume otherwise. They knew each other too well for that.

She smiled bitterly. "At least you're honest enough not to try and deny it."

He ran a hand through his hair, bemused. "I'm still not quite sure what we're talking about, to be honest."

"Oh, Sam, please. I'm not blind."

"Meaning?"

"Meaning if you want to leave me for that bitch, go ahead."

Sam stared at her for a moment, taken aback. How could she know? Come to think of it, *what* could she know? Any infidelity had only been imagined, not real. He had to admit his dreams, if that was really all they were, had been intoxicating in the extreme; more potent than any of the pathetic highs he had known before, whether alcohol or drug-induced. Marianne was more prosaic, that was true; but ultimately, Sam knew he could never leave her for anyone. Fresh tears tracked her face, making him feel like shit. "Didn't think I'd find out, did you?"

"Find out what? Marianne, I haven't done anything. Who the hell are you talking about?"

For the first time Sam saw something more than annoyance flicker across her face. She had thought he was having an affair. Now she wasn't so sure. Sam wasn't behaving the way she had thought he would when confronted with his supposed betrayal. He supposed she'd had visions of him breaking down in a fit of remorse and confessing everything, throwing himself on her mercy. Well, if she thought that, she could think again. Fair enough, he had been neglecting her lately, and she deserved better than that. Sam had even begun to resent her while fantasising (so he thought) about Celeste, but he'd never actually done anything more than that.

But Sam still felt guilty. He hadn't sinned against Marianne directly, this obsession with Celeste wasn't real. Not in the sense that Marianne meant, anyway. But it had seemed real to him, for what seemed like an eternity. In that sense, yes—he had been unfaithful. He had wallowed in the illicit pleasures Celeste had been so eager to offer him. Not only that, he had absolutely revelled in it. It was only now, when Marianne had, in a sense, found him out, that he was beginning to see Celeste for what he thought she might really be.

A dangerous obsession, nothing more.

Sam felt his adoration slip a notch. The decadence he had so relished now seemed downright sleazy—something to be ashamed of.

Marianne was watching him, carefully gauging the expressions that were surely flitting across his face as he worked through his feelings. "Are you trying to tell me you're *not* having an affair?"

"That's exactly what I'm telling you," he answered, indignant.

"Then why have you changed?" Her voice broke as she asked this, although she struggled mightily not to let the tears shimmering in her eyes fall. Disbelief was written across her face, and Sam felt like a complete shit. Did he try to fob her off with what he assumed were the usual excuses, or did he come straight out and tell her the truth, all of it? Sam didn't hold out much hope of her believing him, but he had to at least try to explain. He owed her that much respect if nothing else.

"I'm sorry. I know I haven't been paying enough attention to you lately. But I promise you I'm not having an affair."

"Then why..."

"Shh." Sam forestalled her queries as gently as he could and sat forward on the sofa. Running his fingers through the bird's nest on his head, he tried to gather his thoughts. "Do you remember the woman in the park?"

"What, last month?"

"That's right, the fur freak."

"Of course I remember her. But what has she got to do with all of this?"

"I can't get her out of my mind."

There it was, out in the open, and it sounded pathetic. Sam could feel her looking at him incredulously but couldn't bear to look at her face. The disbelief was almost palpable.

Finally, she said, "I don't know what to say."

Chancing a look at her, Sam saw a mixture of wonderment and disappointment. Wonder, he supposed, that he'd chance a story like that and disappointment that, to her mind, he had just confirmed her worst fear. What was worse, he'd tried to weasel out of it with such a pathetic excuse.

"I haven't been having an affair with her, Marianne. I don't even know her." Sam paused, then. Now came the tricky bit. "I dream about her."

She snorted with laughter but said nothing. From the look on her face, he didn't think she trusted herself to. He got the distinct impression that he was missing something here. Maybe something important. The reply, when it finally did come, was like a bombshell. "Then how did your back get scratched like that?"

For a moment Sam said nothing. He was too stunned to even think, let alone answer her. His hesitation must have looked as if he was desperately searching for the right excuse. The truth, when it came, was less than convincing.

Marianne sighed. "What? You didn't think I'd notice?"

"No, I didn't," Sam said. "Stupid of me." His face was serious as he answered. "The truth is, I don't know. Like I said, I dream about her. That's all."

"I don't believe you. "

"I can't help that. It's true, though."

They sat there, staring each other out. In the end, Marianne gave in first, although Sam didn't know whether that was because she wasn't sure if he was telling the truth or not, or whether she was just sick of the sight of him. She looked away, disgust writ large on her expressive features and made a big show of selecting a magazine from the coffee table and flicking through it. Deliberately flicking the pages over as loudly as she could, too, precisely because she knew that was something that invariably drove him crazy.

Throughout all this, Marianne had become calmer and calmer, the exact opposite of Sam. He felt as if he was standing on a high wire, poised for a spectacular fall. All this accusation and denial was getting them nowhere fast. He'd had enough of it and stood up abruptly, startling Marianne.

"Let's go back to bed, get some sleep. We'll take the day off and talk this through, if that's what you want. Neither of us is in a fit state to carry this on now."

With that, Sam turned on his heel and went back to the bedroom, leaving Marianne staring after him like a wounded deer. He'd taken the wind out of her sails, and she wasn't quite sure how, or even if, to proceed. Sam lay down and pulled the covers round him, more for comfort than warmth, and waited.

It must have been fifteen or twenty minutes before she crept into the room and gingerly climbed into bed, as far away from Sam as she could get. He said nothing, just laid still, reasoning that if Marianne wanted to talk, she would.

She didn't.

Sam dozed for what little was left of the night in a bed that felt as if it had grown enormous. The distance between them was immeasurable, and he had no idea if he'd be able to lessen it.

Or even if Celeste would let him.

Chapter 14

S am woke to an impressive storm outside, invoking images of the previous night's experiences. Wagner was blaring out of the speakers in the living room, accompanied by an impressive collection of pots and pans in the kitchen. Whenever Marianne was deeply upset, she had a tendency to disappear into the kitchen and cook vast arrays of exotic food to the tune of some deeply tortured music, preferably classical. At such times, Sam usually ended up with a terminal case of indigestion.

The matching weather was purely coincidental, or so Sam hoped. He lay there for a while, safe in his cocoon, unwilling to brave the maelstrom in the kitchen just yet.

Marianne, however, had other ideas.

Sam hadn't been awake for more than ten minutes when the bedroom door flew open and a red-haired tornado stormed in, deposited a tray none too gently on the bedside table, and stormed out again, before he even had a chance to say "Good morning."

Gingerly, Sam sat up in bed and inspected the tray. He knew if he didn't want to provoke her any further, he had to put as much of the food away as possible—at least part of everything. The familiar smell of apple and cinnamon pervaded the flat, and he relaxed slightly. She was making strudel. Usually, she only baked strudel when she was feeling happy, so maybe she was beginning to believe him. Accompanying the fare on the tray was a chocolate tisane, one of Sam's favourite drinks—a fact that cheered him up enormously.

Any day which started off with a tisane was okay by him. Beside the tisane lay a plate of scrambled eggs and bacon, with a side plate of warm croissants with butter.

Bliss.

Sam set to with a vengeance, the extent of his appetite surprising him. He'd worry about his arteries later. In the kitchen, Wagner expired and was replaced by some light string piece, Strauss, perhaps. Definitely a good sign. Sam was just polishing off the last croissant when the door opened again, more gently this time, and Marianne stood nervously on the threshold.

"That was spectacular." Sam smiled, and held out the tray for her inspection. He'd already decided he wouldn't bring up the subject of Celeste unless or until he absolutely had to.

She smiled back at him, pleased. Her face was rosy from the heat in the kitchen and her curls had perked up for the same reason. She looked like a teenager, all excited. Then the little electronic timer she kept in the kitchen buzzed. She snatched the tray and darted off, intent on rescuing whatever it was before disaster struck.

Happy and full, Sam lay back down and drifted for a while. He was in that halfway state when you can hear everything that's going on around you, but it all seems far away, too remote to affect you in any way. He was aware of Marianne hustling around in the kitchen (her mood was light enough for golden oldies on the radio now, so things were definitely looking up), the steady drumming of rain on the windows, the odd rumble of thunder—further away each time...

A scream ripped through the warm, cosy cloud and nearly gave Sam a heart attack. He was up and running before it even finished, intent on getting to Marianne. The food in his stomach lying like a lead weight now. In a matter of seconds, he was standing in the kitchen with a sobbing Marianne in his arms, head buried against his chest, arms clutching him so tightly he could barely breathe.

He was shaking.

Sam tried to get some sense out of her, but she couldn't even talk. She just kept on crying. Looking around the kitchen, he couldn't see anything that could have caused this. Everything looked absolutely normal; for a cook-in day, at least. Mixing bowls, wooden spoons, baking ingredients were scattered about everywhere. The sink was full of hot, soapy water. The oven was shut, and there was no sign of any disturbance. No problem anywhere, as far as he could see.

Then Sam walked around the kitchen table and saw apple strudel plastered all over the floor. The baking tray lay not far from it, overturned. Damn.

"Shit, Marianne. What happened?"

No answer, but then he hadn't really expected any. Keeping his arm around Marianne, he ushered her gently out of the kitchen and back into the bedroom, made her sit down on the bed. Then he just sat and rocked her, stroked her hair and waited for her to calm down. He didn't know what else to do.

Gradually, her crying subsided into hiccups and sniffles, and her grip on him loosened a little. Sam handed her a tissue and let her get herself together as much as she could. She would tell him when she was ready.

While she was doing that Sam went into the kitchen and put the kettle on to make her a cup of tea. "The cup that cures," she had always called it; a favourite phrase of her mother's. He certainly hoped it would work this time. While he was waiting for the kettle to boil, he set about cleaning the remains of the strudel away, then washed the baking tray and wiped the floor.

All the time Sam was in the kitchen, he felt nervous, jittery, though he didn't know why. He felt as if someone was looking over his shoulder, planning some undoubtedly malicious trick. She had seen something in here; that much was certain. Sam was extremely relieved to get back to the bedroom, to Marianne.

"Thanks." She accepted the tea gratefully, but refused to look him in the eye.

While he was in the kitchen, she had got back into bed. She sat propped against all the pillows, almost lost under the huge duvet. She looked like a little girl. Sam climbed onto the bed beside her but didn't try to get in. One step at a time. Then he waited.

After a few minutes she leaned closer, laid her head on his shoulder. "I'm sorry, Sam."

"What for?"

She burrowed in deeper, and her voice—when it came—was little more than a whisper. "I believe you now. About everything."

Perplexed, Sam didn't quite know what to say. He'd expected to hear that something awful had just happened in the kitchen, not this. This was totally off the wall, unless...

"What happened in the kitchen, Marianne?"

Now it was her turn to look guilty. She wouldn't look at him, concentrated instead on what was left of her tea. The problem with that was that her hands were shaking. She was gripping the mug so tight her fingers were bone white.

Sam tried again. "What's going on here, Marianne? Tell me."

"I don't know what you mean."

"Oh, yes you bloody well do!"

Anger flared in her expression for an instant but was quickly extinguished by the memory of whatever it was she had just seen. "I believe you, that's all."

"There's more to it than that, love. Earlier, you wouldn't believe a word I said. Then the cooking feast this morning. We both know you only do that when something major has upset you."

"Not always."

"Nine times out of ten. The other time is usually Christmas or a party of some kind and you know it. What happened in the kitchen?"

Sam was getting pissed off now. First, she'd accused him, then she let him off the hook without a word of explanation.

Sighing, Marianne placed the mug on the bedside table and

turned to look straight at him. She looked ten years older than she had only that morning, strain showing in every line.

"I saw her."

"What?"

"I saw her. In the kitchen."

"But there was no..."

"She'd gone by the time you got there."

Since it had taken Sam all of ten seconds to get to the kitchen, and there was no back door, he found that hard to believe. At first, anyway. Then again, it was no less likely than what had been happening between him and Celeste for the last couple of weeks.

Marianne hurried on, desperate to finish, to get it all out in the open. "Like you said, I was busy cooking. The storm was dying down, I put the radio on, I was beginning to cheer up. A bit, anyway. Feeling more relaxed."

Sam nodded, knowing the way this usually worked.

"I put the strudel on the baking tray and opened the oven door..." She stopped for a moment.

Sam was about to press her when she took a deep breath and carried on, a single tear trickling down her cheek. He wanted to kiss it away.

"There was a baby in there."

"What?"

"Just for a moment. It was screaming, wailing...its skin was blistering. It kept waving its little arms and legs and then jerking them back from the walls, but the skin kept sticking..."

Her voice was spiralling higher and higher. She would break down completely any second, Sam knew it. He hadn't even seen it, yet couldn't get the image, sick as it was, out of his head. How must she be feeling? Sam reached for her, but she flinched back, not wanting comfort yet. There was more to tell.

"I screamed and screamed...and then it was gone... I slammed the door shut and..." She came to him then, let him hold her again. Her voice was muffled as she continued, lips feathery close to his chest,

"That woman was reflected in the glass. I couldn't hear a thing, but I could see her laughing."

Sam hugged her close, not wanting to hear the rest. He felt physically sick—the food he had already eaten churning noisily in his stomach. He didn't want to hear any more.

"When I turned around, she wasn't there." She dissolved into long sobs, all control gone, her story told.

Celeste had picked the image guaranteed to upset her more than any other. Marianne had always wanted a large family, and though Sam wanted children too, they had both agreed now was not the best time. That didn't stop her from getting broody now and again, though.

Sam was going to be sick; he was sure. To begin with, this dream seduction had been all-consuming, rapturous. It was probably the most intense experience he had ever had in his life, sexual or otherwise. Once he had begun to see the flaws, however, it had quickly descended into a waking nightmare.

"I've seen her before, as well," Marianne said.

"Sorry?"

For a moment, Sam thought she meant the times in John Lewis and on Hampstead Heath. Then he realised what she was really saying. Celeste had been visiting her, too.

"The night she scratched you, I had a really weird dream. I was in this gothic maze of a house. Everything was black and white. I could hear noises, somewhere close."

Sam flushed, ashamed. He had a pretty good idea of what those noises must have been.

Marianne stayed in his arms, her voice oddly pale, somehow washed out.

"I followed the noises. I went down corridor after corridor, lots of open doors leading into dark, empty rooms. The noises were still going on, but I couldn't seem to get any closer. Then I turned another corner and there was a light up ahead. A door was open, just a little way, and the light was on inside. That was where the noises were coming from."

Sam didn't want to hear this. More than anything, he wished he'd never set eyes on Celeste.

"I went to the door and peeped in. I could see a man and a woman on the bed, making love. The whole room was lit by candles, millions of them." A little flutter of laughter, fuelled by embarrassment, escaped her, making it worse. "I was going to leave. I was so embarrassed." Her voice dropped. It became even more miserable, if that were possible. "And then I saw it was you."

Sam felt renewed tears staining his chest, though her voice was steady enough. He was crying, too, ashamed that she had seen his infidelity.

"I watched you making love to her, Sam. I watched for ages, and then, when you came..." The accusation in that one word was immense, as if completing the act somehow made it worse, more of a betrayal. "She raked her nails down your back as hard as she could. I could see the blood welling up, even from the door..."

This was bad. This was worse than their confrontation the night before.

"Then she looked over your shoulder and smiled straight at me."

Sam didn't know what to say. He had thought Celeste was his secret, his obsession. Now he found out she had been flaunting that fact before his lover, like a trophy.

"Are they the only times?" Sam's voice sounded strangely distant, even to him. Weren't those times enough? He felt disconnected from all this, remote.

Marianne looked at him oddly, but at least she answered. "No. Another time I was in hospital, in labour. I was in a hell of a lot of pain, so I'd asked for an epidural. I remember being angry because you weren't there." She stopped, musing, then continued—seemingly

Marie O'Regan

unaware of the incongruity. "I didn't know where you were, though. Anyway, once the epidural took effect, I couldn't feel a thing. I was lying there, exhausted, cursing you, when a doctor came in. A woman doctor, gowned and masked, wearing really heavy make-up. She examined me but never said a word. I remember thinking how cold she was. At least her eyes were. That's all I could really see, those green eyes."

Sam started, wondering if she realised the significance of what she'd just said.

She carried on regardless. "Then she leant down to one side. I heard her say, 'I'm afraid you'll need a caesarean.' Then she stood up. She lifted her arm up high above her head, and I saw she had a huge, shiny pair of shears. I remember screaming as she brought her arm flashing down... Then I woke up."

Jesus. For a time, they just sat there, holding each other tight, content just to be together, gaining strength from that. Sam felt closer to Marianne than he had since all of this started. It was a good feeling, one he didn't want to lose.

Then it suddenly dawned on him. Why was Celeste focussing on babies with Marianne? He must have stiffened, or something, because Marianne sat up, wiping her eyes. When she looked up at Sam, the expression on her face was that of naked fear together with a sick resignation. She read the question in his eyes and nodded, seeming a little relieved to have it out in the open. She had probably been wondering when it would finally occur to him.

"I'm pregnant, Sam."

She had obviously thought he wouldn't want to know. He'd said —they'd said, all along—that in a couple of years the time would be right. They'd be more settled, have a nice little nest egg to cushion them when Marianne gave up work. Now that Sam thought about it, though, he couldn't help but feel a warm bubble of excitement. He was going to be a dad. He'd be able to take his son (the thought that it might be a girl never even crossed his mind, typically) out to football matches, go and watch him play for his school team—Sam could see it all.

102

Marianne sat watching him apprehensively, chewing her lip.

Realising he hadn't said anything yet, Sam reached for her again, kissed her, felt her relax against him. "How far along are you?"

"Three months."

"Looks like we've got some celebrating to do then, doesn't it?"

Her face relaxed instantly, a beam of pure joy lighting up her face. She had held on to this alone for the best part of two months—worrying how he would react. On top of all that, she'd had the worry of whether he still cared for her. No wonder she'd been so distant lately. She'd been trying to sever ties, to see if she was strong enough to go it alone. In spite of the way it had all come out into the open, Sam was just glad it had. He'd been so wrapped up in himself that he hadn't even noticed whether she'd been sick. Thinking about all that only served to deepen his guilt. It served no useful purpose.

They kissed and made peace. What mattered now was the future, not the past. After a time, they made love, reaffirming themselves as a couple. Together.

Whatever might happen.

Chapter 15

Clive went up to Celeste's room quite cheerfully, balancing her breakfast tray on one arm. It was a beautiful morning, even if autumn was fast fading into winter. Though cold, it was a crisp, clear day, and for some absurd unknown reason Clive felt good to be alive. He was young again, bursting with vitality. He had even relished the kiss of cold air against his naked body when he got out of bed. It felt good to be strong again.

Celeste had excelled herself this time. She looked truly magnificent. She had met someone surprisingly quickly, Clive thought, even for this day and age. He smiled indulgently as he remembered the day Celeste burst into the house the day she met this Paul. She had been so excited, like a teenager again, a sight he hadn't seen for so long. He had felt echoes of her other activities, too, of course. She was teasing someone, infecting his sleeping mind. There was a photographer, too, that would make her famous. Clive had seen the pictures. In his opinion, they were good for nothing but the lascivious drooling of teenage boys, but that was probably the point. Celeste had certainly bloomed since the pictures had been published. Clive supposed it wasn't that surprising, really. She had a much wider circle of admirers this time, thanks to the pictures, and admiration (no, adoration) was what she thrived on.

From Clive's point of view, it had all worked out well.

Celeste was widely adored and revelling in every moment of it. While that lasted, she had no need to resort to tormenting him.

Clive tapped gently on the bedroom door and heard a muffled reply. He opened the door carefully and cried out in shock as the tray was punched out of his grip and went sailing through the air, spraying tea and toast everywhere. His good mood evaporated in an instant. Celeste had been waiting behind the door, intent on tricking him. The honeymoon was obviously over. It hadn't lasted long this time, either, only a matter of weeks. He said nothing, not wanting to antagonise her further. She would compound things soon enough.

"Clumsy this morning, aren't we, Clive?"

He gritted his teeth at the malicious glee in her voice. He would not rise to the bait. "I'm sorry, Celeste."

She watched as he retrieved the tray and placed the pieces of shattered crockery on it, together with the soggy remains of the toast. When he stood to return to the kitchen, she seized the moment.

"The carpet's still wet, Clive."

"Yes, miss. I'll just fetch a cloth."

She smiled beatifically, as if bestowing some great favour. The smile widened when she saw him flinch. "That won't be necessary." He watched her, waiting. Unable to hold back anymore, she laughed openly as she delivered the coup de grâce. "You can lick it up."

Twenty minutes later, Clive bolted for the bathroom. He vomited until he thought his insides might come loose, the pain of retching spreading like fire across his stomach. He was careful to make as little noise as possible, for fear of more punishment. He could hear Celeste laughing.

He was very glad he had made it as far as the bathroom before his stomach had rebelled, or she would have made him lick that up too. It wouldn't have been the first time. He rinsed his mouth with water from the washbasin cupped in his hands, spitting bits of hair and carpet fluff carefully into the toilet bowl. Gradually, he regained control of his stomach, the churning beginning to lessen.

Celeste was still chuckling in her bedroom. Venturing into the hall, he retrieved the tray and headed back down to the kitchen, where he quickly prepared another breakfast. If she didn't get more food, and quickly, her mood would deteriorate even further. He didn't think she would play the same trick on him twice, but he knew she was capable of far worse.

Sure enough, she was prowling around the bedroom like a caged animal, absolutely furious about something. Her earlier good humour about his predicament was now completely forgotten. However, Clive knew better than to question her about the source of her anger. She passed the bedroom window just then, and he saw the thin autumn sunlight wash across her pallid face. It was noticeably thinner, more angular.

She looked five years older.

So that's it, thought Clive. *They are beginning to see through her already.*

She must have read the pity on his face even as she turned towards him, for she grabbed the tray from his hands and whirled away, towards the bed, and the shadows.

"Don't you feel sorry for me, Clive. Don't you dare!" She sat down on the edge of the bed and began picking at her breakfast, studiously avoiding his gaze. "Time to overcome their little guilt trips, that's all."

She ignored his presence pointedly, and he backed out of the room as soon as he thought it might be safe to do so. He didn't want to get involved in all this.

Not again.

Let her get on with it.

Celeste barely even noticed Clive leaving. Her mind was on far more important things. Sam was beginning to fight free; she could sense the guilt he felt each time he was with her. Fleeting images of another had floated through his consciousness the last time they had lain together, blunting the power their union normally gave her.

Marianne.

That had to be the big cow she had seen with Sam that first day. Big, healthy-looking bitch, fit only for breeding. More subtle pleasures were beyond her.

Before now, Celeste had contented herself with sowing the seeds of doubt as far as Sam's affection for Marianne was concerned. She had wanted Sam to become dependent on her. Obviously a more direct approach was now needed. Her mood lightened as she began to formulate her plan for Sam—and for her. Celeste would get Sam back, she was sure. Body and soul. If she couldn't entice him with her charms, she would just have to terrorise him into submission. That might even prove to be more fun.

Paul, however, was a different matter. She had a strange mixture of emotions where he was concerned, something she found more than a little confusing. The prevalent emotion at the moment was one of intense irritation at the torture he was putting himself through, coupled with an unexpected sense of loss. It was all so unnecessary, she thought, unable to conceive of the depth of emotion he must be feeling to mourn so deeply, so completely.

Celeste would have to be careful with the methods she employed to regain his devotion. She was somewhat surprised to find that it was his true devotion—freely given—that she wanted. No, *needed*.

Maybe if she made him feel that he had been unfair, had toyed with her affections, her finer feelings, he would reconsider. The perversity of the image delighted her, and she laughed aloud at the prospect. Its irony did not escape her.

Celeste was well aware of the physical changes all of this uncertainty had wrought. She had seen the deterioration in the mirror. Even if she hadn't, she couldn't deny the shock in Clive's eyes this morning. It was slight, but it was definitely there.

Celeste couldn't afford to be too subtle about this, or to take too long. She couldn't allow any of them get away.

Chapter 16

Paul woke on the sofa to find some obscure film on TV and the doorbell ringing without pause. The floor was littered with the empty dinner containers, and there was maybe half a bottle of Pepsi left. Bewildered, he heaved himself off the sofa and made his way down the hall to the door. He belched heavily as he went, releasing clouds of garlic. He hadn't eaten that much in ages. Paul couldn't remember the last time he had enjoyed—*really enjoyed* —any meal.

Before opening the door, he put the chain on and peered through the peephole.

Celeste stood just outside, gazing calmly back at him, head tilted to one side, for all the world as if she could see him through the tiny hole.

Puzzled, he disconnected the chain again and opened the door. "I wasn't expecting you tonight, Celeste. I thought we were...taking some time."

"Obviously." She pushed past him and headed straight for the living room. Absurdly, Paul found himself resenting the intrusion. Even yesterday, he would have given anything to have Celeste come to his place.

Marie O'Regan

But not now.

Now he felt as if she was invading, an alien presence in his cosy nest. He didn't want her here. She didn't belong. He hurried after her, suddenly afraid of what she might do. Paul knew it sounded stupid, but suddenly he didn't trust her.

When he got to the living room, Celeste was standing by the bay window, arms crossed, staring out into the darkness. Everything about her oozed anger, and Paul hadn't got a clue why.

She'd taken his call ending things quite well, he thought; even said she understood—it was obviously too soon for him to date again. So what was the problem?

"Looks like you've had a nice, cosy evening," she said.

"Well, I wasn't doing anything special. Just crashed out in front of the TV with a takeaway, that's all."

"So I see." Celeste took in the debris littering the floor, but said nothing. She just waited for him to say something, to pay attention.

Paul began to understand. At least he thought he did. "I figured you'd be out enjoying yourself, seeing your friends...maybe meet someone new?" He sat back down on the sofa and watched her, ready to gauge her reaction.

She looked down, unwilling to meet his eye. "I'm not much for friends." Her tone was deliberately nonchalant, but she couldn't quite carry it off. Something more was being hidden from him.

"You must have friends you could see? I thought women liked girlie nights out." He kept his tone light, to match hers, but had a feeling he wouldn't like her answer.

"I told you; I'm not much for friends. Especially women."

"Really?"

"Most women don't like me." She shrugged and stared at Paul as she went on, "I guess they feel threatened." She moved closer, brushed her lips against his cheek. "Not like you."

Paul realised that was exactly how he felt. His skin prickled, and he was cold, suddenly. He couldn't escape the notion that he was in danger here, but didn't know why. This was just Celeste, his ex. So why the fear?

"Celeste, what is this?"

She nuzzled his neck, and he felt physically sick. "What?"

"We broke up, remember? We agreed it was too soon."

She growled, shockingly close to his ear. "You didn't think I meant that, did you? I thought we were just...pausing for a moment, that's all."

He pushed her back, gently, feeling her squirm in his grasp. "I wasn't pausing. I meant what I said."

She smiled. "No, you didn't. Not really." She tried to move forward again, and he was forced to push her back again, a little less gently this time. This time she frowned. "I guess you did."

"Apparently." Paul took a deep breath, tried to keep cool. "I can't do this. I'm just...trying to get back on track, that's all. Can't you see that?"

She accepted the rebuke quietly, although whether that was because she was truly sorry or merely biding her time, he couldn't quite tell. Instead, she left the window and began to examine the bookshelves and mantelpiece, picking things up and putting them back haphazardly, even roughly. She moved to the table by the window, started examining his sketches. The silence stretched out, became embarrassing.

Celeste showed no sign of saying anything further, or of leaving, so he decided to take the bull by the horns. "Look, Celeste. It's late. Was there something you wanted?"

She stared at him, one eyebrow raised. "We're very abrupt tonight, aren't we, Paul?"

He sighed. "Like I said, it's late and I'm tired."

"I know," she answered. "I'm sorry. I just miss you, that's all."

Celeste gazed down at him, seemingly without guile, and Paul found himself wavering. His earlier anger at her teasing games began to dissipate in the heat of her emerald gaze, at the remembered pleasure of not being alone, even if it was only for a little while.

Celeste moved closer again, sat beside him, and this time he didn't hold her back. She hugged him, but didn't go further. "We were good together, weren't we?"

No, he thought, *we weren't.*

But even as he was remembering why he'd ended things, the heat of her body was weakening his resolve. He didn't want to be alone anymore. Not yet, anyway.

Celeste kissed him, then, and he responded, losing himself in the taste of her. She pulled back once more, and even as he noticed the slight sheen of perspiration on her upper lip, she shrugged her coat off, let it fall behind her. She slid off the sofa, and knelt on the floor.

Paul couldn't breathe. He'd resigned himself to ending things with Celeste. He'd actually been relieved to do so. Now, here she was, kneeling before him in a black lace mini-dress that left amazingly little to the imagination. And, God help him, he wanted to sink into her embrace and lose himself there. Was he that weak? He could see the swell of her breasts and even her nipples, poking out of holes in the lace. He let his gaze drop further and saw the area of deep shadow between her legs. The dress itself stopped very high up indeed, showing an extraordinary amount of thigh.

She placed a hand on either side of him on the sofa and leaned forward to whisper in his ear. Her lips brushing against his skin. Her perfume was incredibly potent, making his senses swim.

"I could stay, if you like..." she said. "Just for a while."

It was no good. He was lost. Paul tried to talk, to say something, but all that came out was a strangled croak. It was becoming blatantly obvious that at least part of him was glad to see her.

Chuckling softly, she pressed herself against him, kissed his neck. He was completely paralyzed, though whether by fear or shock he couldn't say. She was definitely the one in control now, and he felt disoriented at the speed with which she had regained the upper hand. He felt her shift slightly, felt the ministrations of her lips, tongue, and teeth as she kissed, licked, and nibbled her way across his chest. His penis felt as if it were being smothered, his jeans had grown so tight. He, too, shifted, trying to ease into a more comfortable position. Her head bobbed lower, kissing his belly now. He felt her fingers, butterfly-light, undoing his jeans and reaching into his pants.

Paul lifted himself a little and she eased his clothes down, discarded them. She stood, smiling, and reaching down, took hold of the hem of her dress and pulled it up and over her head. With a groan, Paul stood up and joined her, ran his hands down her back and cupped her buttocks, pulling her to him.

Then they were kissing. Any lingering disquiet was gone, evaporated in the heat of the moment. She pulled him down to the floor with her, and they lay upon the fur coat spread out in front of the fire.

When had she done that?

Paul stayed poised above her for a moment, gazing down at the perfection of her naked body spread beneath him. Then he lowered himself down and in one swift movement he was inside her, and his thoughts of any kind vanished in the glorious molten heat of her. They became a tangle of limbs, sweating and thrusting, conscious only of the sensations that were growing by the second.

Paul felt himself building to a climax, all control gone. He could feel Celeste writhing beneath him, effortlessly matching his rhythm. Then he erupted in an orgasm so long and intense, he thought it would never end.

His breathing finally slowed down, and he opened his eyes to find Celeste gazing up at him with an amused, even gloating expression. She changed to a more adoring, exhausted look as soon as she became aware of his scrutiny, and she was *almost* fast enough.

All the rage came flooding back, anger at being taken for a fool. Paul was reminded of the reality behind the façade, and he wasn't about to be fooled again. He rolled off Celeste and made for the bathroom, making no attempt to indulge in any of the usual post-coital pleasantries. He wanted her to know he had seen through her. The glow he usually felt after sex was gone and he felt cheap, used. She had played him for a fool and, for a little while, he'd fallen for it.

He got himself under control and wandered back into the living room, having stopped to pull on a pair of jogging pants on the way. Celeste was fully dressed once more and was fixing her face and hair in the mirror above the mantelpiece. Paul saw her reflection before he actually saw her face, and he stopped dead in the doorway, shocked.

The face in the mirror was subtly different. The eyes were harder, more dangerous-looking. The nose was longer and straighter, the cheekbones much more slanted and angular. The mouth was harder too, the lips much thinner, compressed. Overall, the impression was one of haughty condescension, even of cruelty. It hit Paul instantaneously, like a hammer blow, then she became aware of his presence. The image in the mirror transformed in an instant, although Paul couldn't see quite how.

The softer, appealing woman he had been so besotted with gazed back at him, eyes softly welcoming. She turned to face him, a questioning look on her face. "Are you all right?"

"Why shouldn't I be?" She was watching him carefully, wary of how much he had seen.

"Well, you...you rushed off a bit quickly. I just wondered if something was wrong." She seemed so sincere.

"I'm fine." There was no way he was going to make this easy for her.

She turned back to the mirror, continued primping, all the while watching his reflection in the glass. "I don't suppose there's any chance of a drink, is there?"

"Tea, coffee?"

"I was thinking of something a little stronger, actually."

"I haven't got anything stronger. Now, like I said, it's late and I'm tired." He sounded like a complete bastard, and he hated that. But he hated the way she had played him more.

Celeste picked up her coat and pulled it on, every movement screaming her anger. "I certainly wouldn't want to stay where I'm not wanted."

Paul exploded. "It's got nothing to do with that and you know it. We were taking some time, a breather...Then you turn up here and seduce me..." He was almost incoherent in his rage and frustration.

Celeste burst out laughing. "Well, pardon me for outraging your Puritan sensibilities. I didn't notice you complaining at the time."

"You're right. That shouldn't have happened."

"Shouldn't it have?"

Here they were, back to the games again. Paul had had enough, finally. More than enough. "Look, Celeste. This is getting us nowhere. What do you want from me?"

She threw a look laced with pure venom at him, and surprised him by storming past him and heading down the hall to the front door, in complete contrast to her mood only a moment earlier. Flinging the door open with a resounding crash, she stood silhouetted for a moment. Scarlett O'Hara—scorned and vengeful. Ever the actress.

"I just wanted to be loved. What's wrong with that?"

Then the door slammed shut behind her, and she was gone, leaving Paul standing alone in the living room, dumbstruck. There had been real pain in her voice at the end. He didn't think she had been faking that, whatever else had been. It had been too uncontrolled. He had really hurt her. Her parting words came back to him, stung him afresh. What was wrong with wanting to be loved? Nothing.

Except that when she said it, it didn't quite ring true. Oh, she'd meant what she said—he had no doubt of that—but he didn't think her definition of love was what most people would mean when they talked of such things. What she wanted—needed—was more insidious than that. What Celeste needed to thrive was nothing less than complete adoration. And Paul knew now he couldn't give that anymore. Not without losing an aspect of his life before meeting her that was intrinsic to his sense of self. What Celeste wanted wasn't a partner, a lover, but an acolyte. And when she tired of him and went on to the next, as he was sure she would given time, what would become of him then?

He doubted whether she would even remember him. Or if she did, it would be as some passing shadow, a dim memory of some clumsy, over-eager cast-off.

Paul sank back down onto the sofa and buried his face in his hands, let the scalding tears flow as they would, wanting them to sear the last traces of illusion from his heart. He still had his memories of Clare. That would be enough, for now. She at least had offered him a clean love.

And she had loved him back.

Chapter 17

For a few weeks, life returned to normal. Sam and Marianne both booked some holiday time—the last two weeks of December—little more than a month away. In the time leading up to that, both made a concerted effort to pay attention to each other, spend time together, rediscover what being a couple really meant.

Life may not have been perfect, but it wasn't far off it. Celeste seemed to have faded from their lives completely, content with that one last act of malice.

December 15th dawned clear and sunny, but bitterly cold—Sam and Marianne's last day at work for the year. They were determined to make this Christmas, the last before the baby arrived, special.

It was also Marianne's birthday. Sam had booked a table for two at the local Italian restaurant for eight o'clock. Confirmed pasta freaks, they were both looking forward to it. Nearly five months pregnant, Marianne was showing now. Not much, but enough that people realised she was pregnant, rather than just putting on weight. Several well-meaning acquaintances had made jokes about her weight recently, and Marianne had cried each time.

Sam spent the day trying to clear some of his backlog to hand over as little outstanding work as possible to the people covering his cases. The day seemed to pass very slowly, and it was with an enormous sense of relief that he checked the clock for the last time and saw it was five o' clock.

Time to go home.

Sam stepped out of the cocooned warmth of Archway Tower and shivered as an icy wind whipped around the corner, almost, but not quite, taking him with it. The corner of Junction Road and Highgate Hill was notoriously windy, and most people braced themselves subconsciously when rounding it. He walked around and up onto Highgate Hill, shivering. The queue at the bus-stop was enormous as usual. Also as usual, the buses were few and far between. A bus came, but Sam couldn't even get on. It filled up in a matter of seconds, leaving him nearer the front of the queue for whatever that was worth these days. The queuing system was rapidly becoming a thing of the past, overtaken by the helter-skelter of modern life.

Finally, at about a quarter to six, a bus wheezed its way around the corner and pulled to a halt, the doors thankfully right in front of Sam. He let himself get pushed up onto the bus by the horde behind him and managed to board ahead of most of the pack.

Sam swiped his Oyster card, then made his way quickly to a corner seat just behind the exit doors, always a prime target. Sitting down, he pulled his coat around him as tight as he could and tried without much success to see out of the filthy window. Sam looked up just in time to catch sight of a woman in the aisle, staring at him. Then she turned and climbed the stairs to the top deck of the bus. She was wearing one of those black crushed velvet hats, and a black coat, collar held high to obscure the lower part of her face. Her eyes were all that was really visible, but that was enough for him to see he was looking at Celeste.

Sam desperately needed to get back to Marianne, to make sure she was all right. He was filled with the utter conviction that some harm had come to her. He rummaged in his pocket for his mobile phone and switched it on, for once glad that Marianne had made him buy one. The display brightened into life, and he saw that there were no messages—hardly surprising, seeing as Marianne was the only person with that number. She knew he hardly ever turned it unless he was running very late or was worried about her for some reason. His fingers hovered over the keys for a moment as he wondered whether to ring her.

Best not, he decided.

She'd be far more likely to worry if he rang her just to see if she was okay. Rather than satisfying his own fears, he'd just be alerting her to the fact that something was likely to be wrong. Sighing, he turned it off and jammed it back into the depths of his coat.

The bus journey seemed to take forever. Sam could see nothing out of the window except vague details of brightly lit shop windows. Faces swam briefly into some sort of focus then were swallowed by the encroaching darkness, all of which only served to fuel his frustration.

Celeste's face stared back at him from every window, every poster.

Finally, the bus turned into Colney Hatch Lane, not far from home. Spotting the garage just after Pages Lane up ahead, Sam rang the bell. The minute the doors opened, he was off the bus and racing towards Pages Lane, only to slide to a halt for a moment when he saw the woman sauntering along not ten yards ahead. He knew for a fact he'd been first to get off the bus. So how did Celeste get so far in front of him?

She stopped, just at the limit of his vision in the encroaching darkness. Celeste stood silhouetted under a streetlight—same hat, same coat. Sam didn't want to get any nearer to her than he had to. He was desperate to get home to Marianne, but didn't want Celeste to know he had spotted her. As if she needed telling.

She just loitered at the periphery of his vision, taunting him with the mystery of whether she was really there or not.

The entrance to their block loomed out of the night, and Sam resolved to leave this ghost behind. He all but ran up the drive, narrowly missing being hit by a car accelerating away from the flats. He pushed the double glass doors wide open as he raced through them, coat flying out behind him. They crashed backwards against the wall so hard Sam thought the glass would smash. Doors were unlatching, cracking open as people ventured to peep out, see what was causing all the commotion, before ducking back inside and shutting them again. This was London, after all, and it was dark outside. Paranoia was the norm.

Reaching his door, Sam fumbled for the keys, cursing. It took three attempts to find them, let alone fit them into the lock. When Sam finally let himself into the hall, there was no sign of Marianne. No lights were on. The flat was totally quiet. There was none of the usual familiar atmosphere: music playing, dinner cooking. It was nearly half past six now. She was normally home long before Sam. He went into the living room and flicked on the light switch, hoping she'd fallen asleep on the sofa.

Nothing.

He tried the same thing in the bedroom. Again, nothing.

Then he looked in the kitchen, in case she'd left a note—had to go out. Where was she? Sam imagined all sorts of fates that might have befallen her, all involving Celeste.

Sam stood in the hall, chest heaving, looking uselessly from side to side. His face was wet, but he couldn't even remember if it had been raining outside.

He'd lost her. He'd lost Marianne, and the baby. Sam could feel it in his heart, like a rotten, black, festering sore.

The key turning in the lock broke through the haze. Sam turned to the door, fear seeping in past the shocked numbness. What next? What more could he lose?

The door pushed open and revealed Marianne standing in the doorway, silhouetted against the light from the foyer. Sam's last thought before collapsing in a heap was that it had been an epiphany of sorts. He'd won a reprieve.

When he came to, Marianne was kneeling over him, a worried frown on her face even as she wiped Sam's with a damp cloth. "What's the matter, Sam?"

"I thought I saw a ghost." Shakily, Sam attempted a laugh, but it didn't come off very well.

"What?"

Her tone was incredulous, and so he tried to explain, tried to get her to understand. After her experiences with Celeste, she didn't have too much of a problem.

"Maybe you were wrong, Sam. Maybe it wasn't her."

"It was her."

Silence fell—dreams and apparitions were bad enough. They'd both had more than their fair share of those. But what had Celeste actually done, out here in the real world? It boiled down to a glimpse in a store and what had seemed to be a chance meeting in the park. Things had quieted down lately, hadn't they?

Marianne sat back, her face troubled. Her hand went (unconsciously, he thought) to her belly and absently patted it, comforting both her and the nascent life inside.

Finally, she spoke, "But nothing bad actually happened, did it? So I don't see how it could have been her."

Sam got the impression she was only saying this for his benefit. Marianne believed, all right. She just didn't want to any more than he did.

They helped each other up, and Marianne went on, "I think she's had us both in such a state we're jumping at shadows."

Sam nodded reluctantly, not wanting to continue this. Marianne could delude herself all she wanted, if it made her feel better. "I suppose so."

"Come on, Sam. It's seven o'clock. We'll be late for dinner if we don't get a move on."

Reluctantly, he set about getting ready. He had no appetite now, none at all, and just wanted to stay home, safe (he hoped) with Marianne.

Eight o'clock and they were just being led to their table. Sam still wasn't all that hungry, but that was all right. Marianne would probably be able to eat enough for both of them, anyway. Now that she was over her morning sickness, it was as if she felt she had to make up for lost time.

Sam couldn't help glancing around continually. Just to check.

He watched in disbelief as Marianne ordered what seemed like almost everything on the menu, along with a request for a large plate of garlic bread. A recipe for heartburn. Sam stuck to a simple plate of pasta; there was more than enough food coming already if he was still hungry after that. He ordered a lager, and Marianne stuck to Diet Coke. It struck Sam as a bit hypocritical, but she said it settled her stomach. If she ate everything she'd ordered, she would probably need it.

By common consent, they chatted about things for the baby, argued about names, caught up on each other's day. He kept a watchful eye on their fellow diners, but Celeste didn't seem to be around.

Halfway through the meal, something occurred to Sam. He sat back, placing his cutlery back on the plate. "I forgot to ask. Why were you late tonight?"

She wouldn't look at him. "I wasn't that late, only about an hour."

Sam persisted. "Yeah, but still... What happened?"

For some reason, she was reluctant to tell him. Sam could see the evasion in her eyes, usually so forthright.

Marianne shook her head. "Nothing, really. Some of the girls invited me for a drink to celebrate my birthday. What's the problem?"

"Nothing. I'm just surprised you didn't mention it before, that's all." She was being a little too defensive for Sam's liking.

They carried on their meal in silence for a few minutes, 'til she relented, seeing his unease. "I just didn't want to upset you, that's all."

"Why would I be upset just because you went for a drink?" Mystified, Sam waited to see what came next.

"There was an accident at the station on my way home." She sounded carefully nonchalant, but Sam knew her better than that.

"What sort of accident?"

"A woman fell down the escalators. They had to stop everything for about twenty minutes."

"Was she badly hurt?" Sam kept his eyes on his food, not wanting to put her off while she was talking. There was more to this than she was saying, and he needed to hear it all.

"I think so. She got caught up at the bottom." Hearing a tremble in her voice, Sam looked up. She was visibly upset now, the veneer of indifference gone. "She was alive, though, so that's something." A pause. "She was still screaming when they stretchered her out."

"Jesus." Sam didn't know how else to respond.

One thing he had always hated was the fatuous comments people tended to make when confronted by tragedy, like "she was too good for this world," or "at least she's not suffering now." Comments like that were invariably more for the comfort of the one speaking than for the recipient. They didn't mean it that way, but it was the inevitable result. Perhaps the comfort for both parties lay more in the fact that each knew the sorrow was shared and understood. In that way, although the grief was in no way lessened, at least its load was made easier to bear.

Marianne had one more little bombshell to drop, though. "I heard one of the ambulance men saying it looked like she was going to lose the baby, even if they managed to save her."

"She was pregnant?"

"Six, maybe seven months. She was bigger than me, anyhow."

Something in her voice wasn't right. There was something she wasn't saying. Sam looked up, waiting for the clue he felt sure was coming.

Marianne's voice was trembling now. "She was standing right in front of me. Then she fell."

Sam took her hand. "I hate to say it, but thank God it wasn't you."

"I got the impression it should have been."

Startled, Sam misjudged the lager he was about to sip and spilled a little of it down the front of his shirt. "Say again?"

"Like I said, I was right behind her when it happened. I don't know whether it was intentional or not, but I saw a woman's hand against her back—very small and pale, with blood-red nails, very long. Then she was falling."

Sam stayed silent, waiting for the rest.

"She had hair like mine."

Sam didn't doubt that it was Celeste, and she was back with a vengeance. A pall had fallen over the evening. They had been stupid enough to think she'd gone, until tonight. How could they ever have thought it would be so easy?

They fussed with their food and carried on eating with great reluctance, needing to give things time to lighten up a little, if they could. Upset as she was, Marianne still managed to put away a formidable amount of food. Sam finished his linguine and sat watching her, amazed. She finished her Diet Coke about halfway through the meal, and Sam signalled the waiter for another round. When she was finished, she sat back and wiped her mouth, smiling at him guiltily.

Sam grinned. "I'm almost afraid to ask what you want for dessert."

She laughed explosively, ashamed but unrepentant, then clamped a hand over her mouth, embarrassed.

Sam smiled and took her hand once more. "It'll be all right, love. Promise."

She nodded and tried to smile. Sam felt the weight of the night's events lift. It looked as if they would be able to put all this behind them, at least for tonight. Sam signalled the waiter for the menu and, in a considerably lighter frame of mind, they pored over the desserts, both of them opting for their favourite, tiramisu. When it came, Marianne's eyes positively lit up. Neither of them wasted time on conversation. They would have to do something about Celeste sooner or later, but not now. Tonight was *their* time.

Finally, both full to bursting, they pushed the plates away, signalled the waiter once more, and ordered cappuccino.

Now, Sam thought. The time was right. All the shadows had been pushed back a little, at least, and things were good between them. "Marianne."

"Mm?" She was hardly listening to him.

"Marianne, I've got something for you."

Now her eyes lit up. She was like a child when it came to presents.

Sam reached into his jacket pocket and placed the small blue velvet box on the table in front of her. She looked at Sam, and then took the box, feeling it before opening it. She looked almost afraid of it. Gingerly, she opened the lid. He watched her face, trying to gauge her reaction, as nervous as she was.

When she saw what was inside, she gasped. It was a ring, a solitaire diamond. They both knew what it meant. What Sam didn't know was what her reaction would be.

"You're not going to make me ask out loud, are you? Not in here."

Smiling, she shook her head.

"Do I have to ask what the answer is?"

Again, a shake of the head. She wasn't making this any easier. Did she mean no, she wouldn't marry him; or no, he didn't have to ask?

Seeing Sam's discomfiture, she handed the ring back to him, grinning at his expression of dismay. In a voice barely under control, she managed to put his mind at ease. It would be all right, after all. "You do it."

Taking her hand, Sam eased the ring onto her engagement finger. It fit perfectly. They sat there, holding hands, stupid grins on their faces, until a waiter noticed. The next thing they knew, the manager was at their side offering his congratulations, together with a bottle of champagne. The meal was on the house, he'd said.

The manager and two or three of the waiters ("My sons," he'd informed us. "Fine boys. May they be so lucky.") joined them in a toast, then another. Before long the champagne was gone—Marianne's glass was still almost full, she'd allowed herself no more than a sip. They finally ushered the couple out of the restaurant at nearly one o'clock in the morning, amid much hand-kissing and back clapping.

Sam and Marianne went home in a rosy glow, far away from any problems, every day or otherwise.

Sam woke up the next morning with a terminal hangover, a soppy grin still plastered across his face. Last night had been more than worth it. A week ago, he had been in danger of losing everything and was too besotted to even care. No, besotted wasn't the right word—it gave the impression of whimsy, which was far too innocuous. The right word for his condition had been far stronger. He had been obsessed. And for what? For dreams of a woman he had barely met in what passed for normality. Not that Sam had found everyday life to be too normal, lately.

And now, here he was, engaged and an expectant father. Sam looked across at Marianne, still fast asleep. She was smiling, gently, her expression beatific. He could see her hand, diamond proudly displayed, cupping her belly. She looked beautiful. Sam eased out of bed, trying not to wake her. She got tired more easily lately, and he didn't want her to lose any more sleep than she had to. God knew they had plenty of that ahead of them once the baby was born.

Sam made his way down the hall to the kitchen and shut the door behind him so as not to disturb Marianne. Sometimes he surprised himself with how thoughtful he was becoming. He filled the kettle and switched it on, then drew the curtains.

The glare hit Sam like a sledgehammer, intensifying the beat in his skull to a barely manageable crescendo, inducing a rising wave of nausea. It had snowed during the night. A thin, pristine blanket covered the gardens and nestled in clumps on the surrounding fir trees. He had to admit, it was beautiful to look at, even if his eyes couldn't quite cope with it yet.

Turning to the cupboard over the sink, Sam found the industrial strength paracetamol and swallowed a couple dry, grimacing at the taste.

Trying not to retch, Sam grabbed a glass and turned on the cold tap, began swallowing. It took three glasses of water to dilute the stuff stuck to his tongue. But the inside of his mouth still felt less than pleasant, as if his tongue was carpeted with some foul-tasting lichen. The kettle had gone off the boil, so Sam switched it back on and went to the windowsill to get a mug from its tree.

That was when he saw her.

Sam hadn't noticed her immediately because she was swathed in white from head to toe. Even her beautiful black hair was covered, wrapped in a white woollen hat that looked more like a turban. She must have been hiding in the tree line.

Now she was right outside the window. Her face must have been less than a centimetre away from the glass. Her breath plumed in the frigid air, momentarily misting little patches of the window with each breath. The only colour in evidence was the scarlet slash of her lipstick and her brilliant green eyes, staring hungrily in.

Sam dropped the mug, heard it smash distantly on the floor.

She bared her teeth, hissed, and with a speed he found bewildering, she raked her nails down the glass, gouging deep scratches in it. Blood welled in those scratches, and for a moment Sam thought it was hers. Then he saw it was the glass itself. How did glass bleed, for God's sake? Her mouth gaped wide, but the scream came from Sam's lips. Her cry was buzzing in his head—nowhere else. Blood was dripping down the glass, casting Celeste in a crimson glow.

Stupidly, all Sam could think was, *The glass is bleeding! How the hell is the glass bleeding?*

Then she was gone.

Just like that, the only evidence that she had ever been there was a bloody handprint smeared on the now undamaged glass. All traces of the fractures she'd gouged in it were gone...and even the handprint was fading now.

Sam stepped back, shaking, and crunched barefoot on pieces of the broken mug. The pain was hot and immediate, searing up his leg. But at least it made him forget the window and Celeste.

Sam let out a loud yelp and began hopping around the kitchen, trying to reach his foot, which was bleeding worryingly heavily.

It never even occurred to Sam to sit down, which promptly resulted in him falling flat on his arse, adding insult to injury.

Marianne chose that particular moment to appear in the doorway, white with fright. When she saw what had happened, she shook her head, sighed, and went to the bathroom for a towel. She then spent ten minutes picking shards of china from his foot, and disinfecting and bandaging it. Through it all, she had to cope with cries of pain, repeated attempts to escape from her ministrations, and the obligatory sharp hiss every time she went near it, let alone touched it. In short, Sam behaved like ninety-five percent of injured men—he regressed to the age of five.

Sam allowed himself to be led, hobbling, back to bed and left Marianne to do all the clearing up and make the tea, finally.

The whole performance had been purely for Sam's benefit. Bitch.

When Marianne came back into the bedroom ten minutes later with a tray of tea and toast, she had an insufferably smug expression on her face. The indulgent little smile that said, "Men. Absolutely useless, bless 'em."

Sam resisted the temptation to say something scathing and resolved to let himself be pampered for a while. He hoisted himself up onto the pillows and accepted his breakfast with as much good grace as he could muster. He was quite happy to play the clumsy idiot if it stopped Marianne from wondering what had happened, from realising that the scream had come *before* the crash of china, not as a result of it.

Truth to tell, Sam didn't really want to think about it either. Looking at the tray, his appetite returned—something he would have thought impossible. He had scoffed half the toast and all the tea before Marianne even had a chance to get herself comfortable. He quickly finished the rest and lay back, contented, feeling almost human again. His headache had receded into the background and he no longer had the shakes.

Sam watched Marianne daintily consume her share. She was getting through it almost as fast as he had, but with a delicacy he found astonishing. Sam pictured her at nine months and had to smile. If she didn't cut down a bit, soon, she would be as big as a house.

"What?" She had seen his expression and was staring, half smiling and half accusing.

Sam tried to extricate himself as gracefully as possible. "Nothing. I just like to watch you eat, that's all."

"Meaning?"

"Nothing!" Sam protested his innocence heartily, but she wasn't having any of it. He tried one last time. "I just like to see you enjoying your food."

"Especially when I enjoy so much of it, am I right?"

Grinning sheepishly, Sam nodded. Caught. "I'm only thinking of you, love. If you put on too much weight now, you're going to find it very hard to lose afterwards."

"I know. You're right. It's just I'm always so *hungry*."

"Well, switch to fruit or something. It's the only way, really." She nodded. Marianne knew he was right, same as Sam knew fruit just wasn't the same – and it wasn't his decision anyway. Neither of them said anything for a while, then Marianne put her tray on her bedside table and leaned back against the mountain of pillows she had accumulated—closing her eyes.

Sam leaned over and placed his head gently on the swell of her belly—listened to the sound of the baby's heartbeat thudding along like Red Rum. "I wonder what it'll be."

"Hmmm?" Marianne was off with the fairies somewhere, not really listening to me.

"The baby. I wonder whether we'll have a boy or a girl?"

"Does it matter?"

She was listening properly now, Sam noticed. And she was serious when she asked if it mattered. He got the feeling he'd accidentally touched on something that had been worrying her. "No. No, it doesn't matter at all to me. Just so long as he or she is healthy, that's all."

Marianne's hand found the unruly mop Sam laughingly referred to as hair and began stroking it. They lay like that for quite a while, neither wanting to disturb the other. They had found their own private peace for a while, though Sam knew—absolutely knew—it was really just the lull before the storm.

Chapter 18

Christmas Eve. The season of peace and goodwill to all men was upon them, and Sam was trying to quell his more Scrooge-like tendencies. Marianne, however, was in full flow. Christmas was her absolute favourite time of year, and she always revelled in it, happy as a sandboy. Since finishing work, she had thrown herself wholeheartedly into the serious business of making the Christmas cake and pudding. Not to mention the dozens of mince pies she'd secreted in tins all over the kitchen.

Two days ago, Sam had allowed himself to be dragged to the local Marks and Spencer food hall. He had watched in amazement as she systematically denuded the shelves, or did her level best to. Time and again he had tried to get her to see reason. How much food could two people eat in three days? But he knew he was fighting a losing battle.

She took attacks on her Christmas preparations personally, and Sam had learnt early on not to interfere with her fun. Now all the work was done. The walls were festooned with glittering chains until the living room looked like some treasure cave; that or Santa's grotto. Sam was beginning to feel like Marianne's apprentice elf. All he needed was the pointy ears.

Here they were, at ten o'clock on Christmas Eve, and Marianne had finally decided they were ready. They had just finished hauling the last of the presents out into the living room and placing them under the tree. There was nothing else to do.

At least he hoped not. With Marianne, Sam was never sure.

He breathed a sigh of relief when she came into the living room with two mugs of tea.

"What's on TV, Sam?"

"God knows."

In comfortable silence, they flicked channels, searching aimlessly for something watchable. Sick to death of the usual Christmassy fodder—blockbusters they'd both seen before, Christmas specials of the popular sit-coms—they were pleasantly surprised to find something on one of the more obscure satellite channels. It was the tail end of an introduction to some old film, a silent one. ...*of Fire*, according to the announcer.

"Could be worth a look," Sam said. "Something we haven't seen, at least."

Looking at the screen, Marianne answered, "I don't think anyone still living will have seen this one."

Sam said nothing, just waited.

"Oh go on, then," she muttered, and got up, heading for the kitchen. "Tea?"

Sam kept his attention fixed firmly on the television as he answered, not wanting to give her the chance to change her mind, or suggest something like *Love Actually,* one of her favourites. "Please, love."

The interminable title sequences had only just ended when Marianne came back in, placing their drinks on the coffee table in front of them. Sam muttered a thank you and they settled down to watch the film.

Snow was howling through narrow cobbled streets; a dark figure was barely visible struggling towards some as yet unperceived goal. It was impossible to tell what sex they were, let alone any idea of age. The camera closed in on the figure from behind, a large, ornate building of some kind looming ever closer. The music, naturally, was fraught with tension. Sam looked over to Marianne, ready to give in and ask whether anything else was on, and stopped, the words stuck in his throat.

She was transfixed. The only light in the room came from a small lamp on a table beside her. To Sam it appeared as if she was lit from behind. He could see a tear slowly tracking its way down her cheek, glittering brightly. Sam couldn't believe it. It had actually got to her. He'd always believed that the imagery in many of the silent films had a stronger effect precisely because of the silence. Marianne, however, had never been convinced.

This one, however, had got to her. Best to leave her alone, for now.

Gradually, the story unfolded. The figure in the snow had in fact been a woman. Destitute, ill, maybe even dying. She left the obligatory baby on the church doorstep and stumbled away, weeping into the night. The next twenty minutes of the film were taken up with a series of little scenes, sad and uplifting in turn, denoting the rise to maturity of the baby, clearly becoming a girl of outstanding beauty. About half an hour into the film came a scene that brought Sam back to full awareness with a jolt.

The scene opened with the priest in charge of the home calling the heroine into his office. She went willingly enough—viewers were aware by now, thanks to those little narrative "cards" they used to use that the girl was now of an age to find employment. But from the sinister look on the priest's face and the eerie music welling up, it was obvious something deeply traumatic was about to happen.

They didn't have long to wait.

The priest held a chair for her as she sat down in front of his desk, but he didn't move round to the ornate throne that passed for his chair on the other side of the desk. Instead, he gently stroked her hair.

The camera cut to the girl, getting more jittery by the minute.

She looked like a scared rabbit, bracing herself for the moment when she'd have to cut and run. Her eyes darted fearfully from side to side, looking decidedly moist.

Sam sat up, disturbed. This subject matter was a little out of the ordinary for a silent film. Films of that period had usually shied away from anything like this. He waited for someone to burst in, demanding to know what was going on. For another of those narrative frames. Something.

Almost unconsciously, Sam was holding his breath. A quick glance across at Marianne confirmed she, too, was sitting rigid with apprehension. Disbelieving, they watched the drama unfolding before them. Tears were streaming freely down the woman's cheeks now, as the priest's hand left her hair and moved onto her cheek, then downwards onto her neck.

This forbidden contact seemed to trigger something in the priest. Gone was the kindly priest-face. His expression now was that of a lust-filled monster crazed with desire. Roughly, he pulled the girl up to her feet and pushed her back against the desk. There followed a brutal and sickening rape scene that would have appeared gratuitous even in a film made today. It was more like some porn epic.

Marianne was openly sobbing now, tears streaming down her face. She looked as if she was about to be sick.

Furious, Sam reached over and grabbed the remote...and froze as he was just about to switch channels. The girl on the desk had turned her head. She was staring straight at him, lambent green eyes full of reproach. He had just realised what was wrong with that image when she spoke.

"You could have saved me, Sam. I loved you."

Then the lights went out.

It wasn't just the lights. The TV blanked out, as did the little display on the DVD player.

"Power cut."

Sam jumped a little at Marianne's voice, hoarse with unshed

tears, then relaxed slightly. Her voice sounded strained, almost as if she was in shock.

"Maybe it's a fuse. I'll go and look." Sam turned and started to edge towards the door. At least, that was what he thought he was doing. He'd only moved two or three steps when his shins connected solidly with the coffee table and he fell forward, knocking the wind out of his sails and sending cups smashing to the floor. True to form, he'd barely landed on the floor, when the lights came back on.

Sam hauled himself up onto his hands and knees, trying to be careful of any shards from the mugs on the floor—this was getting to be a habit. He rolled over and sat down hard, waiting for Marianne to laugh at him. He was fast becoming an expert in pratfalls. It would have come as a welcome relief, but she wasn't laughing. She was sitting on the edge of her chair, hunched over, face contorted in pain, gripping her stomach.

Sam felt his insides turn to ice. "Marianne?"

"Call an ambulance, Sam. Quick."

He went to the phone and dialled 999, gave the details operating on instinct alone.

Numb, Sam went back to Marianne after putting the phone down, knelt in front of her. He landed in coffee and grimaced. He could see the desolation in her eyes, the panic, and feared the worst. "What do I do? How can I help?"

"I'm bleeding."

Sam looked down quickly, suddenly realising what he'd done. It wasn't coffee he'd landed in after all. There was blood all over the chair, and it was spreading slowly across the carpet. Doing his best to stifle his disgust, Sam placed his hand on her shoulder, held her as she rested her head against him. What else could he do?

Sirens screamed in the distance, growing closer. He just hoped they were in time.

Chapter 19

Walking up Dartmouth Park Hill, he watched the striking green dome of St. Joseph's church looming with a sense almost of coming home. He hadn't been to Mass since losing Clare and the baby, and he'd missed the solace it offered. He had felt calm, truly at peace, for the first time in months, certainly since he had met Celeste. That feeling persisted throughout the comforting ritual of the Mass, right up to Communion. At the ringing of the bell, he filed along the pew and joined the queue in the centre aisle. The queue moved fairly quickly, and he received Communion with a sense of relief. Crossing himself, he resolved to attend Confession sometime soon, complete the catharsis. It was when he turned and walked off towards the side aisle to return to his seat that he saw her.

She was sitting in the side chapel staring straight at him, a mocking grin on her face, green eyes blazing. She looked like a cat contemplating its prey, ready to enjoy the dance.

Quickly, Paul surveyed the surrounding parishioners. Nobody seemed to have noticed the expression on her face, or his. When Paul looked back, she was gone. In her place sat a middle-aged woman, tired and worn-looking. The woman stared at him nervously, obviously wondering what he was looking at. Luckily, he had only stopped for a moment.

Keeping his head down, he made his way back to his seat and knelt, bowing his head as if in prayer.

It couldn't be her. Couldn't be.

He got through the rest of the Mass, mumbling the correct responses purely by instinct, trying to resist the urge to look and see if she was still there. All the while he was desperate to get out, get away from there—from her. As soon as he decently could, he scrambled from his pew and joined the line heading out. He kept staring at the people he passed, flinching every time he thought he saw her. All false alarms, serving only to fix him in other peoples' memory as some sort of lunatic who was shying away from unseen shadows, which no doubt had been her intention all along.

He blundered blindly back down Dartmouth Park Hill almost blinded by tears, all peace shattered.

The following day, he got onto a tube train at Tufnell Park station, southbound—only to find her occupying the seat facing his. With a cry, he hurled himself back through the doors even as they were closing. A corner of his jacket got caught and he only just managed to get it free in time.

Standing there on the platform, chest heaving, he caught sight of those eyes again, incandescent with rage. She was furious. The cheated snarl on her face stayed with him for days. He knew then she was out for blood. The stakes of the game had just risen considerably.

Paul stumbled home, shuddering as if frozen by the time he got there. He made himself a cup of hot, sugary tea (Wasn't that what you were supposed to do in cases of shock?) that tasted absolutely vile and took it into his bedroom. Once there, he pulled the curtains shut and buried himself under the duvet. The sweetness of the tea made him feel physically sick, but he managed to keep it down.

He slept through until the next morning, awaking considerably refreshed. Climbing out of bed, he realised he was still dressed, albeit extremely crumpled, and smiled ruefully. He was going down and down; he could feel it. He just didn't know what to do about it. Time would tell, he supposed.

He slipped out of his rumpled clothes and pulled on a clean pair of jeans and a fresh jumper.

In the kitchen, he put the kettle on to boil. While he was waiting, he turned the radio on and went to the breadbin, intent on some toast. One of his favourite songs, "Shiny Happy People" by R.E.M., was playing, something that was guaranteed to cheer him up.

He was halfway to the fridge for the butter when the music faded and the voice of the DJ came straight at him... "And it looks bright and fine out there on this Tuesday morning!"

Paul stopped as if poleaxed.

Tuesday? How could it be Tuesday?

He rushed into the living room, tea and toast forgotten, and switched on the television, found the news channel. There it was. Tuesday. He'd slept for more than twenty-four hours.

He wandered back into the kitchen to make breakfast, resolving to make the most of the day. He meandered around the flat for an hour or so, putting laundry through the machine, washing up breakfast, generally putting things in order. Things he didn't have to think about.

By about eleven o'clock, all his work was done and he was once more at a loose end. Paul made up his mind to go shopping, numb the senses with a little mindless extravagance. Paul pulled on a jacket and headed off, locking the door firmly behind him. He walked to the end of his road and turned left onto Dartmouth Park Hill, walked up as far as Raydon Street before turning left, and walked along to the bus stop. He was in luck. A bus pulled up within minutes. It didn't look too full, either. He sat in the front left seat, just behind the luggage compartment. Whether it was true or not, Paul always felt as if he got more leg-room that way.

He gazed out the window and let the world go by, barely conscious of his surroundings. All the familiar landmarks washed past, and before he knew it, they were there. Looking at his watch, Paul was surprised to see nearly forty minutes had flown by. The bus was now overfull with people crammed into the aisle all the way to the back, many of them looking balefully at those who had been lucky enough to find a seat, as if their own bad luck had been deliberate.

Then the doors opened and the flood of lemming-like shoppers poured out. Paul let himself flow with the tide until he was inside, then made his way across to Marks and Spencer as quickly as he could, intent on cutting out Mothercare. He couldn't hear to go past such shops now. They brought everything back as if it had happened only yesterday. He headed for the stairs to the left of the food hall, determined to ransack the menswear section. He spent a pleasant forty minutes picking items at random. It had been a while since he'd last bought any new clothes, and what he did have was beginning to look decidedly worn. He found a warm, comfortable black wool jacket and added that to his basket, along with a cherry-red baggy jumper. That would do for now.

He paid for his things, wincing at the damage to his bank account, and moved onto the next shop. There was a Currys next door, and he browsed delightedly through all the gadgets, purchasing a Gameboy, of all things.

What the hell, he said to himself. *Christmas is early this year, that's all.*

It would serve to keep him amused on some of the lonely winter evenings that lay ahead. Paul bought half a dozen cartridges for his new toy and left hurriedly, before he could be tempted again. He'd spent a small fortune already, and he'd only been in two shops. Still, he had to admit it was having the desired effect. He felt more cheerful already.

He stood for a moment, looking at the crowds surging around him, oblivious to anything that didn't involve them directly, and suddenly he didn't want to be there anymore. He wanted to go home.

He picked up a bus quickly enough, but the journey home seemed to take forever. Maybe it was just fatigue. Suddenly he felt as if he could sleep for a week. Maybe he dozed, maybe he was just sensitized somehow, by now. Either way, about halfway home Paul became aware that someone was watching him. Someone just behind him.

He held off looking for as long as he could, afraid of what he might see. The feeling wouldn't go away, though. If anything, it was intensifying. He was going to have to look soon, whatever the consequence.

When he did, all the joy of the day drained out of him as suddenly as if someone had pulled the plug on it, only to be replaced by a dreadful cold.

Apt, he thought. *Dread-full*. It described the sensation perfectly, regardless of the fact that it made him feel as if he were centre-stage in some Victorian gothic play.

Celeste was sitting right behind him. She was dressed all in black (fittingly), which made her skin look even paler, almost translucent. Her dark hair framed her face perfectly, sooty mascara making her green eyes blaze all the brighter. The animosity held within her stare was plain for all to see, if they would only look.

Speechless, Paul gazed back, spellbound, unable to believe what his mind insisted he was seeing. Again, everyone else on the bus seemed oblivious to her presence. Paul realised they probably didn't even see her, at least not in the same way he did. Smiling at his discomfiture, Celeste leaned forward, placing the scarlet slash of her lips close to his ear so he could feel the moist heat of her breath as it caressed his throat and inhale the heady aroma of her perfume.

"I'll never let you go, Paul. Never."

"All change, mate. We're at Archway." The driver's voice was sharp, annoyed.

Paul blinked owlishly and looked around, momentarily lost. Where were all the people? He hadn't even noticed the bus pull in at the depot, let alone stop. They had only been halfway through the journey when Celeste had...

What had she done? He couldn't remember. Was that shock? Or had she engineered that too? The bus was empty.

The driver was shaking Paul's shoulder roughly, impatient to go on his coffee break. Turning quickly, Paul checked the seat behind him, already knowing what would find. Nothing. She was long gone, if in fact, she had ever been there in the first place.

"Come on, mate. I haven't got all day."

"I'm sorry. I must have dropped off," He began collecting his bags, which he had somehow let slip to the floor.

"Yeah, well, drop off the bloody bus, all right?"

Paul nodded, embarrassed, and followed the driver to the front of the bus, still apologising.

It was a long, lonely walk home. Paul didn't trust himself to catch another bus. He was afraid she'd appear again. She was out for revenge now, he thought. It was beginning to look as if he'd fallen into extremely deep water.

Chapter 20

The ambulance had got them to the hospital within fifteen minutes—record time from Muswell Hill to Archway even at that time of night. Everything had taken on a nightmarish quality by then, lent a totally surreal aspect by the sirens and flashing lights. Marianne had been stretchered off the ambulance and they were met by what looked like an entire bloody crash team. There followed a mad rush down corridor after corridor: Marianne crying, doctors issuing hurried instructions, nurses everywhere. Sam just hung onto her hand and kept up as best he could as the strip lights overhead flashed by in quick succession, making the whole thing seem like the inside of some vast kaleidoscope.

They went through another set of doors and a nurse stepped up, tried to disengage Sam's hand from Marianne's. She had a hell of a job. She was muttering something that no doubt was supposed to be comforting, but Sam didn't have a clue what it was. The woman might as well have been speaking in fluent German for all the sense he could make of it. All he knew was that they wanted him to leave Marianne, and he had a terrible fear that if he did, he might not get her back.

Now here he was, nearly five hours later, and there was still no news. Some Christmas. Sam sat there resolutely, not daring to go further than the coffee machine. His kidneys felt as if they were floating, but he wouldn't wander in search of the toilet in case a doctor came looking for him. He felt as if it would be tempting fate.

Finally, at about a quarter to five in the morning, out they came. The doctor was middle-aged, obviously exhausted, and looked as if he wasn't far off from collapsing himself. The nurse looked as if she was, under normal circumstances, quite pretty, with dark hair and eyes. She had a mouth that kept trying to soften but couldn't quite make it. When she wasn't exhausted, she probably looked about twenty-three. Right now, she looked nearer forty.

"Mr. Hansen? Sam Hansen?"

Sam nodded dumbly and stood up, afraid of what he was about to hear.

The doctor saw the expression on his face and smiled wearily. "Your fiancée is going to be all right. We were very lucky."

Sam relaxed slightly and felt himself sway, dizzy at the sudden drop in tension. Then the wording of what he had said hit home, and it all came flooding back. He forced himself to ask the next question, although he was pretty sure he wouldn't like the answer. "And the baby?"

For a moment, the doctor didn't answer. In that time, Sam saw his life fall apart, quite clearly, and in minute detail. No family, not now, and maybe not ever. What if Marianne couldn't have any more children? They'd never really talked about having children before all this, but he was getting kind of used to the idea.

"Relax," the doctor said. "The babies are all right, too."

"*Babies?*"

The doctor broke into spontaneous laughter at Sam's amazed expression.

"Babies. Your fiancée is expecting twins. Actually, I'm surprised it wasn't picked up before. We managed to save all of them, but she has lost an awful lot of blood. It was touch and go for a long time."

"What caused it?"

"We're not quite sure." He frowned slightly, a confused expression on his face Sam didn't like. "There doesn't seem to be any physical reason that we could find. Has she been under any undue stress lately?"

He was fishing, that was plain to see. Celeste crossed Sam's mind, but he pushed that away. "No. No, I don't think so." What could he say? They were being targeted by some sort of erotic ghost? Best to keep things like that to themselves; for now, at least. "Can I see her?"

"Sure. She's being admitted to the ward now. Sit tight here for another ten minutes or so and someone will come and get you."

Sam nodded and gripped the man's hand, shook it hard. "Thank you. Thank you very much."

"Glad to be able to help, Mr. Hansen." He started off, the exhausted nurse trailing behind him, and then turned around again. "By the way, merry Christmas."

Sam muttered the same and sat back down, dazed. It was hard to take it all in at once. Half an hour ago, he'd thought himself bereft, about to lose Marianne as well as the baby. Now he found not only was she okay, but they were having twins! He grinned stupidly as it began to sink in. Marianne certainly didn't do things by halves.

Sure enough, ten minutes later Sam was duly fetched. The nurse who came to collect him was the first unfriendly face he'd encountered here. Again, she was a student nurse, no more than twenty. She was as cold as ice. Sam supposed it could have been tiredness, but he got the distinct impression she couldn't stand the sight of him. She virtually oozed disapproval. As she turned a corner, he caught sight of something glinting at her throat. A crucifix.

Maybe that explained it. Maybe it was something as simple as the fact that she was religious and disapproved of the fact that he and Marianne weren't married, even though she was pregnant. If that was the case, she'd better learn to be more tactful or get out of nursing. It was definitely the wrong profession for someone so obviously bigoted. It probably wasn't the only prejudice she was carrying around, either

Then she went through a set of swing doors, and as Sam followed her through, he found himself in a small private room. She made her way across to the bed and placed her hand on Marianne's shoulder, shook it gently. "Here's your boyfriend to see you."

There it was, the accent definitely on "boyfriend." The nurse made her way directly towards Sam, forcing him to step aside for her. That or be mown down. "You can't have long. I'll be back in ten minutes."

She was stopping just short of being openly antagonistic. Still, considering what Sam and Marianne been through recently, that was the least of their problems.

Sam put her out of his mind and moved forward, closer to Marianne. The door shut behind him just a little too firmly. Taking Marianne's hand, he sat on the chair at the side of the bed. He didn't know what to say, feeling as guilty as he did.

She smiled wearily at him, nervous. "How do I look?"

Sam smiled, relieved. Same old Marianne, intent on looking her best, whatever the situation.

"You don't look bad, love. A bit white, that's all."

That was an understatement. She had no colour at all.

Her skin was so pale it was virtually translucent, and there were huge dark sacs under her eyes. She looked awful and she knew it. Nothing Sam could say would change that. Smiling wryly, she closed her eyes, lay very quiet. A single tear leaked from the corner of her eye.

Sam pretended not to see it, not wanting to embarrass her. He was pretty close to tears himself. He cleared his throat, trying to calm things down. "They said you'll be fine. You just need some rest, that's all."

"But no baby, right?" Now she was staring at him, eager to read his expression.

148

Sam blinked, amazed and a little angry. "You mean they didn't tell you?"

"Tell me what?"

She was badly frightened now, and from Sam's experience of the last few hours, he had a pretty good idea of what was going through her mind. He stroked her hand gently, tried in vain to keep his voice steady. "You didn't lose the baby, so relax."

"I didn't?"

"Nope. You even gained one."

"What?" Hope was dawning, and it gladdened Sam's heart to see it, to see her face softening a little.

"Twins. Both fine."

"Twins?"

"You're beginning to sound like a parrot, you know." Sam was grinning openly now. The expression on her face was comical, a mixture of elation, shock and apprehension. Maybe things would work out after all.

It was the 28th of December and Sam was bringing Marianne home from the hospital. The doctors, after much cajoling—not to mention pleading—had finally agreed to let her go a little earlier than they really would have liked, on the strict understanding that she maintain complete bed rest for at least another week.

This morning, before setting off to bring her home, Sam had hauled all the presents into their bedroom and placed them on the floor beside her side of the bed. Any time she was ready, they could have their fun opening them.

The cab pulled up outside their block of flats and Sam got out quickly, running round the vehicle to open the door on her side and help her out. He paid the driver and ushered Marianne through the doors and to their flat, keeping hold of her bags as he searched in his pockets for the front door keys. Finally, he got the front door open and let her in, helping her off with her coat and leading her through to the bedroom. "Get yourself into bed," he said. "I'll put the kettle on."

"Fair enough," she answered, sinking down onto the bed. He grinned, and made his way through to the kitchen to make her some tea.

He made his way back into the bedroom and stood looking at her, cup in hand, trying to see if she was awake or asleep. Then she opened her eyes and smiled.

"It's good to be back."

"It's good to have you back." Sam moved over to the bed and perched on the edge, afraid of hurting her.

She laughed and grabbed his hand. "I'm not going to break, don't worry."

"I just didn't want to hurt you, that's all."

"Well, you didn't. I'm not sore or anything. I feel fine."

"You're not getting out of that bed."

"Tyrant."

"I made you tea," he said, proffering the cup.

She sighed theatrically, one hand on her breast. "Lovely. The stuff they had in the hospital was actually orange. It tasted as if it had been stewing for a week."

"Are you saying you'd like me to let it stew for a while?"

"Don't you dare!"

She took a sip and then placed it back on the bedside table. For someone who had been dying for a decent cup of tea, she didn't seem all that enthusiastic. "Now, what have you done with the presents?"

"As if you didn't know."

"Well come on, then. Give!"

Feigning resignation, Sam started hauling packages onto the bed. There followed a cheerful half hour of present opening.

For Sam's part, there was the usual selection of socks from various aunts and uncles. From his parents, there was a sweater, suit, and a Marks and Spencer voucher no doubt intended for underwear. His mother would have been far too embarrassed to buy such a personal item nowadays. From Marianne, something Sam had secretly wanted for a long time but always said he wouldn't bother getting, as it was for kids really—a PlayStation.

"Marianne! What on earth? We can't afford..."

"I've seen you gazing longingly at them, and we all know what a big kid you are really."

He smiled, admitting defeat. "All right, you win. Thank you. What did you get?"

"Oh, the usual."

She had been given a couple of bottles of her favourite perfume, L'Eau d'Issey, and some chocolates. From Sam's parents, perfume and the obligatory Marks and Spencer voucher.

Sam gazed in disbelief at the pile of toiletries and other presents littering the bed. "What did they do? Buy up Lush?"

"Looks like it, doesn't it? I can't wait to wallow in a lovely deep bubble bath, maybe the Raspberry Ripple one. What do you think?"

Sam took the bottle she was proffering and unscrewed the cap. He took a quick sniff and handed it back quickly, trying to breathe. "A bit strong, isn't it?"

She giggled and chucked it back on the pile. "That's half the fun."

"You haven't opened mine yet," Sam said.

"I was saving that 'til last." She picked it up and shook it gently, stopping immediately, stricken by the look of horror on Sam's face.

He couldn't keep it up, though. "Only kidding."

She punched him in the arm, exasperated. Nevertheless, she put the box down carefully and started to unwrap it. When she saw what was inside, Sam thought for a moment she was going to cry.

"Sam, it's beautiful."

It was a gold cross and chain. A Celtic cross, to be exact, very ornate. But very delicate.

"I got Father Chris to bless it."

"That's nice. Really nice. Thank you, Sam." She reached for him, and they hugged each other tight, tears very near the surface.

Trying to lighten the mood a little, Sam made a show of checking his watch. "Whoops, time to do the veg. We don't want our Christmas dinner to be late, do we?"

"You haven't forgotten to check how long the turkey needs, have you?"

"Marianne, that bloody thing has been cooking since half past nine this morning. What on earth possessed you to buy a monster like that for just two of us?"

"I thought you liked turkey sandwiches."

"There's a limit to how many turkey sandwiches even I can eat."

She at least had the good grace to look ashamed of herself as she started laughing, confirming Sam's fears. "I could always help."

Sam headed for the kitchen before he started to laugh, shaking his head. "I'm sure you could, love. I'm sure you could."

He washed and peeled all the vegetables, and put them onto cook. He even remembered to check the turkey. Everything seemed to be going okay. When he was finished, Sam headed back to Marianne, who no doubt would have more instructions. "Christmas dinner will be served in about forty minutes. Can I get you anything?" Fatal last words.

"Another cup of tea would be nice."

"Sure. Anything else?"

"Any chance of the TV being brought in?"

Sam knew he shouldn't have asked. "I suppose so. You do realise I'll probably end up with a hernia?"

She smiled enigmatically and waited.

Sam heaved a huge melodramatic sigh and headed for the living room. He didn't mind, really, and she knew it. It would be pretty stupid if he was stuck on his own in the living room watching television and Marianne was in the bedroom with nothing to do but read. It took him nearly twenty minutes to get the bloody thing in there, but Sam managed it in the end.

He left her flicking through the channels and went to make the tea. Dinner was almost ready. It only needed another ten or fifteen minutes. Having made the tea, Sam set off on the trip to the bedroom again. He had a feeling he would be doing that trip time after time over the next week or so.

The rest of the day passed quickly. It didn't take long to eat, then Sam washed up (more giggling), and they spent the rest of the afternoon watching television. At some stage, they both fell asleep.

It felt good to be together again.

Sam woke up to find the room completely dark, except for the static flowing across the television screen, washing them both in its glare. He was absolutely freezing. Madam, of course, had sole possession of the duvet and wasn't about to relinquish the death grip she had on it. Not without a fight, anyway. Sam tried, briefly, but it was no good. She was completely cocooned in it, snoring gently.

He got up and went to the wardrobe, retrieved his old sleeping bag from its depths and took it back to the bed. It had languished there for years. Marianne hated camping. He spread it out and climbed in, zipped it up tight. His own personal cocoon.

Bliss.

Shit!

He'd forgotten to turn the bloody television off. Fumbling for the catch, Sam tried to unzip himself. No good, it was stuck tight. He even tried prodding Marianne awake, but that one was a definite non-starter.

Then the static went. There was no sound at all, and the screen showed nothing more than an indistinct jumble of dark shapes, moving aimlessly. Sam watched apprehensively. It would be just his luck if it had overheated or something and was about to explode.

Then she was there. Incandescent, almost, against the dark background. Celeste stood perfectly straight, arms flung wide, gazing defiantly directly at him, green eyes blazing. She was completely naked, and, to Sam's shame, he couldn't take his eyes off her. She had probably the most perfect body he had ever seen, every contour perfectly in proportion. She had slicked her dark hair straight back, away from a face devoid of any make-up, which only served to emphasise the fact that she didn't need any.

"Miss me?"

The sultry voice wasn't real, Sam knew that, felt it, but still it seemed to echo and resonate around the otherwise silent bedroom.

He shook his head angrily, refusing to acknowledge her.

"Do you love me, Sam?"

Bitch. Still trying to tease him, even now. After all she had put them through, she still thought she could entice him.

Sam turned away and buried himself in the sleeping bag, unwilling to face her any longer. The soft purr of her voice degenerated into noise, bouncing around and around the room in an insane insectile buzzing. Hot tears stung Sam's face, the shame burning into him as he realised that he was indeed still in love with her. "In love" as opposed to loving her, but that was bad enough, wasn't it? At the moment, though, the anger he felt towards her was winning out. Sam tried his best to hang on to that, stoke it.

He had a feeling he would need it.

There was a faint click as she finally allowed the power to switch itself off, and the television died. The darkness in the room became total, hiding Sam's confusion. It took him a long time to get back to sleep.

Sam sat in the living room nursing a coffee. Everywhere was quiet. It was two o'clock in the morning and Marianne needed her rest. The last thing she needed was to be woken up now, especially to hear about his latest encounter with Celeste.

He felt almost as if he was still in that dream house of hers. Everything had that same monochrome, eldritch quality. It was a feeling that was guaranteed to set his nerves jangling. The cruciform pose she had adopted hadn't been lost on him, either. Well, he wasn't about to start worshipping her blindly again. That had been his mistake the first time.

Sam knew now she was never going to leave them alone. She wouldn't be happy until she had regained his complete and utter adoration. If she couldn't have that, she would destroy them totally, or die trying. Sam's mind flashed wilfully back on the sight of her naked body once more, arms outstretched as if in yearning, and he felt his own body responding. Resolutely, he forced the image back, tried his hardest to replace it with Marianne.

This wouldn't be easy.

Chapter 21

Paul sat in front of the television in a daze, barely even registering what was on. He didn't know which way to go now. He knew he didn't love Celeste. What they had couldn't be called love. To tell the truth, she frightened him. Yet he had to admit she exerted a strange sort of fascination over him, too. There was something so unreal about her. She didn't just seem obsessive—there was something weirder, more dangerous. He just couldn't pinpoint what it was. Then again, it might be better not to try.

Paul thought back to the day he had met her, that chance meeting months ago. Or had it been chance at all?

Things certainly seemed to have become very intense very quickly. He tried to remember when he had first been aware that things were getting out of control, but couldn't. What was it she'd said? "I only wanted you to love me. What's wrong with that?" What indeed?

On the surface of it, nothing. Had he been wrong, after all, to treat her like that? To discard her so easily, like some worn out item of clothing? In his confused state, he was beginning to wonder whether he really had tired of her, after all, or whether it had been motivated by guilt. Had it really been because of some sense of disloyalty to his dead wife and child? He certainly felt as if he had neglected the memory of his family. He had done his best to forget them for a while and found it hard to forgive himself for that, however easy it was to rationalise it. He hadn't even been to the grave. Whatever the reason, it had brought to light another side to Celeste, a decidedly dark side at that.

He couldn't hide anymore, anyway. As of tomorrow, he intended to pick up the pieces of his life. He'd arrange to see Bob again. It had been a while. He had commissions to get back to, as well. It was time to put Celeste behind him.

If she would let him.

Even as all this was going through his mind, he gradually became aware that there was something familiar about the face on the screen in front of him. Sitting forward, he turned up the volume, tried to pay attention.

"...could this be the newest supermodel is the question on every-one's lips at the moment..." The presenter prattled on, but it was all lost on Paul. That face... There were certain differences, of course, but he was pretty sure it was her. He had never seen anyone with eyes that green before, and now, all of a sudden, there were two? There were other similarities, too. Something about the cheekbones, high and angular. The screen showed a series of photographs of her in various poses, none of which left much to the imagination. Then it cut to a headshot, with her looking directly into the camera.

A shudder racked him.

For a moment there, he had felt as if she were looking straight at him, *into* him. "I don't need you," the look said. "You missed your chance."

He knew he was being stupid, imagining such things. Yet the feeling persisted.

It had been weeks since Paul's last encounter with Celeste, and he was beginning to breathe a little easier. He was able to concentrate on his outstanding work again, and new jobs were starting to come in. He felt stronger than he had for a long time, and that could only be good.

He'd managed to get through Christmas fairly easily, even though it was something he'd been dreading. Once again, Bob and Annie had stepped in, insisted he spent the day with them. It had passed all too quickly. All right, so he had probably used the beer a little too much to get to sleep once he was home, but on the whole it hadn't been too bad. Paul supposed, in time, he'd learn to enjoy being alone again, but he wasn't holding out any hopes. He had played every computer game he'd bought to death and was already itching to go out and get new ones.

The doorbell rang, and Paul went to answer its summons, opening the front door to find Bob standing there.

"Fancy a pint, mate?" he asked.

Paul grinned. "You don't have to ask me twice," he said, and pulled his jacket down from the hook on the wall. "It's only Thursday, though. Anything wrong?"

Bob shook his head as they headed down the path. "Everything's fine, mate. Annie's visiting her mother for a few days, and I thought we could both do with some company."

"Well then," Paul said. "Let's go."

The evening passed in a blur, and Paul was glad of the company. He needed to get out more, if he was ever going to start coming to terms with things properly. He stared around the warm pub, watching everyone in their little groups, chatting and laughing, and began to feel almost as if he belonged again.

Bob came back from the bar with another pint and planted it on the rickety wooden table. It wobbled, and beer sloshed over its edge on to the table's surface, threatening to wash over the edge.

"Oops, sorry," Bob said as he sat down, already sipping from his own pint. "Must be more pissed than I thought."

Paul smiled, but said nothing—just used a beermat to coax the spillage safely over the edge of the table away from him.

Bob turned and looked over his shoulder, then turned back to Paul, grinning. "I think I may have pulled."

"What?"

Bob had the good grace to look embarrassed. "I didn't say I was going to do anything, did I? I'm married, for one, and Annie would kill me, for another."

"That's true," Paul said. "And she'd take her time." He grinned and asked, "Who?"

Bob gestured over his shoulder. "At the bar. Tall sort, dark hair."

Paul looked in the direction Bob had indicated, and at first couldn't see anyone resembling that description. Then the crowd waiting to be served parted, and he saw her, staring back at him, an insolent grin on her face.

Celeste.

Paul cleared his throat, and asked, "What did she say, then?"

Bob grinned. "Not much, really. Just chit-chat at the bar. Gave me her phone number... You know what it's like."

Paul nodded. "You're not going to see her, though, are you? I mean...Annie."

Bob shook his head. "'Course not. Good for the ego, though. Nice-looking girl like that interested in an old fart like me."

Paul smiled, and both men took a drink before changing the subject. When Paul looked again, she was gone.

Paul didn't hear from Bob for a few weeks after that, and he suspected the worst. He knew all too well how easy it was to fall for Celeste, but was surprised to find that he was jealous. Perhaps, he thought, he'd ended things too quickly after all.

It was a rainy Monday afternoon, and Paul was sitting at his desk, trying to finish a drawing for a book's internal illustration. He hadn't paid too much attention to the title, just read the publisher's brief. Something about fairies, a few line drawings needed on the pages indicated. He'd read through the prose and worked up a few sketches. This was the last one.

The phone rang, and Paul picked it up absently. "Hello?"

The voice at the other end was strained, almost unrecognisable. "Paul? It's Bob."

Paul dropped his pencil and sat back, stared out at the sheeting rain as it poured down his window. "You all right, Bob? You sound terrible."

Bob laughed, his voice bitter. "I expect I do. I've been a fool."

Paul froze. "Oh no, mate. You didn't."

Bob's voice was defensive now. "I didn't mean to. I just needed a bit of a lift, that's all." There was a pause. "I didn't sleep with her, mate, I swear. Just flirted a bit, you know."

Paul said nothing, unsure how to proceed. Bob was his friend, but so was Annie. What if she found out about this? What if she already had? Before he could stop himself, he breathed her name. "Annie..."

"She doesn't know," Bob said. "And if you don't tell her, she doesn't have to. It's over, anyway. I can't see her anymore."

Paul ignored the implied request to lie for a moment, and asked, "Why's that?"

The voice that answered bore no resemblance to his old friend, the cheerful, happy-go-lucky man that was well aware of how fortunate he was to have Annie in his life. "Because if I do, I'll want more.

I'll want to leave Annie." There was a pause before he continued, almost under his breath, "And because I'm scared of her."

The chat went on for a few more minutes, as Paul tried to reassure his friend, to give him comfort, and tried to help him fight for his marriage. Inside, though, he knew things were about to get very bad. He could feel it. Not content with screwing his life up, Celeste had gone after his friend, just to hurt him. To prove she could. If Bob dumped her, just as Paul had, he didn't know what she'd be capable of. And he wasn't sure he wanted to find out.

Chapter 22

Towards the end of February, Paul began to despair. He'd continued to see Celeste in the oddest of places. She featured prominently in his dreams, too, so he was scared to go to sleep. He was finding it difficult to focus on work, and once he'd convinced Bob that he mustn't see Celeste again for the sake of his marriage, he hadn't seen his friend in weeks. Bob was too embarrassed and guilty to leave Annie for long, even for a pint with Paul.

Friday night, Paul was restless. Bob finally called and arranged to come around. He seemed better, Paul thought, more like his old self, but something wasn't being said—at least over the phone.

Paul sat on the sofa, channel-hopping, unable to settle. The wind howled against the windows outside, and shadows of branches whipped back and forth in the firelight. Other, unfamiliar, shadows made him tread warily, unsure of why he was so nervous, suddenly. He told himself it was just people, passersby eager to get home, out of the wind and rain.

A glass tinkled in the kitchen, and Paul sprang to his feet, rushed into the room.

Celeste was standing in the middle of the room, a glass of wine in each hand. She smiled, and offered one to Paul. "You wanted to see me?"

So she hadn't finished with him, after all. She'd just been biding her time.

Paul took a deep breath, eager not to sound too angry, too confrontational. Maybe now they could resolve this, finally. "What do you think you're playing at?" God, he hoped his voice sounded more confident than he felt.

She smiled, moving past him into the living room. That familiar perfume assailed his senses, warming him. "I'm not playing at anything."

He followed her, not even noticing he'd taken the glass she'd proffered. She was taking the mickey now. Daring him. She sounded as if she was innocence personified, but looked as if she was enjoying herself mightily.

"You know I'm not talking about us. Leave Bob alone. Let it be over."

She pouted. "Why should I? He likes me."

"I'm sure he does. But we both know you couldn't care less about him, don't we?"

Celeste's reply was carefully noncommittal. "Do we?"

"Don't start your bloody games with me, Celeste! I know you too well for that."

The ferocity of her response astounded him, drove him back against the wall of the living room as she pressed herself closer, breathed her reply against his ear.

"You don't know me. You only saw what I wanted you to see!"

It sounded all the worse for being whispered, though it came out as more of a hiss.

The lights dimmed, then brightened once more. There was a crackling sound, and the smell of burnt insulation filled the air, making Paul's eyes water.

Was she doing that? How could she do that?

"Would you like me to show you what I'm really like, Paul?"

He shook his head, frantic to escape, but had no choice but to watch, terrified, as her features began to ripple, moulding and remoulding themselves. Her hair, too, remodelled itself constantly, making her look like a modern-day Medusa. Paul saw a wilful seventeen-year-old with masses of dark, wavy hair and a pouting expression. A woman of twenty-two or three with black hair worn in a shining bob, thinner in the face than her predecessor. Then the Celeste he had wooed and briefly won. Next, an old woman with yellowy white hair, face sagging and wrinkled.

Through it all, her eyes never changed. Those bright green eyes stayed incandescent.

He slumped against her as a wave of dizziness threatened to sweep his legs from under him. Her arms wrapped around him. This was all too much. He had known she was dangerous, but this? This was crazy.

Then the Celeste he knew was back, pressed so close to him they might have been dancing. Her eyes, large and moist, looked at him as if they were filled with a world of hurt and reproach. She hugged him tight, all trace of threat gone in an instant.

In spite of himself, Paul felt guilty. His mind was already refuting what he had just seen. It was impossible, just his guilt playing tricks on him.

"I only wanted you to love me. I still don't know what I did wrong."

Helpless, Paul didn't know what to say, could only look at her, totally bewitched and miserable in that knowledge.

"Bob loves me, even if you don't," she whispered. "Why can't you leave it at that?"

Paul struggled to stand upright, pushing her back gently as he cleared his throat. "Because you're using him. We both know it. I just don't know why."

Was that a hint of mockery flashing across her face, so fast it might almost never have been there?

Marie O'Regan

Celeste sounded completely sincere, almost tearful, as she replied, "Maybe I just don't feel the same way about him as I do you."

She looked down, suddenly, flushed, as if unaware of the slip she had just made. Could he have been that wrong about her? Still, Paul wasn't sure. Not yet. She looked up at him, shyly gauging, he guessed, how to proceed.

Thunder boomed outside, and she cringed.

Paul found himself holding an armful of warm, perfumed female. Without thinking, he hugged her close, burying his face in her fragrant hair. She clung to him in turn, love's dream regained. His mind filled with images of the two of them, together, wiping away all traces of his other life. He swallowed the bait that quickly and easily, and the worst part of it all was that he barely even noticed.

He kissed her neck, and whispered, "I never said I didn't love you."

Was he really that lonely?

She looked up at him, then, hopeful.

He fought to keep focussed, to stay free. The flat was heavy with anticipation, and he felt himself weakening. It was too hard, staying alone. Too hard, and Bob had Annie. He'd understand.

It was Paul that broke the silence, putting himself squarely under her spell once more. "We could... We could try again."

He stood staring at the floor, waiting forlornly for the rebuff, slightly ashamed at being that desperate, not to mention transparent. Two little hands stole into his, warming him. He forced himself to look at her and was amazed to see tears welling up in those fabulous eyes. Crème de menthe, he decided. They were the colour of crème de menthe.

He cleared his throat, and continued, his voice suspiciously hoarse, "I'd understand if you didn't want to."

Clare's voice piped up inside him, incredulous, *What are you, crazy?* And maybe he was. He closed his eyes and willed her away. Much as he'd loved her, her ghost was all that he had left and that was driving him mad. He couldn't cope alone anymore.

166

Celeste smiled at him and brushed her lips against his. "Come home with me." The words were spoken firmly, no hesitation allowed.

"What?"

"I said, come home with me. Now."

Shocked by the sudden turnaround, Paul could only nod.

Taking him by the hand, Celeste led him around the corner and up onto Highgate Hill. They walked in complete silence, with her slightly ahead of him, putting slight pressure on him to keep up. He was out of breath before they were even halfway up, something he noted with shame and even a little disbelief. He tried to cast his mind back to the last time he had any exercise. He'd always played squash regularly with Bob. When had that stopped? Before Clare, he thought. Since then, they'd seen each other in the pub, or Bob's house, or not at all. With a shock, he realised briefly just how far he had let things drift.

They reached the top of Highgate Hill by St. Joseph's church and crossed onto Hornsey Lane. Paul barely noticed. He was still trying to figure out how he could have lost touch with things so completely.

Paul knew he was at a crossroads. He could leave Celeste now, even if it provoked another onslaught. He could find another job soon enough, he thought, even another flat if he had to. He could pick up the pieces of his old life if he tried. There would be problems, he knew that.

Or he could carry on, try again with Celeste. He had already come halfway to convincing himself that their previous split had been largely his own fault. What was that saying? She was...unlike any other person he had ever met, and perhaps that was part of her charm. There was no hiding that he loved her anymore. It was too late for that. The question was, did he pursue that and take the consequences, or did he opt for the safety of what was left of his old life?

"Hell hath no fury like a woman scorned." Was that why she'd been so vicious, even to the extent of trying to make him jealous by flirting with Bob?

Then they were stopping at a house, and Paul was brought back to reality with a jolt. He hadn't known she came from money. Nothing he knew of her had suggested this. They stopped in front of one of the big, narrow houses that occupied one side of the street just before they hit Archway Bridge, locally known, for obvious reasons, as Suicide Bridge. Before Celeste even found her key to the front door, it opened to admit them.

Paul found himself face to face with a tall, athletic looking man in an immaculate suit. An actual butler! How many people had one of those these days? He stood silently, holding the door, waiting for Celeste and Paul to enter. He couldn't be more than thirty-five and was one of the most beautiful men he had ever seen. That was probably a strange way to describe another man—and not a way Paul felt comfortable with—but it fit perfectly. He was tall, probably six-one or six-two, athletically built. That much was apparent in spite of the perfectly tailored black suit he wore. There was only the barest suggestion that he shaved at all, and his features were perfectly chiselled, as if he had been sculpted, not born.

His eyes, however, were a different matter. They spoke of sights endured rather than merely seen, containing an abundance of sadness. They were the eyes, of an aging demon, worldly-wise and thoroughly sick of everything. He realised the man was staring back at him and lowered his gaze, embarrassed.

Celeste took little notice of him, other than to drape her coat over his waiting arm and issue terse instructions for dinner. She spoke with a practised ease that declared her background.

Paul offered his own coat rather awkwardly and mumbled a thank you as it was taken. The butler nodded, a slight smile playing on his lips at the unaccustomed acknowledgement. Then he disappeared down a flight of stairs, to the kitchen, presumably.

Celeste walked back out of what appeared to be the living room and called down the stairs after him. "Clive! Bring up some coffee."

There was an answering call as Celeste took Paul's hand and led him into what was indeed the living room. A huge log fire roared to the left of the room, making him feel warmer instantly. He looked closer and realised it was in fact a gas fire.

"Not the real thing, I'm afraid," Celeste said. "Something to do with these—what are they called—smokeless zones?"

She spoke as if smokeless zones were a relatively recent inconvenience, Paul realised. Yet they had been in effect since he was a little boy, hadn't they?

He saw her watching him, unsure of his reaction, and hastened to reassure her. "It's great. Flames always seem more warming than a radiator." Embarrassed, he moved over to a huge armchair and sank into it, stretched his feet out before the fire.

Celeste kicked her shoes off and stretched out on the sofa. Paul tried, rather unsuccessfully, not to stare at her legs.

The door opened and Clive appeared, bearing a tray of coffee. A few moments passed with the serving of the drinks and then they were on their own once more. To Paul, the rest of the evening seemed as if viewed through a kaleidoscope, a series of disjointed images, all of which instilled in him a feeling of wellbeing, no matter how strange they were. Staring at Celeste seemingly surrounded by candles across a dining table. Memories of some sort of chicken dish strongly redolent of garlic and absolutely delicious. Back in the living room, laughing and talking over wine—a lot of wine.

They were in Celeste's bedroom, though Paul couldn't quite remember how they had got here. It was a large, airy room, dominated by a massive four-poster bed, swathed in yards and yards of rich crimson drapes, trimmed in gold braid. The bedding was silk and matched the drapes. He was vaguely over-awed, totally unused to such magnificence. He couldn't remember Celeste having left his side during the evening for a moment and was embarrassed to think Clive had been ordered to do this, but the room glowed brightly, lit by thousands of candles in shallow dishes. Every available surface was littered with them, and the air was heavy with the scent of wax and the candles' floral perfume.

Stupefied, he let Celeste lead him to the bed. Standing there, he allowed her to undress him, push him back so he lay atop the sheets. He watched as if drugged as she lifted her black dress (*When did she change into that?*) up and over her head, dropping it to the floor. She was naked underneath, and she was glorious. He found it hard to believe this was happening to him.

Then she climbed onto the bed and lay beside him, ran her fingertips gently across his chest. With a groan, Paul rolled onto his side and gathered her into his arms, kissed her as he ran a hand down her side, relishing the softness of her skin. The feel of her flesh against his was almost more than he could bear.

The night became a tangle of limbs, a delicious heat and soft wetness. They rode on waves of passion, rising and rising until they fell, exhausted—only to rise again a little while later. He was vaguely aware of her voice muttering words he couldn't understand, of sensations of heat and something fogging his mind. But through it all, there was Celeste.

The first hint of dawn was bleeding into the sky as they finally fell asleep, entwined in each other's arms. Just before he slipped into unconsciousness, Paul thought just for a moment that he saw something. All around them were shadows, moving closer. As they neared, Paul saw they were gaining form and substance, gradually becoming figures, indistinct so far but getting clearer until he could make out the faces of half a dozen men, just watching. He struggled to stay awake, to raise himself up onto one arm, but fell back, exhausted, as sleep took him.

Chapter 23

Clive lay on his narrow bed in his quarters adjoining the kitchen and listened to the sounds Celeste and her lover were making upstairs. He buried his head in his pillow, trying to blot the sounds out so that he could sleep. No use. Was he jealous? He couldn't believe he felt that way about a monster like Celeste, but there it was. The thought of the two of them making love was enough to make him feel physically sick, hot anger twisting his gut as he imagined himself in the other man's place—remembered pleasures serving only to fuel the fire.

It was no good. Sleep seemed a million miles away, with all the moaning going on. Sighing, he got out of bed and headed for the kitchen, grabbing his dressing gown as he went. He retrieved a glass from the dishwasher and turned on the cold tap, leaving it to run for a moment. All the while, he just stared off into space, reminiscing over his years with Celeste, the good times and the bad. Surprisingly enough, or perhaps not considering the duality that defined her personality, there had been a plenitude of both. They had established a camaraderie, of sorts, over the years, an understanding. They knew each other too well for it to be otherwise, despite what she had put him through—or perhaps because of it.

So the answer had to be yes. He was jealous, and it was useless to try and hide it. Yet he knew Celeste well enough to know that Paul, whoever he was, was just another passing fad. She might well have convinced herself that this was love, a passion that would burn forever, but that had never been true yet. Clive had yet to see any evidence that she was even capable of more than that, and so he was sure it would cool off soon. It always had before.

Celeste needed to be adored. Of all people, she had better reason than most for such a need. It went beyond mere vanity. It was what kept her alive, kept her young, time after time. He could wait this current crop of admirers out, as he had others in his time. After all, he was the one she really needed, whether she realised it or not. Whenever the latest devotee ran screaming as the last of the scales fell from his eyes, it was always Clive that had to endure. They were tied together in an obscene communion, however unholy. Him, Celeste, and the house, perhaps the most ludicrous element of all. Yet didn't every creature need a lair, a haven? As sanctuaries went, he supposed, the house served its purpose well. If he had to serve Celeste in perpetuity, it might as well be in comfort.

Finally filling his glass, Clive turned off the tap and wandered sluggishly back to his bedroom, turning off the kitchen light as he went. He had left his bedroom dark. He knew that, remembered it clearly.

A silvery glow, so pale as to pass for moonlight, was emanating from his room, pulsing slightly. It couldn't be that simple, thought Clive. And since when did the moon pulse? Every night he made sure his curtains were pulled tight shut, blotting out all possible sources of external light. Otherwise he couldn't sleep. He had been like that since early childhood, he knew; he'd never suffered the night terrors that afflicted so many infants, making them want a light left on. He relished the darkness, the peace he could find within its embrace.

Besides, the light wasn't coming from the window. It was actually centred on his bed. *Could it be a familiar?* he wondered. It wouldn't be the first time they had spent the night time tormenting him, merely for their own tawdry amusements. Or was it for hers? No matter.

Cautiously, he pushed his door further open and inched inside, breathing shallowly for fear of disturbing whatever was inside, or alerting it to his presence unnecessarily. He was being a melodramatic fool. He knew better than most the secret places of the soul, and they could hold no further fears for him. Yet the terror persisted, an unremitting, insistent inner voice screaming a warning. He had had occasion to thank that voice more than once before now. If it was a familiar left loose, he would just have to put up with it. He had learnt that the hard way over the years.

Usually, they would just watch him for a while, amusing themselves like naughty children by opening the windows, pulling the covers off the bed, that sort of thing. If he resisted their amusements or ignored them, they could turn mean. Light bulbs would explode, showering the floor with glass which promptly got trodden on when he leapt out of bed in a fright. He could be stung hundreds of times by myriad little creatures he could never find. They left little welts that wept for days, throbbing virulently, oozing pus and blood until they faded.

Best to let them play undisturbed. It was less painful.

As he crept into the bedroom, Clive felt the strength rush out of him. It wasn't the familiars this time. Half a dozen men were standing around the bed, staring back at him. They looked almost like a negative, the contours of their bodies picked out in traceries of silver that glowed in the otherwise total darkness, like the trail of some giant nocturnal slug.

"It's time, Clive. Time to choose."

The voice was faint, like the whisper of the sea in a shell transplanted from the shore and equally distant. Yet he would have known it anywhere.

Matthew? Could it really be him?

Clive strained to hear more, some instinct prompting him to

remain silent until he knew more of his visitors. Could this be another of Celeste's tricks, designed to trap him into some disloyal comment or suggestion?

"You can be released, Clive. Don't you want redemption?"

Still, Clive waited. When no answer was forthcoming, an expression of disgust came over Matthew's face, and he flickered and began to fade, disappointed perhaps with Clive's apparent indifference.

The remaining shadows roiled, as if unsure of how to proceed, wavering in and out of existence.

Steeling himself for the inevitable retribution if this was indeed a trap, Clive took a step forward, hand raised as if in prayer. "How, Matthew?"

His brother smiled as he saw the recognition in Clive's eyes. "It's not too late. You are not alone." He gestured towards his companions.

Clive saw they were all men, all young, all races—the one common factor seemed to be that they were attractive. He thought he recognised them, some of Celeste's past loves.

Matthew brightened momentarily, a feat which appeared to take some effort, and nodded in approbation. "You see? We abide, as much as we can. We want to help. The time is not quite right, yet. Be patient a little while longer. We will help you when the time comes."

There was a final flash, and they were gone, an after-image persisting for some seconds after their departure. Finally that died, plunging Clive into darkness so absolute that for a moment he thought it had been Celeste after all, and she had struck him blind as a penance for falling prey so easily to his visitors' seduction. Then the familiar contours of the room began to reassert themselves, solidifying as his eyes slowly adjusted to the dark.

Clive made his way carefully to the bed and climbed in, having placed his water on the bedside table. He didn't want it now. He felt too sick, afraid of what might come next. Clive felt the presence of the familiars as they watched, no doubt they were disturbed by the nocturnal visitors' presence, and closed his eyes against the tears he felt welling up there.

Was it true? Could he earn redemption, even now? Clive had thought that chance lost over a century earlier and had long since resigned himself to a life that dragged on and on as Celeste's accomplice. He found it hard to believe it was really possible to change all that now, to move on and find peace, regardless of whether he deserved it. He had thought Matthew lost, never to be seen again, and yet here he was, drawn to his brother so he could help him save their souls and put an end to their suffering.

Clive lay down on the bed and stared at the ceiling, willing the familiars to keep their distance. They were too unsettled to bother unduly about him, and he was grateful for that brief respite. He had a lot to think about and not much time. Sick as he was of seeing the wanton destruction Celeste had wreaked on so many lives in her time, he was painfully aware that he did love her. The question was, did he love what she had become? The answer to that was no—and if, by releasing himself and these men from her attentions, he could free her from her appetites and the price they demanded, then perhaps redemption could be his, after all. Perhaps he could save both their souls, rather than just his own.

For the first time in many, many years, Clive got out of bed and knelt on the cold stone floor, clasping his hands together in prayer. "Please God," he wept, "grant me the strength to save us all. To let these people live their lives free of Celeste's demands. Grant Celeste peace, and grant me the strength to bring all this to pass. Amen."

He lowered his hands and placed his head on the bed and wept for the loss of his soul for all these years, and for the possibility of redemption. If he only had the strength to grasp for it.

Chapter 24

Marianne was watching Sam closely now. Or maybe he was just being paranoid. Who could tell anymore? Sam was beginning to think he was losing his mind, with sanity drifting further away the more he tried to hang on to some semblance of normality.

Why wouldn't Celeste leave him alone?

She'd been hounding Sam for weeks now, invading his dreams whenever she could ever since he brought Marianne back from the hospital.

She was more subtle about it all now, of course. Sam would just catch little glimpses of her, quickly lost. He'd be waiting at the checkout at the supermarket and naturally, when it was his turn, the girl on the till would go for her break, being replaced by Celeste. Or he and Marianne would be sitting quietly in Mass, and Sam would turn to offer the person next to him the sign of peace, only to find Celeste instead of the little old man who had been there only moments before.

Marianne, of course, hadn't seen any of this. Sam tried to hide it from her, but she picked up on it anyway. He was a fool to think she wouldn't. The tenser he got, the more obvious it was. Yet she hadn't questioned it. Sam had a feeling she was happier that way. Her focus now was the babies, and there was no room for such the madness dealing with Celeste invited.

Sam couldn't let her know Celeste was still pursuing him. It was bad enough that *he* was frightened. If Marianne knew, the stress could cause her to miscarry, and that wasn't an option. Sam would just have to go on, as best he could, and hope. For now.

Every night Celeste visited Sam's dreams, cajoled him. He would find himself laying in her bed, terrified, desperately willing himself to be back home, back in his own bed, but it was no use. She would creep onto the bed, strip slowly, and kneel over Sam as she played with herself, hands caressing her breasts, exciting both of them. Even if Sam closed his eyes, it was no use. She'd just lie down beside him and press the length of her body against his, kiss his chest, stomach. Tease him until he just couldn't resist her anymore. And try as he might, he couldn't wake up. Celeste wouldn't let him.

Marianne wouldn't let him near her anymore, claiming it hurt. Sam could understand that. His mind whispered that wasn't really the problem, that his cheating was the problem, virtual or otherwise, but he refused to listen. But it didn't exactly help him to hold out against Celeste. She teased and teased, and the flesh could only take so much, confounded as it was by his daily frustration. Celeste was winning her battle for Sam's affections, piece by piece.

Marianne didn't have long to go before the birth, and Sam found himself having to be a bit careful about what he said. This close to the arrival of the twins, Marianne had attained massive proportions, and to say she was slightly oversensitive about it was understating things, to say the least.

Fed up with being pregnant, and, Sam assumed, unsure of what was going on about Celeste, as far as Marianne was concerned, he couldn't put a foot right. Sam couldn't say he really blamed her. He tried to act as if everything was normal, tried not to rise to her sarcasm, her bad temper. But it was difficult, and he had a feeling it wouldn't get any easier between now and the birth. Sam was still keeping Celeste's attentions to himself, fighting to keep his love for Marianne separate, pure. Unsullied by Celeste's appetites.

Not that Celeste had made it easy. Far from fading into the background, she had actually increased the pressure, seemingly hell-bent on rekindling his obsession, bringing him back into her grasp. Sam got the feeling that if this didn't work, she'd settle for just destroying everything he held dear. The dreams came every night without fail. Every time it was in true thirties style, completely monochrome, Celeste at her glorious silent movie best. And they had all been completely and utterly pornographic. He was exhausted.

"Sam!"

He made his way to the bedroom to see what Marianne wanted. She couldn't even get out of bed anymore without his help. Small wonder, then, that she was so miserable. He found her lying on the floor, trying without success to pull herself up using the covers for purchase.

She scowled at him as he dithered in the doorway and motioned him forward. "Help me up, Sam, for God's sake."

"What happened?" All lethargy gone, Sam hurried over to Marianne and tried to help her up.

"What does it look like? I fell out of bed," Marianne said, as she tried in vain to get up.

He got hold of her and managed to hoist her into a sitting position, no mean feat in itself. From there, she manoeuvred herself into a kneeling position. Supporting herself on the bed, she heaved herself up and plonked herself back down on it, gasping for breath.

Sam hovered uselessly in the background. "Did you hurt yourself?"

"No," she snapped in a monotone, avoiding eye contact.

"Are you sure?"

"I'm fine! Stop fussing!"

Silence.

She seemed uncomfortable, although whether that was physical or a result of snapping at him, Sam wasn't sure. Kneeling down in front of her, he peered up into her face, tried to take her hand. No dice.

"What's the problem, love?"

Nothing.

Sam sat and waited, but she wasn't going to be saying anything in a hurry. Exasperated, he stood up and headed out of the bedroom.

"Sam."

He stopped, waited, back still to Marianne. He was furious. Absurdly, he felt as if he was about to cry.

"Come back, Sam. Please." Her voice was weary, raw, but devoid of anger. The hate Sam thought had lurked there recently was gone, replaced by a sorrow that cut deep. Wearily, he walked back to the bed, sat heavily beside her, and let her take his hand. "We need to talk."

"I've been trying to do that for days!" The anger flashed out before Sam could stop it, and he felt her flinch. She refused to rise to the bait, though, perhaps realising they had reached the point of no return.

"I'm sorry. At least I'm trying now."

The old steel was creeping back in. "You can push me," she was really saying, "but only so far." Sam said nothing, just sat sulking like a petulant child, eyes fixed firmly on the floor.

"Things aren't right between us. They haven't been for a while, now, have they?"

"Tell me something I don't know."

Marianne dropped his hand, virtually pushed it back into his lap. "Cut the sarcasm, Sam. We have to sort this out."

Now Sam looked at her, stung by her tone. "So tell me what's wrong, for Christ's sake! I've bent over backwards to be under-standing over the last few weeks, and for what?" Lost for words to adequately vent his rage and frustration, Sam came to a premature halt. Marianne knew exactly how he felt, of course, and why. All it took was one word for him to realise that.

"Celeste."

Sam flinched. "She's still bothering you?"

She laughed at that. "What did you think? That she'd leave me out of this?"

"I'm sorry. So sorry. I thought I'd be enough."

She blanched at Sam's words, and he realised too late how it had sounded. "You mean now she's got you back."

There it was. Her voice was bleak, containing a world of hurt. Sam could only imagine what images, what lies, Celeste had been subjecting her to. And all along he had thought her safe, as long as he played along with Celeste's demands.

"She hasn't got me back, not really. I'm just..." He struggled to find the right words, the right justification, if there was any. "I'm just going along with her, I suppose. Letting her think she's won. It's you I love, Marianne." She let him take her hand this time. "She's only in my dreams, and I can't get her out."

Marianne wiped her eyes, her voice low as she answered, "I know, I've heard them."

They talked for a long time after that, trying to find common ground. Celeste hadn't just been visiting Sam, after all. She had been invading Marianne's dreams too. As well as having to listen to him moaning beside her as he made love to Celeste, she got to watch, too.

Sometimes Celeste varied it, so that Marianne would dream she and Sam were happy again, making love...until he called out Celeste's name as he climaxed.

Or there had been the dreams where Marianne was in labour, alone in a hospital room. She screamed and screamed for help, but no one ever came. And she could always hear Sam crying Celeste's name next door while in the throes of passion.

And over it all, the sound of Celeste, laughing.

She must have lain awake night after night, afraid to sleep for fear of what she might see, listening to the sounds he made while making love to Celeste. No, that wasn't right. Fucking Celeste. You couldn't call it making love.

Sam stammered, "I don't know what to say, love. Sorry doesn't really cover it, does it?"

Marianne moved closer, laid her head on his shoulder. "No, but it's a start."

They talked about going away for a while, but that wasn't really such a good idea with Marianne so far along. There was no guarantee it would achieve what they wanted. The way their luck was running lately, Marianne would probably go into labour on the motorway.

The one thing they were both sure of was that they didn't want to split up. They couldn't let Celeste win. Sam supposed they were still being naive, even then, hoping that she'd get bored and move onto some other poor sod. Hopefully someone unattached. Except that neither of them really believed that. But what choice did they have?

Chapter 25

Paul spent the rest of the weekend with Celeste—the majority of it, he had to admit, in the bedroom. He couldn't (wouldn't) remember the last time he had been so happy. Fleeting doubts raced across his mind now and then, but he pushed them away, just as he pushed away memories of his previous life and family. They were gone. That was all. He had let his doubts come between him and Celeste once before and look at what had happened then. Celeste filled his mind with pictures of their own desires, and for now, that was enough.

Sunday afternoon they decided to take a walk, breathe some fresh air for a change. The strangely quiet Clive produced their coats once more as if from nowhere, then he stalked straight back downstairs. Paul noticed he had kept his gaze firmly on the floor, almost as if he was afraid to look Celeste in the eye. For her part, she didn't look exactly happy with him, either.

Paul had missed something along the way between those two, that much was obvious. The ill-feeling between them was plain to see. He realised Celeste was waiting for him to open the door and rushed to oblige. She swept through and onto the street, leaving him to follow.

They turned right and walked along the lane, stopping on top of Archway Bridge to enjoy the view it afforded of London. It was a bright day, weak sunshine doing its best to limit the chill. Paul looked over the bridge and saw the traffic hurtling down the Archway Road on its way into central London. He could make out the bright green monstrosity that was the Archway Tavern at the bottom of the hill. Beyond lay the sprawl of London, partially concealed in the haze of pollution that hung permanently like a shroud overhead. Up here, at least, the air was clear. Or as clear as it could be in this day and age.

"Penny for them?" Celeste was watching him, bemused.

"They're not worth it." He'd meant no offence, had just been letting the wool gather. Still, she looked embarrassed, making Paul realise how abrupt he had sounded. He groaned, and tried again. "I just meant I wasn't thinking about anything in particular. Let's head back to The Crown for a drink, eh? It's cold, just standing up here. Or we could go on? There are some nice pubs in Crouch End."

She nodded, saying nothing, but looked happy enough. At least he hoped so. She turned back towards home and slipped her arm through his as they headed back the way they had come, which he took as a good sign. Passing Celeste's house, Paul saw the curtains twitch by the front door. So Clive had decided to watch them. Big deal. He was probably hoping the coast was clear for a few hours. He was glad Celeste hadn't noticed, though. For some reason, he had the distinct impression that Clive was terrified of her.

Then again, maybe that wasn't so strange. Paul had seen her temper once, if only briefly, and he had no desire to witness a repeat performance.

It was dark, as usual, on this side of the lane. The tall houses effectively blocked out the sunlight for a large part of the day, which made it permanently cooler than the north side of the lane. Paul shivered, surprised to realise the cold had no discernible effect on Celeste.

They reached the end, almost, of Hornsey Lane and came out into sunshine once more. Paul breathed a sigh of relief as the temperature rose. Ahead of them lay The Crown to the left, and across the road, St. Joseph's church. It was an impressive sight with its green dome dominating the local view. He'd always meant to visit it sometime, to see if it was as beautiful inside.

Turning to Celeste, he said, "Let's go across and have a look inside."

She looked shocked. "What on earth for?"

"It's supposed to be beautiful. Very ornate, I've heard. I'd like a look."

"Then go on your own."

The venom in her voice was unmistakeable and stopped Paul in his tracks. "What's wrong?"

"Nothing. I just don't like church much, that's all." She smiled tightly, attempting to minimise the blow and pulled him towards The Crown. "You can look in there any time, Paul. Let's have that drink, eh? I'm freezing."

That was patently untrue, but Paul let it pass. So she didn't like churches. That wasn't so unusual these days. Her reaction to it had been extreme, though. Something wasn't right. He knew that. A vague memory of her reaction to finding out that O'Neill's had started its life as a place of worship tried to surface, but he let it go. Surprisingly enough, he found he didn't care much anymore. After all, what had churches done for him recently?

Paul thought back to his wedding, or tried to—but that memory seemed hard to find. He tried to remember his wife's name, but it was gone. A moment later, that memory, too, was gone. It was far easier to concentrate on this relationship than on the past. It hurt less. He felt vaguely uneasy, aware on some level that this wasn't right, but he couldn't seem to care.

Celeste was smiling at him. Paul wondered if she had something to do with his...confusion, and then even that was gone. He wandered on in a daze, content to be led.

Late Sunday night, Paul let himself back into his own flat to pack some clothes, ready to take them back to Celeste's house the next day.

He'd needed one last night in his own place before he moved in with her. He ran a bath as he laid out the next day's clothes in his bedroom. After his bath, he made a cup of coffee and took a book to bed. It took him all of fifteen minutes to fall asleep with his book across his chest, coffee cooling on the bedside table.

On Monday morning, Paul was up at dawn and on his way to Celeste's by eight o'clock with a spring in his step. He felt years younger, and the fact that he couldn't remember actually getting up and going through the motions of washing, dressing, and such didn't bother him at all.

He sat on the top deck of the bus and watched the familiar views trundle slowly by. Even at this hour the roads were clogged, thick with desperate commuters and lorry drivers. Paul stared through the filthy windows, noted the dirt ingrained into the brick work, and reflected on what it must be like to actually have to live on the Archway Road itself. Hell on earth, he would have thought, at least during the day.

He got off the bus and headed for Highgate Hill, eager to reach Celeste's house, to get home. He stopped for a moment, looking up the hill, remembering the weekend. Up there, it had seemed so much cleaner, though he knew that was an illusion. The air was exactly the same. The difference was the sensation of being above it all, in a village, almost.

As he reached Hornsey Lane and made his way to Celeste's house, he saw Bob walking ahead of him, and slowed down. Surely he wasn't going to see Celeste? Angry, Paul moved forward, intent on confronting his friend.

Bob paused for a moment outside the house, but didn't go in. Paul waited, and saw his friend lift his hand as if to knock, and then seem to think better of it. He turned and carried on down the lane, keeping his head down, staring at the ground.

Paul knocked on the door himself, and Clive opened it almost immediately. He'd been watching Bob, Paul thought. Did he know what Celeste had been doing? The butler gave no sign, and Paul put it out of his mind. He was home.

Another knock came, and Paul froze. Clive's eyes widened and he shook his head slightly, and Paul realised he did know after all. Must have known all along, and had probably seen Celeste do this more than once. Clive opened the door, revealing a very nervous Bob, standing there, his face full of hope.

When Bob saw Paul, his face fell. He was furious.

Paul stepped forward. "Bob, I..."

"You bastard," Bob answered. "How could you?"

"It's not like that, I knew Celeste before you met her."

Bob snorted. "As if."

Vainly, Paul wished Celeste herself would appear, would back him up. "I did, I swear. I'd only just finished with her when..."

Bob held up his hand. "Forget it. I don't want to hear your lame excuses." He stalked off, oblivious to Paul's attempts to smooth things over.

Paul heard Celeste, behind him. "Well, that was awkward."

He turned, angry. "I thought you two were finished?"

"We were." She motioned him towards the living room. "I guess he wanted to start things up again." She disappeared, and Paul followed her into the living room, eager for the warmth of the fire, and for Celeste, all thoughts of Bob already forgotten.

Paul and Celeste had been living together for a while now, and Paul was happy for the most part. He missed his friend and regretted how things had been left, but knew he belonged here with Celeste.

So here he was, this Friday evening, sitting in the pub they'd always frequented. The usual crowd were in, and the warmth and noise calmed him, as usual. Celeste was nowhere to be seen today, so he'd decided to try once more to reconnect with Bob.

Around eight, Bob walked in and frowned when he saw Paul at their usual table. He nodded and walked over. "Still with that cow?"

"If you mean Celeste, then yes. Still with Annie?"

Bob looked furious at that. "Of course I am. She's been wondering where you went, by the way."

Paul smiled. "I'm guessing you didn't tell her."

"'Course not." He sat down, his face stern. "Not like it matters anymore anyway, does it? You're with her now."

Paul did his best to ignore the sneer in his voice. He had to keep cool. "I know you liked her, Bob. But you were never going to leave Annie, were you?"

"What's that got to do with it?"

He sounded like a spoilt child who'd had his hand slapped, and Paul felt his temper begin to flare.

"The spark was still there, Bob. Between Celeste and I. Were we supposed to ignore that because you couldn't make your mind up about having a bit on the side?"

He didn't have any answer to that one. Paul hadn't expected him to. Still, the frustration on Bob's face gave him no pleasure, no sense of satisfaction. Bob might start talking to him again, he supposed, but the friendship would never go back to what it had been.

Shaking his head, Bob stood up, ready to leave. "You know what you did, Paul. You can't worm out of it that easily. And what about Clare? What would *she* have said about Celeste?"

The expression on Bob's face as he looked at Paul then was one of pure disgust, an emotion Paul couldn't help echoing at the mention of Clare, her memory suddenly sharp once more.

Bob squared his shoulders then, and cleared his throat before spitting, "She'd turn in her grave if she could see you now." Then he was gone, swallowed by the evening's crowd.

Paul waited for a few minutes, wanting to make sure he didn't meet Bob on his way out or catch up with him outside. Best to give Bob some distance for now, rather than push ahead as if nothing had happened.

Sitting there, watching everyone else having a good time, surrounded by friends, lovers, family, Paul began to wonder whether Celeste was worth all this aggravation. Wouldn't a solitary life be simpler? Then he turned, feeling the hair on the back of his neck prickling. She was standing by the door, watching him, the wind blowing her hair about her face like a dark halo. The green of her eyes struck him forcibly, even at this distance. Relieved that it was only Celeste (his mind had tried, briefly, to convince him of something far worse), with all thought of staying single gone, he smiled and started towards her.

For a moment there, he had been terrified, though it was patently obvious now that there was no foundation for such a feeling. She was watching him carefully, he saw, and felt the fear still lurking, shrieking that it was still there. Whatever the danger was, it was still there.

"Have a nice little chat with Bob, did you?" she said.

"I was just trying to make peace, that's all."

She tossed her head, plainly angry. "I wouldn't bother. He's not interested."

"I had to try."

His tone was placatory, but Celeste was not about to be mollified. She turned away, leaving the pub. Paul rushed to follow and caught up with her in a few moments. For all the attention she paid him, he might as well not have been there. They walked onward, back to Celeste's, the atmosphere strained. They were almost home before she broke the silence.

"So, what did he say?"

Paul sighed, shoved his hands deep into his coat pockets against the cold. "Not a lot. I don't think I achieved much."

Finally, she thawed. He'd obviously given the right answer. Turning to Paul, she stood on tiptoe and kissed him. "I could have told you that. Saved you the trouble."

Peace reigned once more, and Paul held her close, feeling the tension seep out of him. Everything would be all right as long as they just stayed together. That was the talisman. That was their strength.

They reached the house, and Paul put an arm comfortably around her shoulders as she opened the door. Warm light swallowed them both before the door shut behind them.

Bob stood on the lane, staring after them. They thought it would be so easy to leave him behind.

His thoughts turned to Annie, waiting for him at home, and he grimaced. She seemed so...pedestrian next to Celeste. He'd tasted stronger pleasures with her, had lost his heart in the process. And she thought she could just walk away?

He fell into darkness as he walked away, lost in thoughts of revenge.

Chapter 26

March. At last the weather was beginning to turn a little less savage, although it couldn't really be called warm yet.

Marianne and Sam had been to see the parish priest of St. Joseph's church up on Highgate Hill. Their church was Our Lady of Muswell, but Marianne wanted the twins christened at St. Joseph's as it had been her mother's parish. The priest seemed amenable to the idea and so they had set the date for 15th May, when all being well, the twins would be six weeks old.

From St. Joseph's they went across the road and to The Crown, to speak to the landlord and book the function room upstairs. Sam was pleased to find out that they would take care of the catering. That meant one less thing to organise.

They spent a pleasant half hour in the pub after that, relaxing with a drink and chatting. Marianne and Sam had achieved a new closeness recently. Once she had been reassured that she came first, she relaxed slightly, or at least had managed to put Celeste to the back of her mind.

Over the last few weeks, Celeste had begun to target them less and less. With the lessening of pressure, Marianne had blossomed, and the majority of their thoughts were now geared firmly to the future. With the birth getting nearer, the nesting instinct had taken hold of Marianne with a vengeance. The flat was so clean it virtually sparkled, and there was a perpetual smell of Pledge. The second bedroom had been completely redecorated to make a bright and cheerful nursery. Lots of yellow and white, with two gleaming white cots taking pride of place. With yellow bedding, of course. Marianne had done much of the work herself, reluctantly allowing Sam to help on the parts she couldn't reach. Sam was amused to find that, given her current size, this left a fair amount to do.

Draining his pint, Sam started fidgeting, eager to get going now that the business of booking the function room was concluded.

"All right, all right, I can take a hint," Marianne muttered.

"What?"

"Don't give me that. I know you're itching to leave."

Sam tried to protest but gave up when he saw the expression on her face. Smiling, she finished her tomato juice and began to struggle into her coat. She didn't even attempt to do it up. That had been a battle she'd conceded weeks ago. Sam helped her sheepishly, feeling a bit guilty for having rushed her, even though that hadn't been his intention. She was finding getting around difficult enough these days without him making her feel as if she had to hurry. Today's trip, short as it was, looked as if it had worn her out completely.

He lifted her hair clear of her coat and kissed her cheek. "Do you want to get a cab home?"

She smiled and touched his face, then set sail towards the door. "No, I'll manage. Just don't rush me on our way down the hill."

Personally, Sam wasn't sure they'd even make it down the hill, whatever their speed. They walked onto Highgate Hill, blinking owlishly in the sudden daylight. Arm in arm, they started off on the trip down the hill to the bus stop at the bottom. Cars made Marianne sick now, so they went everywhere by bus, which for some strange reason didn't cause her a problem.

Halfway down the hill, Marianne stopped dead. "That's her."

Sam looked up, confused. "Who?"

"Who the hell do you think?" The look she flashed at Sam then was pure venom.

After the truce, he was shocked to see such an expression of hate on her face. Stupefied, Sam could only follow the direction she had pointed in. He already knew what he would see, though. Marianne had been totally enraged, and there was only one person who could engender that sort of reaction from her. Sure enough, there was Celeste, walking towards them with her head down, engrossed in conversation.

Something wasn't quite right, though. The first impression was that it was her, certainly, but there were differences. Most noticeably, her hair. This girl's hair wasn't the sleek black bob Sam knew so well, although it was dark. She was with someone, a man. Immediately Sam was jealous, something he knew was patently ridiculous, even if this was Celeste. He felt nothing for her anymore, except perhaps contempt. And yet jealousy raced through him before he had a chance to swallow it back.

The pair walking towards them laughed, easy in each other's company. Then she looked up and all doubt fled. The shocked expression on her face was only visible for a moment before a mask of indifference came down, but they all acknowledged it. Even the air seemed to still, as if they were in the eye of a storm.

Sam gripped Marianne's arm tightly, not wanting a confrontation. Not here, and definitely not involving Marianne. Celeste drew level and passed by without even acknowledging their presence. Her companion, however, was another matter. He obviously sensed something, but was at a loss as to the source of the problem. As they walked past, Sam heard him trying vainly to get her attention.

"Celeste? What's the matter? Celeste?"

She made no answer that Sam could hear, merely pulled the man close and carried on walking, albeit a little faster. As they reached the top of the hill, Celeste looked back as they turned right onto Hornsey Lane, probably checking to see if Sam and Marianne were following.

Her companion said something else, and she turned away, placating him with some lie, no doubt.

Sam pushed Marianne towards the wall. "Stay here."

Before Marianne had a chance to ask why, Sam was running up the hill after them. Diving into The Crown's yard, he climbed the steps on the other side and looked carefully out onto Hornsey Lane.

Celeste was maybe fifty feet in front, ambling down the lane with her arm around lover boy. Who was he? Sam wondered whether he knew exactly what he was tangled up with. He stayed where he was, wary of getting too close. Who knew what she could sense and how far away was safe? Just before Sam was about to step out and follow them, they turned into one of the houses and went inside. Content, Sam wandered back down the hill to Marianne, who was leaning dejectedly against a wall.

"I've found out where she lives."

Marianne, however, looked disgusted at the triumph in Sam's voice. "What good does that do us?"

Sam shrugged, not quite sure of how to answer. The truth was, he felt a little more in control now, as if he had a measure of protection. "I don't know...yet. It's just a relief to know she's got a house, a life, you know? She seems less dangerous, somehow. I don't know." He knew how stupid that sounded—of course she was real and had a life. He just felt better knowing exactly where that life was, where she could be found should the need arise.

Sighing, Marianne wormed her way under the dubious protection of his arm. "I hope you're right, Sam."

"So do I."

Deflated once more, they made their way wearily home. It was at the back of Sam's mind that she might renew her visits, now, in reprisal. A warning to stay clear.

He hoped not.

Marianne went to bed early that night, completely drained by the day's events. Actually meeting Celeste in the flesh, so to speak, had lent the rest of the day a distinctly nightmarish quality, with both of them jumping at shadows, mindful, perhaps, of imminent retribution. Sam kept trying to tell himself he was being ridiculous, yet the fear persisted, colouring everything with its own sickly hue. Everything had seemed slightly off kilter. Surreal, somehow. Full of hidden meaning and malevolence.

It was a real relief when the day finally drew to a close. They talked for hours about what the best course of action would be. Sam wanted to go to the house, confront her, threaten her maybe, though he had no idea with what. Marianne, naturally, hit the roof as soon as Sam even mentioned it. In the end, he gave in, not wanting to upset her. She'd been through more than enough recently. This close to having the babies, she didn't need any more aggravation.

They were so close to the birth now, to being a family. Sam couldn't get rid of the strange idea that if they could just get through the birth then Celeste's hold would somehow, miraculously, be broken. It was completely ludicrous, he knew, but it was an idea that had somehow achieved its own grim conviction.

Sam lay in the dark, staring at the ceiling, listening to Marianne toss and turn. He was afraid to fall asleep. If he fell asleep, he'd let Celeste in, and who knew what she would do now that he'd found her out? Sam managed to stay awake for a long time, watching and waiting, to no avail. The last time he looked at the clock it was 2:00 a.m., and Marianne was whimpering in her sleep.

Blackness. Absolute blackness. A void so total there could be no conception, even, of its penetration. Sam could still hear Marianne crying softly beside him, but beyond that there was no other sound. He didn't know what else he'd been expecting to encounter, but surely there should be something?

Sam reached out for Marianne, wanting to hold her close, give and receive some measure of comfort, but his fingers closed on cold sheets. That jolted him awake. She couldn't even roll over by herself anymore, so where the hell was she?

Then Sam realised what he was clutching. Satin. Their sheets weren't satin, they were cotton. As soon as he was fully awake, of course, he knew. Celeste had struck again; so awake was the wrong word. Perhaps cognisant was more appropriate. Slowly, the familiar layout of Celeste's dream chamber made itself known, as Sam had been sure it would. He could still hear Marianne crying, though, and that worried him. It was a weary, worn-out sort of crying, as if it had been going on for a long time. Either some part of Sam, however tiny, was still clinging to reality or Celeste had brought Marianne into this again. What was Celeste up to?

Climbing out of the bed, which seemed to have assumed enormous proportions, Sam edged forwards carefully with his hands outstretched before him in an effort to avoid obstacles. As usual in this place, he was naked. The air was filled with rustling, scurrying sounds, filling Sam with revulsion. He hated anything that crawled, slithered, or alternatively, raced along on too many feet. Several times, he recoiled, swallowing the feeling of nausea that hit as he felt something brushing against his leg or the flutter of leathery wings against his face, seeming to linger. The air felt as if it was full of the beating of such wings, the chill from them cooling Sam's flesh. He doubted very much whether the nudity was out of any conscious desire on her part. It had much more to do with keeping Sam off-balance and vulnerable. He had to admit, however grudgingly, that it was succeeding.

She was out to put the frighteners on, that much was plain.

Steeling himself, Sam did his best to ignore whatever was crawling around the floor or flitting across the ceiling, swooping from corner to corner, and inched his way forward. Finally, he reached the door. As he felt around in the dark for the handle, the rustling and hissing reached a crescendo, as if intent on warning him away. Sam hesitated, sure he was about to grip something that was eager to sink its teeth in, take some flesh. Telling himself not to be stupid, he reached out, holding his breath, and found what he was looking for. Sam grabbed the door handle and yanked it open, reckoning it couldn't be worse outside than it was in here. If he was wrong, though...

He refused to think about that.

The susurration stopped instantly, as if it was a tape cut off in mid-play. Bitch. Sam heaved a sigh of relief and stepped out into the hall. He could breathe a little easier now, the panic in check. There was light in the hall, albeit dim. The way forward was lit by candles, guttering here and there along the walls like some mediaeval keep. The crying was louder out here. Sam followed the sound for what seemed like hours, along the familiar spiral hall. At last, the hall opened out into the cavernous circular chamber Sam had seen once before, as he had known it would. Although he had expected to reach it a lot sooner. It had the same glass walls, there was even a storm lashing the cliffs looming in the distance, just like before, causing the waves to crash against the rocks, white foam signalling their impact.

And there, on the floor, was Marianne.

The difference was that this time she wasn't wandering along the cliff top in a billowing white dress, unknowing and unreachable. Her doom was closer this time. She lay sprawled on the tile floor, moaning. Celeste kicked her half-heartedly to elicit another cry. Marianne was just the bait. Sam had a feeling he was about to become the main attraction.

Celeste looked up and laughed. "Well, well, look who's come to visit."

She stood with a foot planted lightly on Marianne's hip, as if daring Sam to confront her. She was holding Marianne's head up by a hank of her hair, so she could see her partner. Marianne was beyond seeing anything by the look of her. She was barely conscious and in obvious pain. Sam wasn't sure of the best way out of this for either of them. If he moved forward, towards them, Celeste might kill Marianne. At the very least, she would do some severe damage just to warn him off.

Marianne hung there, slick with sweat, breathing in short, forced gasps. Sam decided his best bet was probably to try and calm Celeste down. He had to persuade her that they didn't pose a threat. From the condition they were both in, it was hard to see how dangerous she could think they'd be, but he had to try. Celeste looked about as scared as the average pit-bull, but was clearly waiting for him to say something.

He cleared his throat. "Let Marianne go, Celeste. Please."

"Persuade me." She was enjoying this, relishing every moment of the torment she was inflicting.

Sam gestured at Marianne. "She can't hurt you. Leave her be."

Celeste let Marianne fall to the floor and sauntered over to view the budding maelstrom outside. For the moment, Marianne appeared to be out of danger, but Sam knew he couldn't trust appearances. Marianne groaned and clutched her stomach, and he yearned to go to her, but was too scared. What was Celeste up to? He had to keep trying to get her to talk, even though he had very little hope that anything he said or did would change her mind about hurting them in the slightest.

"Why did you bring Marianne here, Celeste? I... I thought this was our place."

She laughed out loud at that, delighted at Sam's ham-fisted attempt to seduce. She had seen it for what it was before he even tried.

"Don't flatter yourself," she said, no trace of teasing now. All Sam heard in her voice was scorn. "Your subconscious fantasies could hardly be called 'our place.'"

Now she moved away from the window, advancing swiftly towards Sam with a feline grace that had him cowering before she had even covered half the distance. She stopped no more than an inch from his face, bared her teeth at him before spitting, "They served a purpose. That's all."

Then she was gone, back to Marianne's side before he could even blink. The taste of her perfume at the back of his throat was the only hint that she had really been that close. Sam released a long, shuddering breath, only now realising how terrified he had been in her presence. Celeste began to torment Marianne again, pulling her hair, flicking her in the ribs with her shoe. She laughed all the while, delighted at Sam's reaction. All designed to tease. Marianne barely reacted, lying on the floor almost unconscious.

Celeste stared down at her prisoner, her expression suddenly sad. "This is the bitch you love, isn't it?"

It was over. Sam swallowed, throat dry with apprehension. The way he saw it, Marianne was going to suffer whichever way he answered. Best just to admit it and get it over with, once and for all. Yet there were ways of admitting such a truth, weren't there? Ways that could try to soothe the sting, if only a little, leaving the loser able to salvage something from the experience.

"What I feel for Marianne is...different."

"But you love her?" Slight emphasis on *her*—everything else spoken in a flat monotone. She wasn't going to be easily appeased. Sam could almost believe that this was the first time anyone had tired of her first. That anyone had tried to break free before she was finished with them, ready to move on to fresh game.

He smiled. "I love her, yes. We have a life together. What you and I had was just...passion."

Good word, that. Passion. It sounded so much better than mere lust, more important, grander. Celeste considered this for a moment, then knelt down beside Marianne, rested her hands lightly on her body—one on her arm, one on her swollen belly. Her head was lowered, her eyes hooded, shadows jumping across her face. Sam couldn't read her expression. Alarm bells went off in his head. Had he failed, ruined everything?

"And you'd prefer a mundane existence with *this...*" She nodded disparagingly at Marianne, who thankfully was unconscious by now. "To a life of...*passion?*" She spat the word back at him.

Sam smiled, nodded—though not without a little regret. The emotion wasn't missed. He saw her register it and assess whether she could use it to keep him. She couldn't, and he saw that fact sink in too.

She smiled back, a softer expression this time, showing only resignation, perhaps a little disappointment. "I can understand that. You tire so easily."

Maybe it was just Sam's bruised ego talking, but somehow he didn't think it was just him she was referring to now. Sam was just a face in a crowd of admirers, and only she knew how many men made up that number. Then she bared her teeth at him in a grin so full of malicious glee that he stepped back in terror. Her face shifted, her hair and features changing so quickly Sam couldn't really be sure they had. Then she was his Celeste again, laughing at his fear. All interest in him as a lover was gone now. He was just a toy she was sick of and was about to discard.

The air around her seemed to thicken and swarm. Sam glimpsed hints of several creatures writhing here and there. It hurt his eyes, and his heart, to look at them. Sam could only watch in horror as she raised her hands high above her head, chanting something unintelligible in a voice rapidly approaching a scream. This was too real. He tried desperately to distance himself... This was a dream, had to be. It wasn't supposed to be able to harm. So why couldn't he wake up?

Celeste's fingers stretched and hooked into claws topped by razor sharp nails. Sam heard the joints cracking as they stretched and realigned. They groaned as her gaze returned to Marianne.

Marianne had begun to come around, and she was trying, without much success, to sit up. She struggled to raise herself up onto one elbow and looked around, groggy. Sam watched the fear etch itself onto her face once more as she realised where she was. She hadn't woken up at all. Slowly, she looked up, and Sam saw her horror as she saw Celeste staring down at her.

Celeste chuckled and stared hard at Sam. "I'm sure you won't mind if I leave you something to remember me by?" Her laughter mixed uneasily with Sam's scream and Marianne's cry of pain in a discordant ululation as she plunged her claws deep into Marianne's belly...

The scream continued as Sam surged upright in bed, chest heaving. He felt Marianne echoing his movement. Then silence. They were both back in bed, *their* bed, and they were both terrified. He grabbed Marianne, held her close as she buried her face against his chest.

Her voice was muffled as she said, "You dreamed it, too."

It wasn't a question. Sam knew exactly what Marianne meant, and she knew it. He could only nod in reply, still panting for breath while she clung to him, one hand on her swollen stomach.

Just a dream. Dear God, just a dream.

Sam kept expecting to feel the first stabbing pains in his chest any second, as his heart finally gave up the right to rise above the constant strain. It was beating so hard he felt it might erupt from his chest at any moment. Sam fancied he could hear it trembling. Like a scared animal, its pulse deafened him as it pounded in his ears. Gradually, they managed to get themselves under control, clinging to each other like bereft children.

Sam eased Marianne back, on to the pillows, smoothing her hair back off her face. "Are you okay?"

Marianne nodded, trying not to cry, her breath still hitching with the strain. "That bitch, Sam. Now she's spoiled even this for us."

It was true. They both knew they'd be spending the rest of the time leading up to the birth worried about what harm she had done. They could rationalise that she had only been trying to frighten them as much as they liked, but they'd still have that fear, deep inside.

Sam rested his head on his raised knee and took a deep breath before saying, "There's only one thing left we can do."

"What's that?" Marianne asked, her voice full of fear.

"I'm going to have to kill her."

Sam wasn't altogether surprised when she failed to argue. Marianne said nothing more, just curled into him and lay still. But he could feel her crying, even though she made no sound. With no idea of what to say to make things right, he stared at the ceiling, reflecting on just how he might achieve his aim.

To kill Celeste.

Chapter 27

"Clive!"

Down in the kitchen, Clive flinched visibly. He knew that tone of voice, and it always promised pain. If not his, then someone else's.

He stood and made his way as slowly as he dared up the stairs. What had he done? He cast his mind carefully back over the last few months, since the whole cycle had started up once more, but could find nothing. Nothing that she could have known about, anyway.

Or could she?

Had she found out, somehow, about the recent night-time visitors? He didn't think so, unless it had been her toying with him in the first place. With Celeste, one could never know for sure. He thought guiltily about his half-formed plans for achieving his salvation and then, remembering himself, tried to banish all such thoughts from his mind. Celeste could skim the conscious part of his mind in an instant, and he knew she still did so now and again, just to keep him on his toes. Thankfully, it took her longer to probe deeper, past the defences he had learned to create.

Over the years he had grown sensitive to the touch of her mind when she did this. There had been no sign so far, this time. She

Marie O'Regan

would not be best pleased to realise her pawn had acquired some protective devices of his own over the years, and he didn't know what she might do to punish him. He was safer while she still believed he was no threat.

Unlike Celeste's, his own powers were subtle, and for the most part, protective in nature. He had absorbed them over their time together, almost unconsciously, by some weird sort of osmosis.

Yet he could feel that he was growing stronger, his control (at least of himself) far greater, a conscious thing now. He just had to hope Celeste couldn't sense it too.

He mulled over more mundane things, looking for more common-place grievances she might have, or might use as an excuse. He had done whatever she asked, been unfailingly polite to the sad and lonely victim called Paul. What else could there be?

He reached the top of the stairs and padded silently across the hall to the living room. He could feel the excessive heat even from outside the door. It was quite cold, but not unusually so. Even so, she had the gas fire blazing at full blast, making the living room feel like a sauna. Celeste was standing by the window, wrapped up in a large shawl, staring blankly out at the garden. Her skin had an unnatural bluish tint, as if she was chilled to the bone. Was she ill, Clive wondered? He didn't know if she could even get sick, whether she was still human enough for that.

He coughed, announcing his presence. When that failed, he spoke as softly as he could, "Ma'am?"

"Don't adopt that noncommittal tone with me, Clive. I know you too well."

"I just wondered what you wanted," he said. Thin ice today. Clive stood there and waited for her to answer, not wanting to push his luck.

"Who said I wanted anything?"

So that was it. She was ready to pick a fight. Desperate for a fight.

Someone, or something, had her worried—a feeling she absolutely hated. So Clive was to be the butt of her frustration, whether he deserved it or not.

I should be used to this by now.

But he wasn't, and he didn't think he ever would be. He braced himself slightly, ready for the onslaught. "You called me, ma'am. That's all." He had deliberately kept his voice even, noting not to betray any emotion.

But Celeste knew him too well for that. She knew he was scared. It was what she got off on. "Don't worry, I'm not going to hurt you."

The weariness in her voice astounded him, and she turned to face him before he had a chance to hide his amazement or modify the defensive stance he had unwittingly adopted. Tired as she was, she smiled at that. The sorrow inherent in that tight little smile wrenched at Clive's heart. Another first. She actually had him feeling sorry for her. Was this real, he wondered, or another of her little tricks?

"Am I that bad?"

She started walking towards him, but stopped and sat in the armchair instead when she saw Clive beginning to back away, tensed for the blow he was obviously expecting to fall.

"Aren't you tired of all this?" Her tone was plaintive, all fight gone.

To Clive, it was as if the Celeste he knew was gone, replaced by some changeling, an echo of the Celeste that might have been, under other circumstances. He didn't know how to react, not to this. If he told the truth, would she fly into one of her famous rages and make him suffer, just for the fun of it? Or was her weariness genuine?

Either way, as Clive saw it, he would be the loser. His instinct told him just to answer her truthfully and take the consequences, whatever they might prove to be. At least then he would know what he was dealing with. "Yes, Celeste. I'm tired. We should have died years ago, both of us."

She looked at him appraisingly, surprised by his bluntness. Then she looked away, into the firelight, a hard shine in her eyes. Clive felt his blood run cold. Almost everything was out in the open now and whatever followed, their relationship could never again be the same. What it would turn into remained to be seen.

What she said next stunned him. It was the one thing he had never expected. The one thing he had thought her incapable of.

"I never thought I'd fall in love, Clive. I never found a man I loved before."

He hesitated before venturing, "Paul?"

Irritation flared briefly, an echo of the Celeste he knew so well, and he stifled a smile as she snarled an answer. "Of course Paul. Who else?"

Clive chose not to answer that question. He knew she was tormenting some other poor soul. Had known it for a long time. What he didn't know yet was who. He had heard her crying out in her sleep, had seen her performing the necessary spells several times, though she had tried to be discreet.

She was acting out the role of seducer again, cavorting through someone's dreams. Clive knew how intoxicating that could be. She had learnt that particular craft by practising on him. They had spent many nights together, wrapped in each other's arms, both in dreams and reality. They had usually been a pleasurable experience, if exhausting.

Now that he knew, Clive felt an unexpected pang that it was Paul Celeste had fallen in love with. A small part of his own heart would always belong to her, he knew, no matter how monstrous she was. He had hoped that some part of her felt the same.

She stared at him, her face bereft. "I don't know what to do."

Another first. He had never seen her confused before, vulnerable. There was a stillness in the air, as if the house itself had become aware of the possibilities. He could feel another presence nearby, listening. Perhaps it was one of the spirits that had visited him. Clive had been right to trust them. Celeste appeared to have noticed none of this, intent on her own dilemma.

They were at a crossroads. Could he redeem her, as well as

himself? Clive had to at least try. His visitors had hinted that there was a chance, however slight, for him. Could there be a chance for her too? Would she even want to earn a reprieve, or was she already truly damned? He tried his best to sound her out, to determine her intentions.

"What would happen if it all stopped now, Celeste? Right now."

Her tone grew icy. "I don't understand what you're getting at, Clive."

"What would happen if you allowed the cycle to run down? If you didn't renew this time?"

Her voice, when she answered, was flat, hopeless. "We can't do that, Clive. You know yourself the period between renewals has been getting shorter. If we don't renew, we've probably got a year left like this. If we're lucky."

A year. How many people's lives had been affected, if not destroyed, by Celeste this time, he wondered? Just so that they could have another two years of youth.

He stared at her for what seemed like a long time, his expression blank, before asking, "Is it worth it, Celeste?"

She didn't answer for what felt like hours but could only have been minutes, if that. Clive felt the old fear begin to resurface. Was she even human anymore? Was he? How much of their souls remained unfettered now, two hundred years after she had started all this? Surprisingly, Celeste was the first to break eye contact, dropping her gaze as if ashamed. He hoped that was true. If she could feel shame, then perhaps she wasn't completely lost.

Her tone when she answered was flat, dismissive. "I don't know." Standing up, she returned to her post at the window. "And I don't much care." She glanced back at him and attempted a smile, but failed miserably. "Not when you consider the alternative."

Interview terminated. Had they achieved something? Who knew with Celeste? Clive turned to go. All he wanted now was to reach the relative safety of the kitchen. He had tried, at least. He had not been surprised to be turned down flat. Disappointed, but not surprised.

"I won't lose Paul, though. Not now."
Words that held a world of hurt for someone.

Once he had reached the kitchen, he sat at the table and forced himself to concentrate, to relax. Now, while Celeste was distracted (he hoped) was probably the best chance Clive would ever have to turn the tables and probe her mind. He had to find out her plans towards Paul and any other conquests she might have.

Breathing deeply, Clive let his mind float free. Focussing on Celeste, he felt the first feathery contact and tensed himself for discovery, ready to withdraw if he even suspected she felt his presence. There was nothing.

He carefully blanked his mind, allowing her thoughts to drift across his own. She was thinking about Paul, agonising over whether to let him go, for his own sake. Clive was surprised to feel the depth of her emotion as she thought of him. So, she really did love him, after all. Clive had half convinced himself it was mere infatuation.

He let Celeste's memories of their romance wash over him and felt his own respect for the man growing. Paul had acted with dignity throughout, and their one true confrontation had caused him great distress. Celeste was well aware of the fact that Paul had made his choice and would never willingly let her go now. Without her, his life was empty.

Clive grimaced.

Without Celeste, Paul's life, bleak as it was, would probably not last long. No one could bear such unrelieved loneliness for long and stay sane, untouched by it all. Amazingly, Celeste had achieved something good in ensnaring Paul, whether she had realised it at the time or not.

Clive probed deeper, trying to find some clue to the identity of her other lover(s). He felt Celeste's mind begin to focus, as if sensing his presence, and forced himself to relax as her mind reached out, trying to discover the source of her anxiety. She remained alert for a considerable time, watching, he felt, for danger, and remaining calm was growing more difficult.

Finally, she relaxed, let her mind drift once more. Sam. He caught the name Sam and zeroed in on her memories of him. He was caught off-guard by the savagery involved. She had brutalised Sam and his girlfriend. Clive caught the name Marianne, along with a glimpse of Celeste's loathing for her. Celeste had terrorised them.

Delving deeper, their faces swam into focus in his mind's eye. They made a pleasant looking couple. Clive especially liked the look of Marianne. She had an honest, open face that spoke of a spirited approach to life, as well as great kindness, tempered with practicality. Sam, too, looked humorous. He was fair with a smiling face. Clive got the impression that the smile never completely faded, except under the most extreme provocation. If he had become entangled with Celeste, Clive had no doubt he wouldn't be smiling much anymore.

Celeste's memories concerning Sam and Marianne began to surface in more detail, and Clive flinched. Whatever they had done to piss her off, they had certainly succeeded. He had seldom seen her unleash such ferocity on anyone. Clive watched the saga unfold, and his resolve hardened.

It was bad enough that Celeste was in the process of destroying yet another couple, but Clive sensed a clear threat to Marianne. No, not her...but her children? She was pregnant. He absorbed as much as he could about them, sensing Celeste beginning to gather herself again. She knew someone was pushing, invading, and he could not remain undetected for much longer. Happy he knew what was necessary, he withdrew, feeling more than a little sick.

Just in time. He heard Celeste moving across the living room floor overhead, and Clive quickly crossed to the sink, filled the kettle. He felt her watching him from the doorway. He carefully shielded his thoughts as best he could and set about methodically making tea, as if he didn't even know she was there.

After a while, she gave up and went away, probably to look elsewhere for the problem. He just hoped she was satisfied that it wasn't him.

Soon after, the front door slammed as she left the house with Paul. He sagged against the counter in relief, his legs suddenly weak.

Time passed, and the front door slammed once more as Celeste returned home. Clive flinched as she came hurtling down the stairs. She stormed into the kitchen with a force that wasn't far short of being elemental. He sometimes wondered why the very walls didn't tremble when she was in one of her rages.

She paced the kitchen, furious, her gaze firmly on Clive as he sat at the table polishing silverware, his expression bland. "He's found me. How could he find me?"

"Who?" Clive asked.

He knew, by now, but he wanted to hear it from her own lips. He wanted her to incriminate herself.

"As if you didn't know!"

The disdain in her voice stung Clive, and he looked down, abashed. So she had felt something, after all. He had been a fool to think otherwise.

Paul chose that moment to venture downstairs in pursuit. He came into the kitchen looking slightly nervous, as if unsure of his welcome. Clive breathed a sigh of relief at the distraction. With any luck, she would forget, at least for a while. He hoped it would be for long enough.

Paul had no need to worry, not yet. Celeste still needed his adoration. In a very real way, he was her lifeline. To poor, besotted Paul, she probably looked just as she always had, but Clive's practised eye detected the first signs of her next decline. Her skin was a little drier than normal. Fine lines were appearing here and there.

There was a brittleness in her every gesture that Clive knew all too well by now.

Things would have to come to a head soon.

Paul stood in the doorway, stammered a bid for her attention. "Celeste?"

Instantly, she was all sweetness and light, the innocent in need of protection. "Paul, come in. I just needed a word with Clive."

He licked his lips, his throat dry. "Yes, I... I heard."

Celeste turned to stare at him, then, curious. "Oh?"

The danger inherent in that simple little comment was palpable, and Paul tried his best to become even more diffident, if that was possible. He concentrated on the silverware, while watching Clive and Celeste dance around each other.

Celeste eyed Paul appraisingly. Her devoted little subject was beginning to show a regrettable degree of protectiveness. Was it to be allowed, or slapped down now? She decided to let it pass for now. But he would bear watching. There was nothing more restricting for her than a man defending his woman, in this case herself.

As if he could.

Then again, should it prove necessary to replace Clive, then Paul could well be the ideal candidate.

"It's nothing, Paul, really. Just an old boyfriend I'd rather forget."

Smooth, Clive thought. But would Paul swallow it?

"I wouldn't worry. The woman with him was very pregnant. I should imagine you're the least of his worries at the moment." He'd swallowed it, all right; hook, line and sinker. And in his principled little world, he couldn't imagine anyone cheating on a pregnant woman.

Celeste smiled, feigning an expression of relieved gratitude. Ever the doting female.

Clive had to force himself not to laugh as Paul placed a hand on her back and guided her proprietarily back upstairs. If only he knew. Shaking his head, Clive moved to the kettle and switched it on. They would want him to bring coffee very soon.

Marie O'Regan

When Clive took the coffee up to the living room a few minutes later, all appeared to be normal between them. But Clive caught Paul watching Celeste pensively now and again, his expression hurt.

He's begun to see, thought Clive. *Something's not quite right. He can see that much, anyway.*

The question was, what would he do about it?

Clive lay in bed later that night, waiting. He knew Celeste had invaded Sam's dreams again. She was hungry tonight for more than any one man, even her beloved Paul, could provide. He could feel the echoes of it in the air, together with a sort of expectant emptiness. Clive had become very finely attuned to the vibrations of the house and Celeste over the years.

He sensed Paul, sprawled next to Celeste's body in the main bedroom. Snoring heavily, he had no idea of whom, or rather what, he had had the misfortune to fall in love with. He laid beside her, exhausted, content to dream of the love they had just shared.

Clive could feel the spirits that inhabited this place, swarming around. They were agitated tonight, bloated on the psychic energy Celeste was expending to stay in Sam's subconscious. Distantly, Clive could just sense Sam. The fear emanating from him was strong tonight.

He tried once more to zero in on Sam and Celeste. The images grew sharper, and he recoiled, sickened, before he was enmeshed in the night's fantasies.

Then he felt another, more welcome, presence begin to permeate the room, and opened his eyes, weary of the myriad intrusions. Sure enough, there they were again, at their head a face Clive remembered very well. It haunted him every night—Celeste's first conquest, Clive's brother. Tonight he appeared young and strong again, standing tall and proud at the foot of Clive's bed. Clive felt the first flutter of hope beat hesitantly within him, the power he had sensed before had increased a thousand-fold.

Matthew's lips moved, but the sound was inside Clive's head,

212

where Celeste couldn't hear it. *"Time to be strong, Clive. Help him find it."*

He didn't need his brother to spell it out any further. Sam had finally been pushed too far. He had already sensed as much. Yet he said nothing, merely waited for Matthew to finish. Celeste's presence began to strengthen, as if she was waking up. There was no more time to talk. Not tonight.

Matthew began to fade, but before he faded completely his voice came once more, *"Make sure it burns, Clive. Burns to the ground."*

Silence descended.

To Clive, it felt as if the rain lashing down on him as he stood on Suicide Bridge staring down was trying to wash him from the face of the earth. He had become an abomination, aiding Celeste in her damnable pursuit of adoration. Maybe he was even worse than her, feeding parasitically off of her monstrous appetite. He knew how wrong it was. Such knowledge had been ingrained in him from an early age by his family, his parents and his grandmother. Church people, all of them, and they had raised him to know and love the Lord. He thanked God every day that they had never known what he had become. His fear of Celeste had always been too great, and he was by no means sure he had overcome it yet.

He stood there for a long time, fighting the might of the storm to stay safely upright atop the bridge. He wasn't even sure, really, that it wouldn't be better if he just gave up the battle.

Would it bring Celeste down, he wondered, *if I just jumped now? Would it be enough?*

He groaned, knowing he couldn't bring himself to do it. He didn't have the strength.

Suicide.

Such an ugly word for an end to pain. Yet it could not be

condoned. He knew that. To commit suicide was to commit a mortal sin, or so he had been taught. He had enough sins already on his conscience without the added burden of that.

Looking down at Archway Road, he saw the traffic moving sluggishly below him, headlights glowing. They seemed to Clive as if they were mocking him, daring him to have the courage to jump. With a sinking heart, he realised he didn't have it anymore, if indeed he ever had. Ironic as it seemed, he preferred to meet his end at Celeste's hands, if need be.

Turning his head to the right, he could just make out the outlines of the house. What had started as a new home, full of promise (even if only of escape) had quickly become a living tomb. Two hundred years was a long sentence by any standards, and he was mortally tired. Jumping couldn't solve anything, even if it did seem like the easiest option.

He didn't even know whether, when it came right down to it, he would be able to die. For all he knew, Celeste might be able to resurrect him as some half-dead monstrosity, retaining only enough humanity to be able to serve as before—a zombie, like his brother when he died and Bess resurrected him. They were tied irrevocably, and for the end (for any of them) to be final, they would all have to be destroyed.

The most he could do was try to save Sam, Marianne, and Paul. There had been too many victims already, and he drew the line at harming the unborn. His decision made, Clive walked slowly back to the house. It had never seemed such a long and lonely journey.

Chapter 28

For Paul, the incident on the hill had been distinctly unnerving, sowing a seed of disquiet that would not be pacified.

One minute he and Celeste had been enjoying a pleasant walk home, chatting about the usual inconsequential things. He had been happy, all the worries of work a million miles away. The next minute this man had appeared on the path in front of them, changing everything. The look of shocked recognition on Celeste's face had been unmistakeable, though she had concealed it quickly enough. If looks could kill, he thought, that man should have keeled over on the spot. The look she gave the woman accompanying him was, if that was possible, worse.

It had crossed Paul's mind that she'd looked as if she would have killed them with her bare hands if she could, but he'd hastily brushed that aside as overreaction, jealousy, even. There was obviously something between these three. He would probably never know what. The illusion of closeness that he had been building up crumpled in an instant as the full realisation of how much he didn't know, didn't *want* to know, hit him. And hit hard.

And then there was the expression on their faces when they'd caught sight of her for the first time. That had been fear. He was sure of that. Abject fear.

Why?

He remembered Celeste's display of fury in his flat when he had asked her to leave. He had managed to convince himself that that had been at least partly his fault for the way he had treated her. Was that really true? He couldn't actually remember anymore. He wasn't so sure now. Why had the couple on the hill been so scared?

Paul woke feeling utterly drained, almost as if he had been drugged. He thought back to the previous night's activities and grinned. Celeste had been exhausting, making love as if driven. She had climaxed four times before he had managed to get anywhere near orgasm. There had been a feeling of desperation about the whole thing that he had begun to find more than a little scary. He had gazed into her eyes, seen the passion there, but hadn't there been something else, underneath?

He had closed his own eyes then, not wanting to guess. Then he had felt himself approaching climax and sacrificed himself to it. It had probably been the most intense sexual experience of his life, and it seemed to go on forever. He had slumped on top of her as if dead, and had fallen asleep in seconds, one arm draped across her.

There was no sign of her anywhere, now. She wasn't upstairs, or in the living room or study. The house was totally silent. Had everyone gone out, he wondered?

The sound of a door closing quietly came from downstairs and Paul grinned, relieved. So that was where she had disappeared to.

He headed eagerly downstairs. His eagerness didn't last long.

Celeste was standing in the centre of the kitchen, hand on her hips as she looked around the room. She was absolutely furious about something. He walked purposefully forward, a smile on his face, intent on defusing the situation.

"Celeste?"

She whirled on him, and Paul instinctively flinched. She stopped herself with an obvious effort and smiled. "I was looking for Clive."

Celeste checked Clive's room and leaned on the door, her face thoughtful. "But he's out."

Paul followed her, intent on getting to the heart of this. "Is that a problem?"

She stared at him for a moment before replying, her face solemn. "Depends on where he's gone, and for how long."

"Did you need him for something?"

She smiled, eager to get off the subject of Clive and his where-abouts. "No, not really. Just checking up on him."

She left the kitchen and wandered back upstairs, her expression troubled.

Paul followed more slowly. He was obviously missing something here. She was more concerned about Clive than she wanted Paul to notice. Why was he so important? What had he done? She stood staring out of the hall window. Her earlier depression seemed to have been lifted from her whole. For the life of him, Paul couldn't see what she was so cheerful about. Rain lashed the windows, and thunder rumbled in the distance. The sky had a distinctly yellowish colour to it.

She smiled at the weather. "He won't have gone far. Not in this."

Paul kept quiet, hoping she would elaborate. Almost under her breath, he heard her whisper one more word. "Safe." She'd forgotten he was there, it seemed, all her thoughts on Clive once more.

Ironically, he was jealous. He knew it was stupid. Had seen the way she treated Clive, after all, but there was no getting away from the fact that he felt slighted. He joined her at the window, intending to bring it out in the open, once and for all.

"What's going on, Celeste?"

He had to know what the big secret was, what there was between her and Clive. His imagination whispered all sorts of intimacies and would not quiet. She stiffened, and when she turned to face him, he finally saw the danger he was in, even though she was still smiling.

"Be careful, Paul. You can't know everything."

Paul felt his face begin to burn, frustration and shame building up, turning his stomach to acid. He didn't have to take this. Turning, he took his jacket from the hook and made to leave. Taken aback, he saw she already had the door open and stood, waiting, her expression cold.

He didn't need telling twice.

Paul stalked across the hall and through the front door in silence, eyes carefully averted. He kept waiting for her to apologise, back down. He was waiting for that right up until the moment the front door slammed behind him.

Paul began the long walk home heedless of the torrential rain that had soaked through his clothes in an instant, trickling down his neck and plastering his hair to his skull before blinding him. The water filled his shoes, too, so that he walked in a pool of cold water. He was oblivious to all this, intent as he was on trying to forget Celeste, with her jet black hair and fierce green eyes.

He was trying so hard to forget that he never even noticed Bob as he came hurriedly out of The Crown and followed him down the hill at what he thought was a safe distance.

Paul was bone weary when he let himself back into his flat, his head spinning. He didn't know whether he was coming or going anymore. He stood in the darkened entry hall breathing in huge racking gasps. The heating had been left on, and the air was warm and stale. He felt the chill that had sunk into him, and began to shiver. He stripped quickly, there in the hall, leaving his clothes puddled on the floor as he made his way into the bathroom, where he ran the shower as hot as he could bear, standing thankfully under the cleansing spray.

Gradually, the shivering stopped and he felt more in control of himself. He towelled himself dry and wandered into the bedroom, where he pulled on a warm tracksuit and sweat socks. From there, he headed for the kitchen to make some coffee. Halfway there, he stopped, head cocked. And listened. *Felt.* There was no sound, and the flat felt all wrong, somehow. Empty.

What had happened to his life? He had no idea. All he knew was that he had to choose, Celeste or this—before it was too late.

Funny, he mused, as he wandered aimlessly from room to room, coffee all but forgotten. *All this seems like another world now.*

He felt as if he were walking through an old photograph, everything seeming like a distant but well-loved memory. He moved into the bedroom and, picking up the framed wedding photograph that that he kept on his bedside table, sat heavily on the edge of the bed. The time he had spent with his wife had been the happiest years of his life. Now it seemed like a different life altogether, and he didn't think the gap between the two could ever be breached. He couldn't imagine life ever being that simple again.

Celeste blew either hot or cold, sometimes frighteningly so, but tranquillity was not in her nature. Should he phone her, or go back? The thought of waiting to see if she would calm down was scary, but he liked to think he still had enough pride not to just crawl back like a whipped pup. The accuracy of the analogy wasn't lost on him, either. He had to have some self-respect left. He knew if she called, he'd come running. His pride didn't stretch far enough to resist her for long. But he hadn't sunk low enough to crawl. Not yet, anyway. Who knew how low he would sink before she had finished with him?

Oh God, what if she was?

The thought of facing that loneliness again filled him with dread. He had only just come through that the last time. He didn't know if he could do it again.

He had a choice. If he broke up with Celeste—and his mind whispered fervently that he should—then he would be alone again, and he didn't know if he could face that a second time.

You've got friends, he thought. *Good friends you've let slip. Get in touch.* But what if they, stung by his indifference, had cooled towards him? He couldn't blame them, and truth to tell, he was mortally afraid of finding out.

But if he stayed?

All his instincts were screaming at him to stay away. She was bad news, he'd had an inkling of that this morning. If he went along with her then it would be a dark and dangerous ride, one that could conceivably be the end of him. That much he was certain of. Any intimate relationship with Celeste would inevitably lead to his ruin. Perhaps part of him even sought that. In a way, even that would be a relief.

Yet he did love her. Perhaps it was better to say he was obsessed with her. If she called, he would come running, without a doubt. For the sake of his own self-respect, he just hoped she called. After a decent interval, of course. Then, the niceties observed, he could lean on her strength once more, be carried along, comforted.

God, had he sunk that low?

He lay down on the bed and stared at the ceiling, pretended he wasn't really crying. Thunder crashed intermittently in the distance, the resultant lightning flickering in varying degrees across the bedroom. He preferred it dark. It was easier to hide from the truth.

The storm went on for hours, echoing the turmoil Paul felt. He agonised over which way to go, but found himself no nearer an answer.

Gradually the light filtering through the shut curtains began to brighten somewhat. The incessant drumming of rain on the window slackened a little, though it didn't stop entirely.

Crossing to the window, Paul pulled the curtains wide and stood looking down at the street before him, pavements slick with rain. People were beginning to venture out again, hurrying down the street as far away from the roadside as they could get, desperately trying not to get splashed by passing cars. He had noticed the odd, yellowish cast to the sky earlier, and now it lent a threatening aspect to the panorama unfolding before him. The view seemed bleached of colour, almost. It came to him, suddenly, that the odd lighting lent the view the air of one of those gangster comics he had been so fond of in his youth. It looked like something from *The Untouchables* or something.

There was even a man sheltering in a doorway opposite huddled inside his coat to keep warm. It was too dark to see what he was watching, and Paul smiled shamefacedly at the paranoia he had felt briefly. Why would anyone be interested in watching him? It was just another poor sod sheltering from the sudden deluge.

He laughed out loud, startled by the manic quality he detected (good word that, undetected, his mind whispered), but it only made him laugh harder. Was he having a breakdown? Again? If not, he was probably perilously close to it.

A loud bang startled him out of his hysteria. He stood quietly, waiting to see if it would come again. Probably one of the neighbours. Had he really been laughing that loud? Now he felt more like crying, the hysterical quality of his fear scaring him even more. He was tempted to go back to the window, check if the man in the doorway was still there. Or whether he was lying slumped in the street with his lifeblood draining away, sucked in by the waiting gutters. He might even catch sight of the waiting gunman. For in his mind, he saw, with perfect clarity, that the bang had been too loud, too sudden, to be anything other than a gunshot.

The banging came again, more insistent this time. Paul sagged with relief. It was only someone rapping on the front door. He was halfway down the hall before it occurred to him that perhaps he had relaxed a little prematurely. After all, he didn't even know who was out there yet. He hadn't checked the doorway, to see if its occupant had gone.

The ludicrousness of the situation embarrassed him and he laughed once more. Here he was, just short of his forty-third birthday, in the middle of his own private melodrama. Shaking his head in disbelief, he reached for the door handle. As if on cue, the thunder clapped once more as he opened it, right overhead, making him jump visibly.

It was Celeste.

On some level, of course he had known it would be. Or had prayed as much. He stood dumbly, staring at her cool beauty, drinking it in.

She smiled wearily at his confusion. "Aren't you going to ask me in?"

Paul looked at the floor, unable to meet her gaze. "I wasn't sure you'd want me to."

She pushed past him, made her way down the hall to the living room. "If I didn't want to, darling, I'd hardly have come all this way in the rain, now, would I?"

Was he seeing things? He stared after her, unsure of the truth of what his mind insisted he was seeing...

Couldn't be.

As Celeste walked down the hall, it seemed to darken around her. It was as if she was draining the power from the air itself, even from the electric lights. She wasn't even wet.

Then she turned back to him and smiled. "Coming, darling?"

That was all it took for him to fall, he realised. He could he placated, bought if you wanted to put it that way, as easily as that. He shut the door behind him and followed her down the hall as the fog in his mind descended, dimly aware that it was too late for hesitation now.

He had made his choice.

Paul walked into the living room to find her comfortably ensconced on the sofa, smiling broadly, as if she had known all along exactly what he thought and felt. His pride struggled to reassert itself, if only briefly, and wouldn't allow him to make the first move. He stood at the door, awkward as any sixteen-year-old angling for a date. His throat felt dry, his voice unable to pass the obstruction he felt there, even though he knew it was simple fear.

"Come and sit down, Paul, please."

She patted the cushion beside her, and Paul found himself moving hesitantly forward. He made himself sit stiffly at the edge of his seat, though he ached to bury his head against the soft curve of her neck and beg forgiveness, for whatever she wanted, even if he didn't understand why. He felt her hand on his thigh and closed his eyes, prayed for strength.

"I'm sorry, I shouldn't have taken it out on you." Her voice was honey soft, no hint of the venom there had been this morning.

Still Paul said nothing, not trusting himself to speak.

"Look at me." A hint of steel now.

He turned slowly, looked at her. She had been crying. Her eyes were red and swollen. He forgave her everything in that instant and was lost. He pulled her close, breathed in the aroma of her hair that always smelt to him of sunshine, of *life*.

"It's all right. I shouldn't have pried."

"There wasn't anything to pry into. I was just angry that he'd gone off without saying anything, that's all."

He shushed her. "Never mind that now. Let's just forget about it."

She kissed him then, and he picked her up in his arms and carried her into the bedroom, all thoughts of his previous life gone. They made love, and to Paul it was a catharsis, a reaffirmation. His life was with Celeste now, if she'd only have him. Right or wrong, he needed the strength she gave him. He couldn't be alone again. Afterwards, they slept, tangled in each other's arms. They were content, for the moment, just to be together.

Outside, Bob waited in his doorway, ever vigilant. For a while there, he had thought Paul had recognised him. He had stared down at him so strangely. For his part, Bob could hardly believe the change in his sometime friend. He looked years older, on the verge of madness. His movements had looked jittery, distressed, and he had kept running his fingers claw-like through his hair. To Bob, it had almost looked as if he was trying to wrench it out by the roots.

Then his attention had been diverted, somehow. He supposed he must have heard something, though he couldn't think what could have scared him so.

And there she was.

There was Celeste, walking straight towards him. No, not to him. To *Paul*. The old resentment flared again, strengthening his resolve. He actually felt the pain of it physically, as if something sharp was embedded deep within him. He had watched her stepping daintily between the puddles as she picked her way across to Paul's door. Before she had started banging on it, though, she had done something Bob found extremely weird. She had turned around and stared straight at him, though he would have sworn she couldn't have seen him from the direction she had come. And she had laughed.

Now he watched, and waited. They had to come back out. It was only a matter of time. He had caught sight of them together for a moment, as Paul had passed the living room window with Celeste in his arms. It had been obvious what they were about to do.

He could wait.

When Paul woke, the storm had finally abated. There was no sound of rain, and the wind had died. He realised with surprise that he was absolutely starving and sat up to look at the clock on the other side of the bed. Four o'clock, and he hadn't eaten anything all day. No wonder he was hungry.

Celeste was fast asleep. She lay curled up in a little ball, a contented smile on her face. Paul eased out of bed as gently as he could, trying not to wake her. He pulled on his dressing gown and headed for the kitchen, where he started the coffeemaker and scrambled some eggs, made some toast. He hadn't even realised he was humming until he heard Celeste laughing in the doorway.

"Nice to see you so happy."

A little embarrassed, he grinned, gestured towards the table. "Breakfast is served."

"It's a little late for breakfast, isn't it?"

"Yeah, well, we didn't get a chance earlier, did we?"

She said nothing to that, just sat at the table, picked up a fork, and began playing with her eggs. Not wanting to sour things, Paul poured the coffee and sat down facing her. After a few minutes, the atmosphere began to lift, and they gradually eased into more natural small talk.

The time flew by, and he felt himself relaxing more by the minute. Here was his life, complete. He had it all.

"Paul."

Celeste's voice broke into his reverie. He looked up, bemused. He'd lost track again. That was happening more and more lately, and he was beginning to worry about it.

"Let's go back to my place. Let's go home."

As if in a dream, he nodded and began to clear up the plates.

Celeste watched him closely as he washed up, then went and dressed as he distractedly pulled clean jeans and a jumper on. He was a good man. He had a good heart. Maybe this time it could last. Could Clive be replaced, she wondered? He had long ago ceased to be of interest to her, had faded into the role of manservant. He was another one who could have been a true partner, had it not been for the disapproval she had often sensed emanating from him. There would be a reckoning with Clive, she knew. She could feel it coming. But Paul... Paul was a different matter. She had him now. He'd made his decision, and all else would fade away.

Paul would do whatever she asked in time. He just needed to be broken in gently, encouraged. In time, she felt sure he would come to accept what she was, and they could be true partners.

Then he was ready and came to her with a smile on his face, open and loving. Her heart warmed at the sight of him, a sensation she could only marvel at. It had been a long time since she had felt like that about anybody.

She took his hand and led him towards the front door. "Come on, let's go."

They let themselves out of the flat and stood for a moment on the doorstep, squinting slightly in the daylight, dim though it was. There was probably less than an hour of daylight left.

Celeste tensed suddenly. Danger. Something was coming, fast. She whipped her head around. There.

Paul turned around, curious, becoming aware for the first time that something was wrong.

Bob was rushing towards them, face twisted with rage. He was shouting something, his mouth working furiously, spittle dripping from his mouth, but the words were jumbled, incomprehensible. Paul stepped in front of Celeste, eager to try and calm things down before Bob did something irrevocable. The daylight seemed to have bled from the sky in a rush, the weak yellow glare from the streetlights lending Bob a vaguely demonic aspect, like a force unleashed from Hell.

Bob reached into his coat pocket, and Paul went cold. He had a knife. Suddenly Paul was sure of that. He could almost taste it, and a burning sensation was starting up in his belly. That was where Bob was going to stick it, he knew, right in the gut. All of this went through his mind in seconds, even as the sweat on his forehead turned to ice and his bowels turned to water.

Bob had achieved a speed that was terrifying, and Celeste had pushed Paul aside as if he was no bigger than a small child. As he fell against the railings, she moved in front of him. Was she laughing? Groggily, Paul watched it unfold, but he still couldn't believe it. Celeste surged forward, seeming to glide. The air around her seemed aflame, crackles of static electricity leaving a stench of ozone. Bob had stopped running now. The anger was draining from his face, only to be replaced by a sick dread. Paul had time, just, to be glad he was behind Celeste. He didn't think anyone could survive looking at a beauty that terrible. Bob couldn't. One only had to look at him to see that.

Bob raised his hands above his face in a warding off gesture and stepped back, just a little, off the curb. Paul could hear him muttering a constant litany of negation, "No, no, no..." He stepped back once more. It was enough.

With a cry of triumph, Celeste brought one arm up in an oddly orchestrated gesture, as if she was summoning something. In reply, a battered Ford Escort that had been parked about fifty feet away screeched into action and bore down on Bob so fast that Paul barely had time to register its movement or lack of driver before it hit Bob with a sickening crunch of blood and bone. The car burst into flame on impact, enveloping Bob in a ball of fire. For a few seconds, Bob struggled, a grotesque parody of the man he had been moments earlier, melting even as Paul watched, his features running into a molten mess. Paul would never forget the expression on Bob's face as he went down. He hoped never to see anything like it again.

Then it was over.

Celeste still stood in front of him, but she no longer had the power to terrify. She was just Celeste again and had hidden that fearsome *other*. She raised her hands again, this time aiming them at Paul.

He felt, really felt, his heart stop. Then she smiled, and it leapt in his chest again even as he smiled shakily in answer. She lifted her eyes to the night sky and began to chant, starting low and gradually rising. The air around them began to thicken, shadows creeping forward. Their surroundings became a dim blur, even the blaze in front of them faded to nothing.

He felt sleepy, suddenly, bone tired, and fought to keep his eyes open. He rubbed his eyes and shook his head to clear it, and when he looked at Celeste again, the mist had cleared and they were standing outside her house on Hornsey Lane. His stomach felt a little sick and his head throbbed relentlessly, the way it normally did whenever he had had a shock or been badly upset. Yet he could think of nothing that could have set it off. They had been in the flat and then... Then they had been here. That was all. Wasn't it?

Celeste reached an arm around his waist as if to support him, her face full of concern. "We'll get you something for that headache, darling, just as soon as we get in."

He nodded, and waited for her to unlock the door. He felt chilled suddenly, and wanted—no, needed—to sit down.

Celeste took his hand and led him into the house, made him lie down on the sofa. He was asleep in seconds, all tension forgotten.

He was home.

Chapter 29

After Celeste's last little escapade, Sam watched her house as closely as he could. He called in sick at work the next morning, telling them he had gastroenteritis. He figured that should be good for at least four or five days. Hopefully that would be long enough. Marianne hardly seemed aware of his leaving. She had fallen into a deep depression, and Sam couldn't reach her. She wouldn't allow it and seemed to have already decided he wouldn't be coming back. Finally, he gave up and left, leaving her in bed. It was probably safer that way, at least for now.

Sam got in the car and drove off with barely a second thought, hardly noticing the other traffic. Miraculously, he didn't hit anyone or anything on the way. Reaching Hornsey Lane, he parked the car in a little alley on a diagonal from Celeste's house, and waited.

And he watched.

For the first three days, Sam only left the car to wander further back the alley to take a leak. He had a few cans of Coke in the car and a lot of snacks: Mars bars, doughnuts, that sort of thing. He hardly noticed anything other than the comings and goings from Celeste's house, although he didn't see her at all. The guy Sam had seen with her on Highgate Hill appeared a few times, trotting here and there like some adoring pup. And a black guy went to and fro, doing the shopping and whatever other chores he might have. He appeared to be a house-keeper or something, maybe thirty-five years old.

After three days of this, Sam took to going back home late at night, to get some sleep. Celeste was leaving them alone for now, something he found less than reassuring. Marianne never questioned where he'd been, or asked whether he'd seen Celeste, something he didn't think was altogether healthy. She seemed to have erased every-thing worrying from her mind altogether, concentrating only on the impending birth. Sam felt as if she'd even relegated him to the periphery of things. He tried to talk to her. Every night, he tried to break through the apathy, but it was no good. As soon as Sam even got close to the subject Marianne would plead exhaustion and retire to bed. By the time he followed her, she was either fast asleep or doing a bloody good impression of it. So he gave up trying. Time enough to move forward when the problem was solved once and for all. In the meantime, she was happier in her little cocoon. So be it.

Every morning, after Sam had showered and shaved, Marianne would hand him a pack of sandwiches and a flask of tea without a word. As soon as it was safely in his hands, she was gone. Just like that. That was to be the extent of her involvement, apparently.

The first time Sam saw Celeste, she was with her boyfriend. Sam did nothing, just watched. He didn't want to hurt the guy unless he had to. Sam preferred to think of him as another one of her conquests rather than a willing accomplice. He didn't even see how he *could* be an accomplice. The right time would come, if Sam was patient. With Marianne in the state she was in, Sam thought he might as well have lost everything already. Time was all he had right now, and who knew about the future.

On Sunday, a full week after the last encounter Marianne and

Sam had with Celeste, things appeared to be coming to a head. There Sam was, parked quietly in the little alleyway, when the front door opened and a man came out. He wasn't sure which one, not in this light. It was five o'clock in the morning, and the sky was just beginning to show the first hint of daybreak. Whoever it was had their head down, muffled into the raised collar of a voluminous black coat, hands buried deep in the pockets against the chill. He glanced up as he passed Sam, allowing him a brief glimpse of his face. It was the man he thought was the housekeeper, and he looked haunted.

Sam had ducked low as soon as the housekeeper had raised his head, and he didn't think he'd been noticed. Staying hunched forward over the wheel, Sam watched the man's progress. He stopped when he reached the bridge and stood in the middle looking down. Suicide Bridge, the locals called it. Was that what he was planning?

Sam looked back to the house, to see if he was being watched. The last thing he wanted was for Celeste to spot him now. Nothing.

Should he talk to him? Sam had no guarantee he would even listen. Sam's mind was made up for him as the skies opened, and the rain descended with the force of a sledge-hammer. One moment it was silent, the next it sounded like a horde of drummers practising on the roof of the car. Sam stayed where he was, content to wait out the storm. The guy didn't look as if he was going anywhere for a while yet.

The housekeeper didn't even seem to notice the rain. He just stood there in the middle of the bridge, looking down at the Archway Road far below. The traffic at this hour was minimal. If the fall didn't kill him, there wasn't much chance just yet of a passing car finishing him off. Somehow, though, Sam didn't think he'd do it. He just stood there, shoulders hunched, apparently lost in thought. It looked as if Sam would be stuck there for a while.

Sam stifled a yawn and wound the window down a crack to let some fresh air in. After ten or fifteen minutes, he wound it back up again. It wasn't reviving him, just making him bloody cold. Sam turned the heater up a little and settled back into his seat, made

himself comfortable. Sometime after six o'clock in the morning, he
fell asleep. Thankfully, for once he didn't dream, but slept long and
peacefully. The sound of the passenger door opening woke Sam up in
a rush, and he cricked his neck as he forced himself upright. For one
sickening moment, Sam hadn't a clue where he was, and his first
thought was that Celeste was back.

"What the..."

"Please, Sam, relax. I am not here to harm you." The man got into
the car and sat down heavily, slamming the door behind him.

It was him, the housekeeper. That was some comfort, anyway, if
only a little. How the hell had he known who Sam was? Sam could
have kicked himself for falling asleep. He wouldn't have noticed
anything even if Celeste had run stark naked down the lane,
screaming all the way. It was full daylight now, even though it was
still pouring rain, the sky a dull yellowy-grey. It lent everything a
diseased look. Sam's visitor was soaked through. There was already a
little puddle of water on the floor around his feet and from the look of
his coat it had soaked up a lot more. That thing was going to stink in a
while, not to mention what it was doing to the upholstery. Sam
noticed he was shivering, teeth clenched against the cold and moved
to turn the car heater on full.

"Thank you, Sam."

"How do you know my name? And who are you?"

Smiling, albeit only slightly, the stranger stared straight ahead.
"My name is Clive, and you would be surprised at how much I know.
Celeste has been...visiting you. Visiting your dreams, seducing you.
Am I right?"

"How..."

"Trust me. She's been doing this for a long time. The Louise
Brooks obsession is a holdover from the twenties."

That jolted Sam. That just wasn't possible. "Wait a minute.
The twenties?" He'd known she was weird, but the fucking
twenties?

Clive turned to face Sam suddenly, all traces of humour gone.

Sitting beside him was a desperate man. Who knew what he could be capable of?

"Am I correct? About the dreams?" His voice was like flint, compelling respect if not outright fear. The time to humour him was long gone. This was business, his tone said. *Get on with it.*

"Yes," Sam replied, sullen. "Yes, that's right."

"I thought so. You're not the first, of course." His gaze became unfocussed as his thoughts seemed to take him to distant places. There was sorrow in his voice as he continued, "She's even used me for that purpose in the past."

So now Sam knew. All his little illusions shattered. It hadn't been about her loving Sam at all, or even wanting him. It had never been about that. He had just been another notch on her belt, someone to scratch an itch. Visions of the two of them cavorting danced briefly through Sam's head, tormenting him further. He put them away as fast as he could. His illusions, tattered though they had been, were now gone. Sam didn't need the added aggravation. But that still didn't answer how this guy knew about him.

Sam's voice cracked as he asked, "So that's all it is? It's all just the sex?"

Clive smiled. "I wish it were that simple. No, it's how she survives, Sam. How she stays alive. Not because of the sex, more because of the adulation."

Sam stared. "How she lives? What the hell does that mean?"

Clive stayed silent for a moment. He sighed and looked straight ahead, at the house, as he answered.

"It began in the southern states of America, at the tail end of the eighteenth century."

Sam snorted.

Clive's tone grew harsh as he went on, "Listen to me. You need to know this, if you are to defeat her, or to be any help at all."

Chastened, Sam muttered, "Sorry."

Clive said nothing, but went on with his tale. "I'm from Louisiana, Sam. I was born a slave and grew up to be a servant in

Celeste's father's home, a butler. Celeste was...shall we say, a little wild." He smiled at Sam. The man was trying so hard not to laugh at that one. "She was obsessed with being loved, always needed more attention..."

"So what happened?" Sam prodded.

"Bess happened." Sam stared at Clive, confused, but Clive went on, his expression darkening. "Bess was an *Obeah*, a practitioner of voodoo, or vodun as it was first known in the old country. Celeste had heard about her and once her curiosity was aroused, well, there was no stopping her. She went to Bess and asked for the power to make men love her."

Sam stared at him in disbelief. "That's it? That's what all this is about?"

"No, Sam, not just that," Clive replied. "Bess tricked her. She gave Celeste the power to make men love her, that much is true. But she also made it so Celeste would fade and die without their 'attentions.' She wanted her to learn, I guess, that sex is not love. She can, and has, ensnared so many men, destroyed them—but she has never found one that could really love her, at least not until now."

Sam thought for a moment. "The guy she's been knocking about with lately? He loves her?"

Clive nodded. "Paul, yes. I think she hopes that his love will redeem her, that she won't need anyone else if she only has his love." He turned to Sam. "I don't believe that's true. I think she'll use him up as she has all the others. And when he's gone, when he's either escaped or is dead, then she'll fade again, until she can find more admirers. She cannot die, though, as long as she has me...and the house. Fading is the most I've been able to hope for, until now." He was silent, then, lost in thought.

All those years... It would be unbelievable, Sam thought, had he not experienced her wrath himself. "You've told me all about your life with her, Clive. But that still doesn't explain how you know all about me."

Clive rubbed his eyes with the heel of his hand and sighed.

"Think about it, Sam. All those years together, participating in her rituals, living in that house... It's like we're linked now, she and I. More than even she realises. A while ago, she came home very upset. 'How did he find me?' she kept saying. I knew what that meant. I'd already sensed there was someone significant, as well as the usual transient adventures. I had your name, but not much else. From then on it wasn't too hard to tap into her dreams. Locking on to you was easy after that."

Sam stared at him wordlessly. The air in the car seemed almost suffocating, suddenly, the heat blasting out from the car's vents making him feel sick. This was too much, way too much. "Clive, do you realise what you're saying? You're becoming like her...learning from her." Sam didn't say it, but foremost in his mind was the thought that before long, to all intents and purposes, Clive could almost *be* her.

It was a long time before Clive answered. "That's the most frightening thing of all, Sam. That's why we have to end this. Now, before it's too late—for both of us."

Sam swallowed. All that time he'd been working himself up to the point of being able to confront Celeste, even kill her if he had to, but this was way beyond anything he'd expected. He couldn't let that happen to Clive. For one thing, he seemed decent and wanted to end the cycle. For another, the thought of a second being like Celeste was truly horrifying.

He nodded vainly, trying not to think of Marianne. Celeste had it in for both of them now, had even threatened the babies. If Sam backed down now, at the end (or at least within sight of it), then they were all lost. He couldn't let that happen. He sat back and listened as Clive started to explain what they had to do...

It must have been mid-afternoon before Celeste finally left the house. Sam and Clive had watched the boyfriend, Paul, storm off just before twelve o'clock, and saw Celeste slam the door behind him. The storm was still in full flow then, both inside and out.

Sam was dying to take a leak and starving hungry, but neither he nor Clive dared to leave the car. It would be safer to lay low for a while, see what she did. If they were discovered now, it would be over, for all of them. There would be no confrontation—at least, not one worthy of the name. She would wipe them out without even stopping to think of what Clive's destruction would mean.

Sure enough, two hours later, Celeste stormed off, presumably in pursuit of Paul. Sam wondered what it was about this man that made Celeste love him, rather than just treat him as one of her conquests, to use up and then discard.

"Come on." Clive was off and running towards the house before Sam could say a word, leaving him no choice but to follow.

Swearing under his breath, Sam got out of the car, locked it, and set off after Clive. He had the distinct impression he was in this way over his head, but by now that was nothing new. Sam checked the road as he passed into the house. The way was clear, not a soul in sight. As Sam passed through, Clive slammed the door shut and locked and bolted it. They were safe for now.

Motioning to Sam to follow him, Clive headed off across the hall and down some stairs. These let out into a warm and cosy kitchen, equipped with what looked like every gadget going. Sam thought of Marianne with a pang, of how she would have loved a kitchen like this.

Clive opened a door off to one side, and disappeared into the adjoining room. Sam followed him quickly, not wanting to be left behind. He felt like a schoolboy, going into a haunted house on a dare. Stupid, really. But he wasn't about to be left alone. Sam found himself in what appeared to be Clive's own quarters. The room was quite small, almost monastic in its simplicity. Clive was kneeling beside the battered, metal-frame single bed, reaching underneath. He withdrew a battered looking leather briefcase and set it on the bed. From it, he carefully withdrew a slim wallet, equally worn, and passed it to Sam.

"What's this?"

"Your protection."

Clive sat on the bed and watched Sam.

Gingerly, Sam opened it, wary of what was inside. Incredulous, he looked at Clive for confirmation, stifling the urge to laugh out loud. This had to be a joke. Inside was a simple piece of white cotton cloth. "*This* is going to protect me?"

"This is a relic. It is very powerful."

Sam looked cynical, waited for Clive to elaborate. He was going to have to be convinced.

"Sam, Sam...," Clive said, shaking his head. "You will be the death of us all. Now for me, that would come as a blessed relief. I didn't think you would be so eager." Sam said nothing, just waited, and after a moment Clive went on. "The cloth is a fragment from a priest's robe. A very special sort of priest, one schooled in a much older religion. That's as much as you need to know. Just trust me and believe."

"I guess it can't hurt," Sam said, and put the cloth in his shirt pocket. He wasn't really convinced, but what the hell. It might even do some good. Clive obviously believed it, that would have to be good enough. "Now what?"

The relief on Clive's face was evident. Sam felt his fear lift a little. Maybe that thing did have some juice, after all.

He was surprised to see Clive smile as he said, "Now we hide you. Tonight, I'll come and get you, and we'll set the fires."

Sam stared at Clive, shocked. "Hang on a minute. Fires? And hide me where, exactly?"

He'd annoyed Clive, he could see that, but what else was he supposed to do? No one had mentioned fires before. Not to him.

Clive scowled, and said, "What do you suggest? You knew she would have to be killed. This is the only way. We can't just kill her. The house has to be destroyed as well."

Sam watched Clive for a moment, before replying, "It's not just Celeste and the house though, is it? It's you as well. You'll die."

Clive's answering smile was heartbreaking in its simplicity. "That's true—but trust me, I'm more than ready to go. I need to find peace, if I can. I need to atone."

Sam nodded. Clive had already explained all this. He didn't ask what Clive would do once the fires were set and he'd got Sam out of there. The pact he'd described had three "cornerstones" of sorts—Celeste, the house, and Clive. For the destruction to be complete, Clive had to die too. Sam hoped that Clive would achieve the redemption he so desperately wanted. He got the impression that before all this, Clive had been a good man. At heart, he still was. He didn't want to see anyone else suffer. He prayed Clive would be rewarded for his part in all this.

Sam followed as Clive stood up and made his way back to the bedroom door. Clive paused in the doorway and looked back. "This way."

Sam followed him back up into the hall and then upstairs again, to the first floor. Neither of them made any attempt at conversation. The atmosphere was far too tense for unnecessary banter. The air was leaden, and Sam was finding it hard to breathe. It was as if the house itself was trying to drain their resolve, suck them dry. He did his best to ignore it and pressed on after Clive, who didn't seem to have noticed anything untoward.

They went into what was obviously Celeste's bedroom. Sam looked around at all the crimson and gold, the rich fabrics. He realised the monochrome chamber they had inhabited so enjoyably had been purely for his benefit, and in all probability had only existed within his own mind. The vision of Celeste that Sam had coveted for so long died, then, the glamour blasted. The woman who inhabited this room was a very different creature from the one of his imagination.

Clive stood by the fireplace and beckoned to Sam to join him. The pressure Sam had felt eased the moment he'd entered the room, as if whatever infested this house was powerless here, in Celeste's haven. Sam thanked God for that. He was sweating a bit, but with luck Clive would put that down to nerves. Sam didn't want him to know he was already struggling. He didn't want to admit it to himself, either.

Maybe Clive already knew, for he took Sam's arm and pulled him forward roughly, right up to the hearth. He gestured at the fireplace. "Up here, quick."

"What?" Sam drew back, resisting Clive's pull. "Where?"

Clive glared at him. "I said, up here!"

Sam leaned forward, peered up the chimney stack doubtfully. Stepping back, he said, "Clive, I can't hide up a bloody chimney. Not until nightfall. What if she lights a fire? And won't she know I'm there anyway?"

Clive smiled, his patience wearing thin. "It hasn't been lit in years. There's a priest hole up there, Sam. You'll be able to sit down quite comfortably. And it's warded, I made sure of that. She won't be able to find you."

Sam looked at him, disbelieving. "A what?"

Clive sighed. "A priest hole. It's warded. This house is old, Sam, very old. It dates back to Cromwell's times. Lots of big houses then had priest holes, places where men sympathetic to the Crown could hide from Cromwell and his men."

"And the warding?"

"That, I confess, was me. I spent a long time working out how to conceal that hiding place from her. I never knew when I might need it."

Sam peered up the chimney again, trying to make out any detail in the darkness. He could just about make out a stone shelf of some kind, about two feet above the level of the mantel, probably around six feet off the floor. "It doesn't look very wide," he said. "Are you sure it will hold me?"

"Yes, I'm sure." This time, Clive had gritted his teeth as he strove to reassure him, and Sam shut up. He had a feeling he was pushing his luck. "Now get in." He pushed Sam forward, eager to get him hidden away, safe from sight. "There's a little alcove up there, partially walled in. You'll be fine, although I admit there's not much room to move around."

Resigning himself to the inevitable, Sam nodded and was slightly amused to see the look of relief on Clive's face. "Okay, but I've got to use the bathroom first."

Clive showed Sam where the bathroom was, muttering to himself all the way.

Just as Sam went through the doorway, he remembered something else. "I, uh, I don't suppose there's something to eat, is there?" He was definitely pushing his luck. Sam had the feeling that if he asked for anything else, Clive would shove him up there bodily.

Clive took a deep breath before answering. "I'll make some sandwiches while you're in the bathroom. You'll have to take them up there with you, Sam. She could be back any minute."

Sam wasn't so sure, but there was no need to aggravate Clive any further. He used the bathroom as quickly as he could, taking care to leave everything exactly as he found it. Clive was waiting for him in the bedroom once more, a satchel in his hand. He wasn't even out of breath.

"Bloody hell. You were quick."

"We can't afford to waste time. Now up you go." Clive shoved the satchel into Sam's hands and watched as he slung it over one shoulder, trying to make himself comfortable. Then Sam moved across to the fireplace and peered in. Turning his head, Sam could just make out an iron rung, very rusty, presumably meant to give him a leg up. There didn't seem to be any more rungs beyond that. He hoped the rust wasn't too bad. Sam could just imagine hoisting himself up only to have the rung crack under his weight, the jagged edge ripping his leg wide open on the way down. Not for the first time, Sam found himself cursing his over-active imagination.

He was just about to get in when something occurred to him. "Hang on. This is Celeste's room, right?"

"Right. What's your point?"

"I get she can't find the hidey hole, thanks to you. But how the hell are you going to get me out of the house without her noticing? She'll be able to find me once I'm out of it, right?"

Clive shook his head and smiled.

Somehow, Sam found that less than comforting. He knew, or thought he knew, that Clive was on his side. But there was an element of that smile that struck him as downright predatory—like the smile of a shark as it gazed longingly at a particularly succulent fish.

"Believe me, Sam, you don't live alongside someone like Celeste for two hundred years without picking up the odd little trick here and there. I can get you out without waking Celeste. Once the fires are set, however..." He shrugged his shoulders, an oddly expressive little gesture.

Sam finished the sentence for him. "All bets are off."

"Exactly."

Sam nodded and manoeuvred himself into the fireplace, trying his best not to acknowledge the claustrophobia he could already sense bubbling up. He placed a foot on the rung and heaved himself upward into the darkness, scrabbling for purchase on the stone ledge. Sam's heart came up into his throat as he began to slip backwards, but then his fingers caught and he managed to boost himself up and onto the ledge. Sam got himself onto his knees and rolled under what looked like an outcrop of brick. Now the darkness was total, unrelieved by light filtering in from anywhere. Feeling his way around, Sam found he was in a narrow chamber maybe two feet wide by three or four high. It was a bit of a tight squeeze, even for him.

His stomach rumbled, and he remembered the bag Clive had

given him. He manoeuvred himself into a sitting position and fumbled with the buckles, cursing his scraped fingers and wishing he had some light. Once Sam got the satchel open, he was overjoyed to find what turned out to be a torch—one of the big square ones.

Sam turned it on and played the beam of light around his little cell, for that was what it turned out to be. Nothing. Just a musty little cell set into a chimney, years of dust built up on the floor and in the gaps between bricks. The bricks themselves were burned almost black. Sam found himself wondering how it would feel to hide here with a lit fire below while soldiers searched for you.

Rummaging further in the bag, Sam found a package of chicken sandwiches and a can of Coke. Sighing, he settled down to eat, careful not to let his food touch the dusty floor. He wondered if Marianne was okay, if she had any inkling of what he was up to or whether she even cared anymore.

He forced himself to swallow a bite of his sandwich. It tasted like cardboard. There was nothing to do but wait. And try not to think.

Clive hoped against hope Sam didn't dislodge a cloud of soot onto the wooden floor. He'd never be able to get rid of that before Celeste came back, and he doubted very much whether she'd believe it was a bird stuck inside the chimney. He heard Sam scuffling his way onto the ledge and sliding back, then nothing. Good. They might get lucky after all.

The room looked clear. He could see no sign of their activity, and left the bedroom quickly, closing the door behind him, just as she always left it. Checking the bathroom, he was pleased to find everything as it should be.

The familiars were distressed. He could feel them whirl and eddy in the air around him. They at least realised something was going on. He could not afford to let them alert Celeste to the danger she was in, but could he calm them alone? In the past, it had always been Celeste they obeyed, not him. Yet he could sense his own power building. Maybe he was strong enough, at that.

Clive stood perfectly still, eyes closed, with his arms held high above his head, palms up. He had watched Celeste do the same thing a thousand times. He gathered together the energy he could feel inside him, focussed it, concentrating on maintaining and exuding a sense of calm. For a long time, they continued their aimless motion, roiling agitatedly about him, obviously disturbed by this unexpected turn of events. His was not a force they were used to obeying. Still, Clive persisted, and gradually their disquiet lessened. It was working. He felt a little more optimistic now. When he sensed they were calm once more he gradually released his will, dissipating the force he had been holding in as gradually as he could.

Good enough.

He made his way back down to his room and changed into dry clothes, put his case back under the bed, chuckling. He hoped Sam had swallowed his story about the relic, had some measure of faith in it. It had cost him one of his favourite shirts. Clive was a great believer in the power of faith. He was also a firm supporter of placebos. Hopefully this one would do some good, giving Sam the extra strength he needed.

Time would tell.

Realising he hadn't eaten yet either, he made himself a plate of chicken sandwiches and a pot of tea, then sat down to his food. He turned the radio on and smiled as it spouted the usual cheerful mindlessness, though he was paying scant attention to it.

If Celeste comes in now, he thought, *she'll see everything just the way it usually is.*

His mind tried to whisper that she'd know, that he'd forgotten to hide some small thing that would give them away, but try as he might he couldn't think of anything that he might have missed.

He spent what remained of the afternoon sitting rigidly at the kitchen table. To Celeste, he was sure he would look as he usually did. But the simple fact was that he couldn't move, even if he'd wanted to. He was filled with dread of what Celeste would do should their attempt fail. Her retribution would not only be terrible; Clive was sure she would make it last.

As it happened, it was nearly seven o'clock at night before Celeste returned. He heard the front door open, the murmur of voices in the hall, and the stasis broke, although the fear remained. He forced himself to stand and made his way upstairs to greet them as usual, fighting to quell the tears that continually threatened. As he stepped out of the stairwell and into the hall Celeste whirled to meet him.

She deliberately kept her back to Paul so that he couldn't see her expression. Her eyes, however, told the true story. To Clive, her eyes flashed hellfire.

"Where were you, Clive? We missed you." In order to keep Paul sweet, Clive surmised, her tone was carefully modulated to show just the right mix of concern and irritation.

"I'm sorry. I felt a little unwell when I woke up and thought that perhaps some fresh air might help."

"All this time?" If she had noted the similarity to another excuse, given at the start of all this, she gave no sign. Clive took heart from the fact that she had no idea when he'd returned to the house— couldn't know how long he'd had to do anything she should worry about.

He endeavoured to look suitably penitent. "When the storm broke, I took shelter. I decided it would be best to wait it out." He stole a glance at her, then, and continued, "I hope you didn't need me for anything?"

She considered that for a moment. Clive was fairly sure she didn't believe a word of it, but all he needed was for her to give him the benefit of the doubt. To delay their confrontation until tomorrow; a day that, if he was lucky, they would never see.

The seconds ticked away as Clive held her gaze, determined not to be the first to break eye contact. Celeste would take that as a sure sign of guilt. Then she would punish him without further hesitation, and to hell with what Paul saw. She watched him equally carefully, trying to stare him down. Yet Clive endured.

Finally, she tired of it and turned back to Paul. "Come on." She tugged at Paul's arm and ushered him brusquely into the living room, her tone a little terse. She knew she was missing something, maybe something important, but was content to let it lie for now. "We'll expect dinner within half an hour, Clive."

Paul looked apologetically over his shoulder at Clive, but had no chance to speak.

Then they were gone, and Celeste slammed the door shut in Clive's face as a last petty little victory. It would serve to appease her for a while. Clive permitted himself to relax slightly, then. He was safe, at least for the moment, and if all worked out the way he had planned, tonight was all he had to worry about.

He made his way down to the kitchen to prepare dinner, as she had demanded. She could have her little amusement tonight. He doubted she'd find much pleasure in her future.

Celeste prowled the living room, reminding Paul of a caged animal. Her hair flew out around her in a maniacal halo of sorts, crackling as if charged with electricity. He wouldn't have been surprised to see sparks flying out into the room. Still, he said nothing, just sat in an armchair and pretended to watch television. He had the feeling that something momentous was in the air. The time to back out was long gone, if it had ever really existed. He would just have to trust Celeste to be his lifeline and anchor him so that he could weather the storm he sensed building around them.

Finally, she remembered he was there and confined herself to the edge of the sofa. Even so, she gave the impression that she was about to burst forth like some malevolent force of nature, unleashing disasters hitherto unimaginable. She had her fists clenched tight and sat hunched over her knees, fighting to maintain control. She looked ill, suddenly white and drawn, years older, somehow.

Paul raised his hand and hesitantly stroked her arm. "Celeste? Are you all right?"

She flinched at the sound of his voice, as if she had forgotten he was even there. Surprise gave way to irritation, quickly stifled. "Of course I'm all right. Why shouldn't I be?"

Her tone was almost accusatory, and Paul quickly moved to placate her. The last thing he wanted right now was a fight. He had a feeling she would tear him limb from limb. All she needed was an excuse, and he wasn't about to give her one.

"No reason, no reason. I was just worried about you, that's all."

"How sweet." Her tone, however, suggested it was anything but.

Paul subsided once more, not wanting to provoke her further. Then the door opened and Clive entered with the dinner, obviating the need for further conversation.

Paul accepted a tray, nodding his thanks. Clive seemed edgy, too, almost as if he was waiting for something.

Aren't we all, Paul thought to himself.

Clive had obeyed Celeste's order for dinner to be ready within half an hour, he saw, impressed at the man's speed. He stared forlornly at his pasta, wishing he had an appetite.

Celeste accepted her food with noticeably less grace, still furious with him. She waved Clive away and he escaped gladly, leaving Paul to fend for himself.

This is ridiculous, Paul thought. *I'm scared of being alone with my own girlfriend.*

Yet didn't he feel as if he had good reason? Celeste was watching him as she stabbed at her pasta with a fork, making him uncomfortable. Paul concentrated on his food, forcing it down even though he wasn't really hungry. He downed his wine in one gulp and poured another, hoping to get drunk quickly enough that he could fall asleep and get out of this atmosphere.

Paul had a splitting headache, too, which unaccountably wors-
ened every time he cast his troubled mind back to their journey here.
He couldn't remember the trip at all, and that worried him badly. For
now, though, he was content to let the memories stay buried, if it
meant that the dull thud in his head would just stop, once and for all.
He even wished Celeste would leave him alone, something he found
hard to credit.

No such luck. Celeste had finished eating and was now giving
him her full attention, well aware of his unease. She stroked his arm
as she watched him eat, as if realising how far she had let him slip
from her grasp. But he was determined to resist and plodded on with
the remnants of his meal, forcing himself to concentrate on the plate.

He felt himself getting more and more fuddled by the drink.
Sleep was finally closing in. Sighing, he placed the plate on the floor
and poured himself another glass of wine. Sitting back, he relented
slightly and let Celeste lie against him, circled by the crook of his
arm. She snuggled down, content, and he sighed with relief. Sleep
was winning, and he welcomed it, intent on just getting today over
with. Maybe tomorrow things would have returned to what passed
for normal between them.

Vague, disconnected images of Bob shouting, the screech of
brakes, followed by mushrooming flames kept flitting through his
mind, but were quickly banished. He just wanted to fall asleep, make
today go away.

Dimly, he heard Celeste muttering something strange under her
breath and belatedly tried to concentrate, but the words eluded him.
His head was throbbing now, great waves of pain that threatened to
crush what little sense he had left. He couldn't remember the last
time he'd suffered a headache this bad, if ever. He gave up the battle
to listen to what she was saying, to understand. Miraculously, it
seemed, the pain eased a little. He couldn't make any sense of what
was going on, but dimly sensed it might well be dangerous to try.

Something was happening, though, whether he was capable of
understanding or not. The air seemed to be thickening, somehow.

Her chanting echoed by a multitude of whispers hovering at the edge of his awareness.

Paul wasn't drunk anymore. He sat there, too scared to move, as the room began to change before him. He could see the light shifting around Celeste, as if something was hovering there, but he couldn't tell exactly what. The room itself seemed dimmer, somehow, by comparison. She stood and motioned to him to follow her, her movements appearing to be oddly slowed, as if viewed in slow motion.

Paul struggled to his feet, the air like treacle around him, and obeyed. He felt like a puppet caught in the grip of some malevolent puppet master. Yet he still loved her. He had made his choice, after all, and he would stand by that whatever happened. He had no stomach for the alternative.

Paul watched her rear view as he followed her, hypnotised by the sway of her hips (carefully exaggerated, he was sure). He could feel himself becoming aroused, which was what she had planned all along, of course, though why she should have thought it necessary to stoop to this he couldn't imagine. Had she put something in the wine, he wondered? She disappeared into the bedroom and he followed happily, eager now, all thoughts of resistance gone.

Celeste would save him. That was all he wanted, or needed, to know.

Chapter 30

Below them, Clive watched the bedroom door close and smiled to himself. Everything was falling into place. He would give them ten minutes and then start putting his plan into action. They should be in full flow by then. It had taken him a long time to learn this particular little trick. He had watched Celeste do the same thing many times over the years, but she would have been shocked to know that he had used the same ability on her at least twice before now. It was just a minor skill, as her magic went. He had seen far worse. What he was going to do was freeze time for a while, just for ten or fifteen minutes. No, that wasn't it, exactly. He would be freezing Celeste and Paul. Time itself would flow unabated, leaving them suspended safe in their cocoon for a while, that was all. He doubted whether even Celeste could freeze time itself, no matter how much she might want to.

Ten or fifteen minutes should be enough time to get Sam from his hiding place. Celeste and Paul were fully occupied, so she shouldn't notice the slight build-up of power, if he was careful. She'd be too busy gathering her own. Once the fires were set, she shouldn't notice the danger until Clive had released them and she had finished with

Paul. If she did, Clive would have to try and hold her off by whatever means necessary until they were safely out of her considerable reach.

Clive knew his time was drawing to a close. He'd resigned himself to that long ago. He just had to stay alive long enough to get Sam and Paul out of the house, safe from harm, before the whole lot went up. His own life was long overdue. He was surprised at just how relieved he was at the prospect of it being over. He just prayed that he would have done enough, earned the redemption he longed for.

Not long now. Sam wouldn't be affected. He'd seen to that. The priest hole had been cleansed and protected earlier. He was still expending some energy maintaining that screen, but he was keeping the flow of power as diffuse as possible. So far, so good. He fervently hoped Sam had found some measure of faith, however small, in the "relic" he had given him. Every iota of strength he could pull together would be needed before the night was out, of that he was sure.

Finally, he completed the spell and listened. There was no sound. The house was silent. He just had to trust that it had worked. If it hadn't, and Celeste had become aware of his attempt, she would make sure that he suffered for a very long time.

Clive crept up the stairs, unnerved by the preternatural quiet of the house. He couldn't even sense the spirits that habitually hovered near Celeste, though whether that was a good or bad thing, he couldn't be sure. He couldn't escape the feeling that they were just biding their time, waiting for the right moment to swoop down and batten onto him.

When he reached the bedroom door, he stopped and, holding his breath, put his ear against the door. He couldn't hear anything but his own pulse, pounding in his ears. Opening the door a crack, he peered in and breathed a sigh of relief. It had worked. There they were, frozen in the middle of their love-making. He just hoped he could hold it for long enough. Clive moved quickly over to the fireplace and called to Sam, who appeared moments later, dusty and wary, and more than a little unsteady. He looked a little wild-eyed,

Clive noticed, and was obviously glad to be out of his dark little bolthole.

Give it a while, Clive thought, *and you'll wish you were safely back up there.*

"It's time?"

Clive nodded, and headed straight back down to the kitchen, confident that Sam wouldn't linger. Clive had to smile when he looked at Celeste, naked astride a bemused looking Paul, caught in freeze-frame for the moment, at least. Hopefully there would be no more victims, however willing they were at the time.

Sam tried desperately not to look at Celeste as he left the bedroom. He was surprised to find that the sight of her naked, frozen in the act of making love to another man, still had the power to sting. He turned his head away and hurried after Clive.

When Sam arrived in the kitchen, he found Clive already hard at work. He had a wooden crate full of rags on the kitchen table, and he was busy pouring lighter fuel over them liberally. He fished something out of his trouser pocket and threw it at Sam, who caught it deftly. A box of matches.

"Where do we start?"

Clive fished out another crate filled with rags from under the table and placed it next to the first, continuing to pour lighter fuel all over them.

"You take the first crate and start stashing rags in doorways down here. Sprinkle some lighter fuel over the carpets as well."

Sam nodded and picked up a spare can of lighter fuel, put it in his pocket. Clive did the same, and headed up the stairs.

Sam took the ground floor, while Clive carried on up the stairs and began placing fuel-drenched rags in the doorways on the first floor. He placed at least half a crate-full at the base of the stairs to the second floor. There would be no escape for her that way. He sprinkled lighter fuel plentifully over the floor and walls, making sure the staircase was completely drenched.

He heard Celeste and Paul moving in the bedroom once more as he laid the last of the rags and grinned. Things were coming to a climax in more ways than one, but it was too late now for Celeste to stop him. And she sounded far too preoccupied to hear him making his way back down the stairs.

Nearly over, thought Clive. *Thank God.*

He reached into his pocket and pulled out the matches. Took one out of the box and struck it, held it, mesmerised, and stared at the flickering yellow flame. He heard the soft whoosh of flame from downstairs and smiled. Sam was doing his job.

All was going as planned. He dropped his own match and stepped quickly back, watching the flames climb, licking hungrily at the walls. The carpet became a sea of flame in seconds, the blaze rushing away from him like some incandescent tidal wave. It wouldn't take long to bring an old house like this down, a fact for which he was profoundly grateful.

He looked over the balustrade and saw Sam downstairs in the hall, gazing up at him, and smiled in thanks. Sam was nervous. No, he was *scared*—jittering from side to side, trying desperately to stay away from the encroaching flames. They leapt at him from the shadows, lending him an almost demonic aspect. Clive smiled grimly. Without Sam's help, he doubted whether he'd have found the strength to go ahead with this. He just hoped they both earned the freedom they so badly needed.

A sudden whoosh of flame burst towards Sam. Clive watched

aghast as the flames crept forward, encircling him, cutting off any hope of escape. He had to help him.

He raised his hands, as if in benediction, and started mouthing something inaudible. The front door blew off its hinges. Cold air rushed in, making the blaze dance and weave, opening a corridor that would allow Sam safely out of the house. He saw Sam flinch, the shock evident on his face as the full force of Clive's power pushed him forward, towards his only way out. To his credit, Sam resisted, intent on seeing this through to the end. Clive couldn't blame him for that, and indeed, he admired him for it. But to allow him to stay was to watch him die, and he couldn't have that on his conscience.

Clive closed his eyes and called for help, heard Sam's cry of fear as his prayer was answered. Opening his eyes, he saw Matthew taking form behind Sam, saw him wrap his arms around him and pull him bodily out of the house and into the blessed safety of the night air. The expression on Sam's face couldn't have been more shocked had he seen the grim reaper himself. Maybe he had, at that.

At least, thought Clive, *he'll live to tell the tale.*

Clive brought his hands firmly together and the doorway collapsed, sealing them all into the inferno. He had to hope Celeste wouldn't be able to stop him now. Raising his arms, he opened his mouth to pray. Time to die.

The irony, for Clive, was that he had never felt more alive. Even the air around him seemed to ripple in response to the surge of power coursing through him. His skin crackled with what felt like electricity. The air tasted like fine wine. He could hear every sound, every whisper, within the house and even just outside.

For a moment, he lingered, almost tempted to live and enjoy this power he'd finally found. Then he remembered Paul, and his smile faltered. He had to try to save him.

As if in answer, the bedroom door blasted open and Celeste stood framed in the doorway, barely containing her fury. She was youth personified now, literally blazing with power. Sparks crackled around her, energy eager to find release. She gestured at Clive and a bolt of pure power shot towards him, throwing him backward. He landed hard and struggled up onto his knees, shielding his eyes as best he could. He could see Paul standing naked behind her, backing away from her in terror. Clive was seeing her as she truly was for the first time, and he had to admit it was an awesome sight. He realised how ineffective his own power was when pitted against hers and almost gave up then and there. But what choice did he have now? He groaned, and summoned up what power he could, forced himself to a standing position. He braced himself, ready to fight.

Celeste frowned as she looked around at the ruins of her home. Turning to Clive, she spat, "What have you done?"

Her voice was thunderous, and Clive could see familiars whirling about the bedroom ceiling, wailing in pain. It seemed to have drawn Paul into madness already. He was cringing in a corner now, batting at himself and moaning as if beset by a cloud of bees.

Clive steeled himself, made himself stand up tall. He didn't want to look as scared as he felt. He cleared his throat, and replied, "I've ended it. Once and for all."

Celeste threw back her head and laughed, the derision in her voice as she gestured at the flames almost more than Clive could bear. "Did you think this would defeat me?"

She seemed almost delighted at his effrontery, and Clive prepared himself for a long battle, intent on denting her confidence. He had to be right!

"I know it will. When the house goes, so do we. We're tied together, we three." He stumbled, then, as the floor rippled in response to the pulse of energy that shot out of Celeste at Clive's reply. "You told me that yourself, remember?"

As if in answer, a chunk of plaster fell from the ceiling and plunged down into the hall, shattering into smaller pieces as it landed, only to be followed by another and then another. The fire had reached the top floor and had taken a deep hold on the house. It was too late for them to be saved by normal means, and he didn't think Celeste had enough power to restore the damaged wood, even if she could quell the flames.

Celeste snarled, precious little humanity left. Finally, she realised the extent of the threat, and her reaction was that of a caged animal. She prepared to leap. She heard Paul whimper behind her, and turned to him. Her expression softened in an instant. She bent and stroked his head, murmuring soft words of comfort. Clive was stunned.

So she *had* loved him after all. Celeste would never willingly allow him to get Paul out of the house. She would keep him with her until the bitter end, whatever the outcome.

Paul was crying. He raised his wet eyes to Celeste's and grabbed her wrist, whispered, "I love you." Then he dropped his head again, too scared to do more. Celeste groaned.

The triumph Clive had felt as the flames took hold fell away as he saw their affection. Belatedly, he saw what Celeste had been planning for Paul. She didn't just want to use him up, like the others—she loved him and wanted him by her side, forever. He was Clive's replacement.

If he couldn't stop them, Clive's death would be for nothing.

Raising her arms, Celeste turned to Clive and began to chant. The air around her began to glow, brighter and brighter, and the spirits swarmed. They hovered above her head, flitting around the ceiling as if pulled there, only to circle aimlessly. Clive felt his clothes being pulled, the sharp nip of teeth on his cheek, drawing blood. He could feel two or three of them, at least, that had worked their way beneath his jacket. They bit through his shirt, doing their best to burrow through into the soft meat underneath.

Clive ripped his jacket off, intent on knocking away the last of the filthy things. They were sluggish, easily dislodged. They had already had their fill.

He did his best to quell the rising nausea and stripped off his shirt to inspect the damage. Celeste had returned her attention to Paul, assuming Clive to be no further threat.

It wasn't too bad. The wounds, although messy, weren't that deep. He hauled himself to his feet and found himself standing beside his brother, who had come to his aid now that Sam was safely outside. With Matthew by his side, the battle resumed.

Clive began to chant a spell of his own in turn, drawing his own will together in an attempt to protect himself from further attack. He was no longer fool enough to believe he could beat her outright by herself. The best he could now hope for was to hold her off long enough to ensure the destruction of the house by fire. Once he was reasonably sure he'd defended himself adequately from further attack, he concentrated on trying to reach Paul's mind. His thoughts drifted towards him, reached out to try and make contact with Paul's own—and were driven back when Celeste unleashed a bolt of pure energy.

He fell to the floor, exhausted. No use. He would have to try and reach Paul physically instead, although he was far from sure he could even do that.

The familiars intensified their efforts, but were largely kept back. He wouldn't be able to maintain this level of concentration for long, though. Clive began laboriously edging his way forward, intent on reaching Paul before it was too late. But first he had to get past Celeste.

Then Matthew was there, adding the force of his own power to Clive's. The spirits recoiled, not powerful enough to permeate their combined strength.

Celeste, shocked by Matthew's appearance, had ceased her chant once more. She stood slack-jawed, gazing at him in a mixture of amazement and terror.

Clive struggled to gather the last remnants of his power together and seized his chance. Raising his arms, he levelled them at her, and a blast of pure force hurled her backwards. She collided with Paul, and the pair of them smashed straight out through the bedroom window.

Clive rushed to the window and looked out, his brother—as ever —by his side. To his amazement, Celeste hung suspended before him in mid-air, falling glass and bits of wood miraculously avoiding her only to land on the garden below. Paul clung to her arm, scrabbling desperately for purchase. With one hand, Celeste was doing her best to maintain the fragile grip she had on his wrist. With the other, she was holding Clive and his brother back—the agony on her face broke Clive's heart. If she let the shield drop, they'd defeat her in seconds, and she knew it.

He watched her struggling to save her love with tear-dimmed eyes, sorry for the inevitable outcome. She was crying too, loathe to give up the struggle even though she knew she couldn't hold her beloved Paul much longer. Her devotion was heroic. Her determination to hold onto him to her last breath was etched into every straining sinew—but she was weakening.

She cried out in pain, and dropped a little before struggling back up to window level. "Help me, Clive! You can't do this!"

Clive just stared, sorrow etched across his face. "I can't help, Celeste. I'm sorry."

Celeste growled, and pulled Paul further up so she could wrap an arm around him. Paul was almost unconscious, barely aware of what was going on. Although, whether that was due to shock or injury, Clive couldn't see.

"Why have you done this?"

"You know why!" Clive answered. "We've lasted way too long, and all you do is hurt people."

She snarled at him and shouted, "I kept you alive! You'd have died without me!"

"I wish I had," he said, and now his voice was quiet. "I should never have helped you."

"I just wanted to be loved," she sobbed. "What's wrong with that?"

Marie O'Regan

Clive shook his head. "What you do isn't love," he whispered. "You know that, if you're honest with yourself."

"It's what I asked for," she answered, and now she was sobbing harder, the shame of what she'd become written on her face. "It's all I asked for."

Clive nodded. "I know." He reached his hand out towards her and implored, "Pass Paul to me. Let him live, at least. I can get him out of here. I promise you that."

Celeste shook her head, staring wildly as she searched for a clear place to deposit her lover, to keep him safe. There was nowhere left. The garden was filled with broken glass and flaming timbers. The bushes themselves were on fire. Sobbing, she begged for their lives. "Please, Clive. Please. You can't do this to me."

Clive said nothing.

All at once, Paul roused himself. He stared at Clive for a moment, then nodded and reached for Celeste's arm with one hand. He stroked the hand that held him and tried to loosen her grip.

With a wail, Celeste struggled against him. "No, Paul!"

He just smiled and kept easing his hand out of her grip. She was weakening, and they both knew it.

Clive dimly heard her cry out. Then Paul let go.

He fell like a stone, and Clive heard a sickening thud as Paul hit the concrete far below.

Celeste screamed, a desolate sound full of pain and loss.

Clive ran to the window, and saw Sam in the garden, moving to Paul's side. He saw Sam feel for a pulse then sit back, shocked, his hand covered in Paul's blood.

And he had to be dead. There was no way he could have survived that fall. His face was a mask of blood, and as Sam pulled himself together and turned Paul over, Clive saw a piece of window frame protruding from his chest. His head swung freely, like a rag doll. His neck had been broken. Clive regretted the loss, but took comfort in

258

the fact that at least he was out of her reach now. He would find peace.

There was a scream, then Celeste hurled herself back through the window frame, straight at Clive. All thoughts of protecting herself and Paul—holding her shield against Clive—were gone now. She wanted retribution for Paul's death. No matter how honest and genuine their love had been, they could not have saved each other. Their union had been doomed from the start.

Celeste stopped just in front of Clive, her face completely transformed by hate. "You'll die too," she spat at him. "You fool."

Clive was taken aback, although he knew he shouldn't be. She had never hated him before. Teased him, tormented him, but never *hated* him. He was surprised to feel a pang of hurt at that. He backed away as she advanced on him, listening to the death-cries of the house. Doors fell in, windows shattered in the heat. He could hear the house groaning as it succumbed to the flames. Surely it would soon crumble.

Matthew reappeared, and Clive sighed with relief. He stayed close to Matthew's protective figure, glad that he had come now, in time for his brother's death. His own power was fading fast, his strength all but gone. What was left would have to be enough. Clive's death had to be by fire, not at her hand, for the destruction to be complete. Desperate, he tried to stall her, praying the flames would have time to finish the job before she did.

"You can't kill me, Celeste."

She hovered even closer, the blazing aura that now surrounded her shot through with streaks of black, flickering. She couldn't quite reach him, though. He still had enough power to hold her off.

"Give me one good reason why not," she said.

"You need me."

She laughed scornfully, her form wavering slightly now. Her power was waning, the force she had been wielding to such deadly effect flickering in and out of existence, as was his. She had aged badly even within the last few minutes, and her features were sagging, her hair wispy and white.

Clive gathered the reserves of his strength together, holding it in for one last blast when it was needed.

Celeste continued to try to advance on him, seemingly intent on tearing him apart with her bare hands. "Need you for what? Suicide?"

"Without me you'll die, Celeste. Your existence will be completely and utterly wiped out. You know that. Paul's gone now. He can't help you."

All the while he was talking, Clive was gradually backing away from her, doing his best to stay out of reach. Matthew still hovered beside him, although even he appeared to be fading a little now. He felt the banisters digging into the back of his legs and stopped. He could go no further.

It was hotter here, outside what was left of her bedroom. The destruction was near total. Flames licked voraciously up the blackened walls and even across the ceiling. The stairs were gone. The hall continued as far as the first step...which was a long one now.

All the others had collapsed into the stairwell and were now no more than a blackened mess of timbers heaped on the ground far below.

The floor beneath him was smoking, and he felt the first pains as the heat seared the soles of his feet. He could actually see smoke rising from his shoes—or what was left of them. The banisters gave a little, and Clive leapt forward just before he would have fallen as they finally splintered and broke away. The inside of her room, he saw with awe, was still virtually intact, even though the window and the external wall were shattered. In there, she had managed to maintain the façade of solidity. Her sanctuary would be the last to fall victim to the flames.

He saw that the reality of the situation had sunk in at last, and Celeste was no longer coming for him. Rather, she was staring at what was left of her home, unable to believe it was being destroyed.

He was safe—for now. But would she be able to stop him from killing himself? With his brother's help, he hoped not. The familiars had long since given up the battle and were frantically looking for a safe place to hide. Clive smiled in satisfaction at their plight, secure in the knowledge that there were none.

They would all perish together.

His clothes hung off him in shreds. The many scratches, bites, and burns on his body stung in the heat. Every ragged, tortured breath seared his lungs. If he didn't throw himself off now, the fire would finish the job for him—but not quickly. Already the pain was agonising. Clive was ashamed to realise that, even after all of the night's events, he was too much of a coward to willingly face the flames. When the time came, he would jump.

They didn't have long. He heard sirens in the distance, coming closer. He didn't think they would be able to save the house, though. Not now. He leaned heavily on what was left of the banisters, and felt them give, just a little, beneath his weight. He was drawing heavily on his reserves now, the last of his strength nearly spent.

Celeste had sunk to the floor and was gazing reproachfully at him. "Why, Clive?"

She actually looked hurt, not believing how he had betrayed her.

He sighed, and stood straighter as he answered. "Because I got sick of watching people being used and then cast off. Because I'm tired. Because it's long overdue. All those reasons, Celeste, plus…it's the right thing to do."

Her expression hardened once more, disgusted, he realised, at what she saw in her own twisted way as his weakness. "Maybe *you're* tired. I'm not ready to go yet!"

She reached for him, and he drew back, stumbled as his foot went over the landing's edge.

She seemed to realise the precariousness of Clive's position, then, and grew wary. He sensed her gathering what little strength she had left to hold onto him, to stop him from falling, and knew it was now or never. Whirling, he hurled himself out over the edge of the landing and into the air. He felt Celeste's frantic attempts to stop his fall, to save him—and herself. But he managed to evade her grip. She howled in agony, unable to conceive of losing, *dying*. He felt her efforts to maintain her grip intensifying, and for a moment his descent actually stopped, leaving him hanging there in mid-air. Was she going to win after all, he thought, even after all this? Despair took him, then, and tears streaked down his worn face as he contemplated the hell she would put him through for this.

It would go on forever.

Then he felt her hold cut off, quickly and cleanly, and he began to fall freely once more. Turning as he fell, he saw Matthew standing with his arms wrapped around Celeste, who was desperately trying to get free, to get past him so she could stop Clive from dying. Too late.

The last thing Clive saw was his brother hurl Celeste back into her room, then turning to him and smiling, applauding a job well done. Then his smile faded, and he crumbled into the dust.

The breath was forced from Clive's body when the floor met him with an almighty bang. Clive saw an explosion of light and felt his back break from the impact, myriad other bones splintering in their turn. He felt every injury in exquisite detail. The flames licked eagerly towards him. His face blistered in the heat. He smiled benignly for all that, content. It was nearly over, now.

He had always thought it a cliché, but there before him was a tunnel, stretching off into the distance, and he could see a bright light at the end of it...and oh how it called him. He could see his mother, smiling as if in welcome, and just behind her... Clive wept, tears trickling down to the floor even as his tortured body gave up its battle to stay alive and allowed his spirit to float free, borne on his final breath. Behind her was his brother, Matthew, healthy once more and smiling proudly, his arms open wide in welcome. So his actions on that day so long ago had done some good after all. Clive looked back at the blackened husk on the floor that had held his essence captive for so long and then turned and went to his family. The house faded behind him, even as he travelled upward, and his long torment was finally over. He was at peace.

Cheated, lying on the bedroom floor in a heap, Celeste roared in agony as she felt Clive pass, feeling the last of her power finally desert her. The bargain she had struck was broken, irrevocably, and now she alone was left to pay the price. As she stood to meet her fate, the fire engulfed her at last. Her hair shrivelled and crisped, and she was consumed with terrifying speed, her flesh quickly returning to the dust she had to cheated all this time.

The house was beyond redemption now. Sam, back on the lane, away from the fire and the fury, sat on the ground and watched from the opposite side of the road, hunched over, sobbing as he watched it burn. He watched as the roof fell in, and as the walls crumbled and fell, unaffected by the fire brigade's best efforts. No one came out. Finally, a huge cloud of smoke and flame erupted from the ruins of the house, as if the building itself was coughing out all the badness inside, and then it was done. And still no one came out. Gradually, Sam realised Clive had done it—he'd won. Celeste was gone and wouldn't be hurting anyone anymore, but the cost had been dreadful.

Sam clasped his hands together in prayer as he hadn't done for years, and raised his tear-streaked face to heaven. "Dear God, please look after Clive. And Paul. It wasn't their fault. Amen."

It wasn't much of a prayer, but it was the best he could manage for now, so it would have to do. He wasn't much of a churchgoer, and the words came hard, but they were true, and they were sincere. He hoped they'd got what they wanted.

Sam put his head on his knees and wept. It was over, and he was the only one left alive. He could go home, back to his life, and to Marianne. When he'd got his emotions in check, he struggled to his feet and walked towards the alley where he'd left the car. It seemed like days ago now. Miraculously, no one had keyed it, or tried to steal it. The car sat there patiently, waiting for him. He dug his keys out of his pocket and reached forward to put the key in the lock. For just a moment, he saw Clive reflected in the glass, staring at him—a young, healthy Clive, happy now.

Sam nodded, and the reflection faded.

He opened the door and got in, put the key in the ignition. As he gunned the engine, he heard a sigh and watched as a river of embers sparked across the night sky, lighting his way, fading as they went. His mobile buzzed in his pocket, and he jumped at the unfamiliar noise. Dragging it out, he fumbled with the buttons and held it to his ear. "H...hello?"

"Blimey. Miracles do happen." His wife's voice was warm, and he sagged with relief.

"Marianne?"

"I had a feeling you might be coming home," she said. "Thought I'd ring and check. Nearly died when you answered the damn thing. It's *never* on."

Sam laughed and wound the window down a little. "Yeah, well, you're right."

"I am?"

She was trying to be cheerful, trying to sound unconcerned, but Sam knew she was scared. She'd just been distancing herself, in case they lost and she was left alone.

"Is it over, Sam? Are you okay?"

"Yep, I'm fine. And you were right. Miracles do happen." He paused for a moment, staring back at the ruins behind him. "I'm coming home now, love, safe and sound. Hope the dinner's on?"

. . .

He didn't wait for her reply, just ended the call and turned the phone off. He threw it on the back seat and pulled out of the alley, turned towards home, towards Marianne and his soon-to-be-born children.

Home is where the heart is, he thought, and smiled as he pictured Marianne, waiting for him. *Never a truer word...*

Acknowledgments

I've been working on this book for a long time, and thanks are due to Gillian Redfearn, Alexandra Benedict, Angela Slatter and Mike Carey for providing much needed encouragement; to Ken McKinley and Kenneth Cain of Silver Shamrock Publishing both for accepting *Celeste* and for their support and hard work on bringing this book to fruition, and to Kealan Patrick Burke for the amazing cover art. And by no means least, thank you to my children for putting up with me writing in various corners for so many years, and to my lovely husband, Paul Kane, for his belief in me and for being my first reader, and for his never-ending encouragement and support.

About the Author

Marie O'Regan is an award-nominated horror and dark fantasy writer and editor based in the Midlands. She has had stories published widely in such magazines as *Dusk, Dark Angel Rising, Here and Now, Midnight Street,* and in anthologies like *The Alsiso Project* (winner of Best Anthology, British Fantasy Awards 2004) from Elastic Press, *When Darkness Comes, Amazzoni* in Italy and *Amazonen* in Germany, *Bite-Size Horror, Terror Tales of London, Noir, Best British Horror, Hauntings, Terror Tales* and *The Mammoth Book of Halloween Stories*, alongside Richard Christian Matheson, Simon Clark and Peter Straub. Marie also served on the British Fantasy Society Committee from 2001-2008, starting as Editor of *Prism*, their newsletter, and going on to edit *Dark Horizons*, their fiction magazine, acting as Membership Secretary and Site Editor at various points as well as assisting Paul Kane with Special Publications and acting as Chairperson of the British Fantasy Society for four years (2004-2008), where she worked on projects involving Clive Barker, Neil Gaiman, John Connolly, Ramsey Campbell and Stephen Gallagher. In addition, she worked on the British Fantasy Society's FantasyCon Committee for several years, and acted as Co-Chair with her husband, Paul Kane, for FantasyCon 2008 –

featuring Guests of Honour such as Dave McKean and Christopher Golden – and FantasyCon 2011, with Guests including John Ajvide Lindqvist, Peter Atkins, Brian Aldiss and Christopher Paolini. Marie and Paul were also part of the Committee for World Horror Convention 2010, worked on FantasyCon 2012 in Brighton (featuring guests like Mark Gatiss, Robin Hardy and James Herbert) and were also part of the World Fantasy Convention 2013 team. Marie is also currently Co-Chair of the UK Chapter of the Horror Writers Association, along with her husband, Paul Kane, and is organising ChillerCon UK (formerly StokerCon UK), which will take place in Scarborough in 2022, in association with the Horror Writers Association.

Her first collection, *Mirror Mere*, came out in Spring 2006 to much acclaim, with authors like Muriel Gray and Kelley Armstrong calling it 'satisfyingly nasty' and 'a delicious batch of tightly written, shivers-up-the-spine chillers'. She has worked as a freelance genre journalist for some years, contributing articles, reviews and interviews to magazines such as *Writing Magazine, Writers' Forum, Fortean Times, Dreamwatch* (now *Total Sci Fi Online*), *Rue Morgue, Shroud, Dark Side, DeathRay* and *Rue Morgue,* and also tutors students for *Writers' News* distance learning course, as well as working for their critique service. Although hers is not the finished version, she provided the first two draft scripts for a short film based on the life of Dick Turpin, which was produced in 2008. In 2012 Marie reached the longlist for the 50 Kisses screenplay competition, and has twice reached the penultimate stage of BBC Writersroom Drama submission windows.

In September 2009, Pocket Books (Simon and Schuster) published her first co-edited anthology, *Hellbound Hearts,* an anthology of stories based on the original novella, *The Hellbound Heart,* by Clive Barker, that inspired the movie *Hellraiser. Hellbound Hearts* features stories by Steve Niles, Mick Garris, Sarah Pinborough, Nancy Holder, Christopher Golden & Mike Mignola, plus Cenobites Barbie Wilde, and Nicholas Vince; with a foreword and original cover art (featuring brand new Cenobite 'Vestimenti') by Clive Barker, introduction by Stephen Jones and afterword by Doug 'Pinhead' Bradley. This was short-listed for the British Fantasy Award for Best Anthology.

In early 2011, McFarland Publishing released a book of interviews co-authored by Marie, called *Voices in the Dark*; 25 interviews with genre authors, directors and actors such as John Carpenter, Stuart Gordon, William Malone, Mick Garris, Joe Hill, Betsy Palmer, Zach Galligan, Mike Carey, Steve Niles, Neil Gaiman, James Herbert, Peter Medak, among others.

In March 2012, Constable and Robinson published Marie's co-edited anthology, *The Mammoth Book of Body Horror*, featuring stories from the likes of Stephen King, Graham Masterton, Brian Lumley, and many more. In September 2012, PS Publishing published Marie's co-edited anthology *A Carnivàle of Horror – Dark Tales from the Fairground*, featuring stories by Joe Hill, Ray Bradbury and John Connolly. Also in that month, Constable and Robinson published Marie's first solo anthology, *The Mammoth Book of Ghost Stories by Women*, with stories by the likes of Muriel Gray, Sarah Pinborough, Sarah Langan and Nancy Kilpatrick. This was also nominated for the British Fantasy Award for Best Anthology. Marie's story 'Someone To Watch Over You' (*Terror Tales of London*, ed. Paul Finch) was reprinted in *Best British Horror 2014* (ed. Johnny Mains, Salt Publishing), and her short story 'Listen' was included on the World Fantasy Convention 2014 complimentary USB drive collection, 'Unconventional Fantasy'. Her novelette, 'The Curse of the Ghost', was published by Hersham Horror in March 2015, and her short story 'The Cradle in the Corner' (previously published in *Hauntings*) was reprinted in January 2016's *Obsidian: A Decade of Horror Stories by Women*, edited by Ian Whates and published by Newcon Press. A collection of short fiction, *In Times of Want* (featuring an introduction from Sarah Pinborough) was published in September 2016 by Hersham Horror Books, and a novella, *Bury Them Deep*, was published in September 2017 from the same publisher. An anthology of ghost stories edited by Marie, *Phantoms*, was published by Titan UK/US in October 2018; an anthology of crime stories, *Exit Wounds,* also from Titan UK/US and co-edited with Paul Kane was published in May 2019, and an anthology of dark fantasy stories inspired by the mythos of *Alice*, titled *Wonderland* (shortlisted for British Fantasy and Shirley Jackson awards), as well as a number of short stories in various anthologies, and a collection, *The Last Ghost and Other Stories*, from Luna Press was released in April 2019. Marie and Paul's latest co-edited anthology from Titan, *Cursed,* dark fairy tales based around the theme of a curse, was released in March 2020. Marie also co-edited a charity anthology, *Tricksters Treats #3*, with Lee Murray, released by Things in the Well press – recently shortlisted for an Australian Shadows Award. Marie also proofreads and copyedits for PS Publishing Ltd. She is currently working on a number of projects, including a collection due for release next year, a screenplay and some original short fiction. Her first novel, *Celeste*, is due for release in January 2022 by Silver Shamrock Publishing. She is also Managing Editor of Absinthe Books, an imprint of PS Publishing dedicated to the novella. Absinthe Books' first three titles – by George Mann, SJI Holliday and Laura Mauro – were released at the end of 2020. Three more titles – from Angela Slatter, Cavan Scott and Jen Williams – are planned for 2021.

More about Marie can be found on her website, www.marieoregan.net.

ADDITIONAL BLURBS:

 "I'm incredibly impressed. It's beautifully crafted, elegant work. She's extraordinarily talented."

— Clive Barker – best-selling author of *Books of Blood*,
The Hellbound Heart, Imajica, and *Abarat*

"Marie O'Regan writes punchy and vivid short fiction in which the reader is disarmed and then dismayed with almost surgical ruthlessness. Nothing here can be trusted; not the world you know, nor the people around you, nor the ground on which you stand. Not even, when she's got you backed into a corner, that final hiding place you call your self."

— Stephen Gallagher – author of *White Bizango, The Spirit Box, The Kingdom of Bones*

"Marie O'Regan's stories are deliciously, satisfyingly nasty, and it's refreshing to read someone who so obviously relishes the genre concocting her unique tales with vigour and lack of pretentiousness."

— Muriel Gray – bestselling author of *The Ancient* and *Furnace*

"Marie O'Regan brings a much-needed female perspective to the modern dark tale; her hard-edged spin on traditional horrors makes her a genuine talent to watch."

— Christopher Fowler – Bestselling author of *Old Devil Moon* and *Ten Second Staircase*

"Marie O'Regan's stories contain a slow burn intensity that really get under the skin. They offer slivers of domestic life where moments of brutality are never far away. This is a stormy, feral and darkly beautiful collection by a powerful new writer."

— Conrad Williams – author of *The Unblemished, One, London Revenant, Game* and *The Scalding Room*

"A delicious batch of tightly written, shivers-up-the-spine chillers."

— Kelley Armstrong – author of *Bitten* and *Haunted* on *Mirror Mere*

"A very satisfying read and if you are looking for imaginative story telling that is disturbing and sexy at the same time, then like me you will enjoy this book."

— Mick Garrity – Jeff n' Joys Newsletter, *Jeff n' Joys Genre Bookshop*

"Marie O'Regan's 'Alsiso' is a frankly disturbing story, although very well executed, of a man who starts to hear voices, slipping into madness and alienation from his wife."

— Djibril - for *Future Fire*

"*Can You See Me* by Marie O'Regan reads like a ghost story of sorts, but one in which there is no ghost, except whatever spirits are conjured up by guilt and remorse. The male protagonist is "haunted" by a ditched girl-friend, a woman with whom he was involved in an S&M relationship. O'Regan cleverly keeps the matter of Claire's corporeality ambiguous for much of the narrative, juggling the various strands in a way that constantly wrong-foots the reader, with the true state of affairs revealed only at the end. At the story's heart is a keenly felt subtext, embodied in the titular plea of the "abandoned" woman, for recognition of individuality, to stop using other people as a means to fulfil one's own needs."

— Peter Tennant – reviewing for *Whispers of Wickedness*

 "Marie O'Regan is featured author, and probably the best known and most accomplished of the magazine's contributors. In *World Without End* she cleverly builds what at first blush appears to be a simple tale of a young girl losing her teeth into one of global apocalypse. You can take this in several ways – as simply an externalisation of the girl's feeling that tooth loss is a monumental catastrophe, or as an actual scenario in which the macrocosm reflects the microcosm (and tempting to wonder if the girl represents Gaia). Either way, the idea is intriguing, and the story well written, managing to hold the attention all the way and make us suspend disbelief."

— Peter Tennant, reviewer – for his Myspace blog

Printed in Poland
by Amazon Fulfillment
Poland Sp. z o.o., Wrocław
14 August 2022

5fffbdc4-7e64-4e94-8f92-1b60c73d43d0R01